ALSO BY LAURENCE HENDERSON

Major Enquiry

With Intent

Sitting Target

Cage Until Tame

# The Final Glass

# The Final Glass

## LAURENCE HENDERSON

ACADEMY
CHICAGO PUBLISHERS

All the incidents and characters in this novel are entirely fictitious and no reference is intended to any actual person, living or dead.

Published in 1990 by
Academy Chicago Publishers
213 West Institute Place
Chicago, IL 60610

**Library of Congress Cataloging-in-Publication Data**

Henderson, Laurence.
    The final glass / Laurence Henderson.
       p.     cm.
    ISBN 0-89733-350-0 : $18.95
    I.  Title.
    PR6058.E493F56     1990
    823'.914—dc20                90-39548
                                      CIP

This book was printed and bound in the USA on acid-free paper.

For Alex Auswaks

Now that the darkness is falling
And nothing is what it seemed,
We'll raise the final glass of all
To our lost dreams.

—Song

# Note

On Easter Day 1916 the General Post Office building in Dublin was taken over by the Irish revolutionary movement, who declared themselves to be the provisional government of a new Irish Republic. To the British, fighting for their lives on the battlefields of Europe, this was an act of treachery and, after besieging the Post Office building, the British executed the seven signatories of the declaration.

The ensuing War of Independence ended in 1921 with the partition of Ireland into the Protestant north and Catholic south, with the south being granted self-rule. In 1948 southern Ireland formally declared itself to be the Irish Republic and seceded from the British Commonwealth.

The Republican movement has always maintained its belief that the whole of Ireland should be within the Republic and has intermittently campaigned to bring this about. In 1969 there were several civil rights demonstrations in Northern Ireland to demand equal rights for the Catholic minority. The Protestants reacted violently and the Republican movement was born anew. There followed a split within the ranks of the IRA. The ruling group became known as the Official IRA (the "Stickies") and the splinter group who believed in bringing about their aims by terrorist violence became the Provisional IRA (the "Provos"). In the decades since, the Provisionals have become the most durable and sophisticated terrorist group in the world.

# The Final Glass

# One

The big Leyland double-decked bus spun its way up the darkened street, past shuttered shops, a few late restaurants and a darkened cinema: other traffic was sparse and only solitary walkers braved the rain. The traffic lights at the top of the street were green, but there was a bus stop a few yards before the lights and the bus pulled into a kerb beside it, sending up a great swirl of water from the swollen gutter. The driver pulled the lever which operated the doors and a single passenger stepped down onto the pavement.

The bus driver released the lever, the doors shut abruptly with a sharp hiss as the airbrakes were unlocked and the bus pulled away from the kerbside in a savage surge of power, the driver making a bid to reach the traffic lights before they changed. The man who had stepped from the bus walked up the wet pavement towards the intersection. The driving rain had blackened his coat and soaked through the knees of his trousers by the time he reached the corner. He brushed the rain away from his eyes and looked in the direction that the bus had taken, but it was no longer in sight. There was no other traffic and he turned to walk in the opposite direction.

Inside the bus, the conductor moved down the aisle of the lower deck, bracing his legs as the bus accommodated to the changing pitch of the road camber. He swayed towards a heavily built black woman who sat on one of the side seats, holding two plastic shopping bags between her straddled legs. The conductor smiled deeply at her as he brushed against her outer knee, but after the first sharp glance, she ignored him and he moved forward to grasp the chromium rail at the bottom of the stairs.

The street that they were now speeding through was part of the business section and completely deserted. The high office blocks and their blank glass reception areas intensified the darkness between the isolated streetlamps, and the driver put his headlights up to full power. The rain shone in the main beam like strands of silk constantly swept aside by the big wipers. The rain hit against the side of the bus with extra impetus as it was driven by the air cross-currents that funnelled down from the tall office blocks.

The driver had been bothered all evening by a faulty catch on the side window of his cab, which, although it held the louvre shut, still permitted water to siphon back over the sill and to drip onto his elbow. He was bored and the dampness of his sleeve increased his irritation. He glanced at his wristwatch: 11.24; it was his final run, and with a clear route he should reach the depot in plenty of time for the official sign-off at 11.42. He would be home shortly past twelve and that would be another miserable split shift over and done.

A horror movie was starting on the slotch box around midnight, but he could not be bothered: a sandwich, a look through the evening paper and then to bed. He eased the pressure of his right foot on the accelerator, waiting for the big gear box to change down and then, without conscious thought, moved the steering wheel slightly to allow for the change in the road surface as he guided the big Leyland into the final stretch.

It was the Broadway now, and the advertising signs made it unnecessary for him to keep his headlights on the main beam. The windows of the big stores blazed out their enticement to non-existent passers-by. The driver yawned and idly speculated about his wife and whether she was still waiting up for him or was already in bed, her comfortable body curled round like an old Turkish slipper into her favourite position for sleep. He raised his hand to check a second yawn, and as he lowered it the bus seemed to lurch; he thought he heard a low rumble, a peculiar sound, like the rising of a great wind. The lower edge of the driving wheel was cutting cruelly into his groin, and he had the sensation of his body being suspended in mid-air as the windscreen came forward to strike him squarely across the temple. The roof of the top deck of the bus burst open and a spear of flame flickered out between the torn metal edges. Both nearside wheels mounted the kerb and tilted the bus fifteen degrees, but it continued on at the same speed with its nearside wheels on the pavement. The bus continued until it struck a concrete lamp standard; the impact smashed open its radiator and sent it broadside across the road to mount the opposite pavement and then head-on into the main window of a television showroom.

The bus ploughed forward into the window display until the buckled metal of its top deck jammed against the concrete lintel spanning the window. The big diesel engine strained forward, urged on by the right foot of the driver, before it stalled. The splintered glass and chips of concrete rattled down onto the pavement and then, slowly, the noise faded and the only sound was that of the falling rain.

# Two

The first vehicle to appear on the Broadway after the crash was a single-crewed patrol car driven by the uniformed P.C. Derek Mathews. In the passenger seat slumped Detective Constable Geoffrey Sheehan, already signed off duty, but who had cadged a lift from Mathews rather than lay out good drinking money on a mini-cab. Sheehan had a heavy strapping on his right leg where he had been kicked by a couple of football hooligans he had assisted in arresting at the Paxton Road end of the Tottenham Football Stadium. He was drowsy because he had spent the hour beyond his duty turn in the station club, taking a lot of whisky with very little water. It took him several seconds to realise what it was that Mathews was pointing out to him.

"Up there on the pavement."

Sheehan peered through the windscreen and saw nothing; it was still opaque from unswept rain. The passenger half of the windscreen was not properly cleared by the wiper blades. Sheehan wound down his passenger window and put his head out into the rain. "What the hell's happened?"

"I can't see the other car," said Mathews.

"Could be a skid."

Mathews used his handset to radio in to the station. Sheehan opened his door and stepped out onto the wet pavement, limped up to the bus and wiped away the rain from the glass inset of the door and peered at the distorted scene inside. He banged on the door, but nothing happened. He went back to the car where Mathews was still talking to the station.

"There's at least three just lying there," Sheehan said.

"It's all news to the shop; we're first on the scene."

Sheehan groaned.

"You could walk up the crossroads, might pick up a bus, could get on the twelve-twenty," Mathews said.

"I'm lumbered. You'll need the full circus for this one; he's well stuck into that shop."

Mathews put away his radio and got out of the car and they both went back to the bus. Sheehan was already drenched, the rain having driven through his cotton raincoat, jacket, shirt and singlet. There were vague shapes moving within the bus, one of them pushing against the door. Mathews added his boot and the door moved inwards about an inch, but the locking bar still held. Sheehan put his own weight against the door and cupped his hands to his mouth close to the gap.

"Down the end, get it . . . the other end of the bus; pull the emergency handle."

"Wha-a-a. . ."

"Get down the end and pull the bloody handle."

The figure lurched away. The emergency door was narrow and a high step from the pavement. The man who had opened it was around fifty, wearing an old brown overcoat. He stood in the doorway nodding his head and trying to say something, but nothing emerged.

"Just sit down." The man remained upright, with his mouth hanging open until Sheehan pushed him gently down onto the nearest seat. He went up the aisle: a man was slumped head first over the back of a seat, his chin resting on the chromium bar. Sheehan pulled him back; the man was breathing, but there was blood at the corner of his mouth. Sheehan laid him down on his left side, checking that his tongue was free.

Mathews came onto the bus pushing forward up the central aisle through the jumble of scattered bags. The conductor had his head in the aisle and his feet halfway up the stairs. Mathews heaved him round; there was a lot of blood on his face and a deep cut along his hairline. Close to the stairs lay a large black woman, her brown coat and blue skirt wrenched high on her sturdy thighs. Mathews turned her onto her side and felt her head; there was a large swelling on the left side of her face. Two torn plastic bags lay amidst a litter of tinned food, burst packets of soap flakes and cereals.

Sheehan squeezed past Mathews and crunched his way through the scattered cornflakes to deal with the man who was staring at him from the seat immediately in front of the driver's cabin. The man had his feet in the aisle and had twisted around in the seat so that he could look back along the bus. Gauntly thin, he sat very erect as he looked through very clear light blue eyes. Sheehan put his hand on the man's shoulder.

"What's the matter? Where are you hurt?" The man widened his eyes a fraction as Sheehan put his hand across his shoulders, gently probing for a possible wound. "Just lie back, on your right side."

The man obediently lay down on the seat and closed his eyes. He gave the sigh of an exhausted child; his arms fell in front of him and his fists opened. Sheehan peered through the glass divider and saw that the driver was slumped across his wheel. Sheehan thumped his fist against the glass and then remembered that he still had his truncheon in the pocket of his raincoat. He hit the armoured glass as hard as he could, but it made no impression: it would need a sledgehammer to get through.

He went back and helped Mathews lift the black woman out of the aisle and back onto her seat: as soon as they released their grip she slid off again. He left her to Mathews.

He stumbled over the conductor and went up the slow spiral to the upper deck. A broken chromium bar dug into his shoulder and he used his pencil flashlight to find the last few steps. His feet crunched into broken glass and the thin torch-beam showed him the crushed indentation at the front of the bus where it had struck the concrete lintel of the shop's window. He moved forward cautiously, trod in something, slipped and fell onto his left knee. Aiming the torch-beam downwards, he saw that he was kneeling in a pool of blood. Something that could be a woman was under the seat close to him; he tried to lift her up, but her clothing had caught. There was a strange smell, acrid and sweet.

He went back to the stairs in a crouch and aimed the torch-beam to the rear of the bus. It was a shambles and he looked with mounting disbelief as the thin beam showed him the scorched upholstery, charred flesh and fractured metal.

"Jesus." He stumbled down the staircase and almost trod on the face of the recumbent conductor. Mathews still had the fat woman by the shoulders. "What's up there?"

"It's a bloody shambles. The whole bloody roof's gone, back and front; what the hell's happened?" Sheehan looked at his watch and then shook it to make sure that it had not stopped; it seemed impossible that only four minutes had elapsed since they had sent in the call. Then he heard the wailing note of the emergency siren and tried to peer through the opaque windows into the street outside.

"Here they come," said Mathews.

They came in a blaze of headlights and a cacophony of klaxons: sixty tons of fire tender lit like a Christmas tree, closely followed by two police cars and three ambulances. Sheehan met the leading fireman at the emergency door.

"The driver will need to be cut out and you'll need to force that platform bar."

The section officer nodded and moved past him into the bus, taking up a lot of room with his helmet, boots and bulky oilskins. He glanced at the litter, stepped over the conductor and went up the stairs. He came down again very quickly.

"Couldn't you smell it?"

Sheehan sniffed. "What, oil?"

"Oil be buggered, that's gelignite."

Sheehan felt the blood rush up his body from somewhere at the bottom of his spine. He looked at Mathews who looked back at him with his mouth agape, but before he could say anything the fat lady jerked suddenly upright, opened her eyes, took one look at Mathews and then opened her mouth and screamed with the full power of her magnificent lungs.

# Three

Following the intense activity during the night, the commander of the Anti-Terrorist Squad called for a full briefing of all squad members at midday. When the squad had been assembled, Commander James Shenton himself entered the squad room; the metal desks had been pushed back to form a square around the half-circle of pieces of pinboard that had been set up on easels close to the windows. The blinds had been dropped and all the lights were on.

Shenton passed through the assembled men and indicated that they should sit down; he perched himself on the edge of one of the metal desks and took out his pipe and tobacco pouch as a signal that smoking was in order. Shenton was not a particularly tall man, but he was heavy-shouldered and now—somewhere in his middle forties—he wore his iron-grey hair cut rather short. With his ruddy complexion and blunt nose, he looked like a football club manager. He had only recently been appointed as commander of the Anti-Terrorist Squad, but his reputation as a murder squad investigator had already given him an enviable record of success.

In contrast to Shenton, the executive officer of the squad, who had been holding sway temporarily, was very much of the newer breed. Detective Chief Superintendent Maxwell was a sleek, slim man, wearing a perfectly cut brown suit, discreet checked shirt and kipper tie. A forty-year-old, bright-eyed organisation man of proved intelligence and administrative ability.

Shenton put a match to his pipe and then looked behind him and dropped the spent match into the empty coffee cup that one of the squad members pushed towards him. He nodded to Maxwell. "Let's see what it comes to."

Maxwell raised his clipboard. "Apart from the driver and the conductor, there were thirteen passengers; seven of them got on the bus the last time it had a major stop, at Mario's Café. Four of them stayed downstairs where there was only one other passenger. The other three, who wanted to smoke, went up to the top deck where there were already five other people. None of the passengers on the lower deck were killed; various lacerations, bruises and all shocked, but they should all be out of hospital in a couple of days. Four of the people on the top deck were killed outright and the other four were seriously injured; two of them are unlikely to regain consciousness.

"On the board we have the names of the passengers and crew as they were positioned in the bus at the time of the explosion: starting from the rear of the top deck is the first mystery. That man was sitting on the right-hand side of the aisle two seats from the back; he received the worst injuries because he was the nearest to the explosion.

"Two seats ahead of him was Carmen Smith, aged forty-five, a ward orderly who had just come off duty. She was struck in the back and left side by fragments of chromium bar which had been blasted from the seat in front of her; nothing of interest there, all personal belongings, except for two hospital towels.

"Next, Graham Southerby, forty-one, powerhouse worker on his way to work at the Tendon Generating Station. He was killed by a metal bolt which hit him in the back of the head. In his snap tin were four cheese and tomato sandwiches, bar of chocolate and a tit magazine. In his jacket, a plastic bag of shag tobacco, cigarette papers, two boxes of matches, penknife, pools coupon and three five-pound notes.

"On the other side of the aisle, a married couple with their little girl: Frank Harvey, twenty-nine; his wife, Geraldine, twenty-three. Mrs Harvey had their eighteen-month-old daughter asleep on her lap. They had spent the evening with Mrs Harvey's widowed mother and were on their way back to their flat which is in the tower-block by the bus terminus. Mr Harvey was fatally hit in the side of the head by a carriage bolt; he was sitting by the window. His wife is half a head shorter than him and it must have passed over her head on its way. The blast threw her forward; the baby was on her lap and got crushed between her mother and the back of the seat in front. The baby sustained a fractured skull and broken neck; Mrs Harvey had most of her ribs fractured and both eardrums ruptured: she is also in traumatic shock. She will recover, physically.

"The man sitting two seats ahead of the Harveys is the second mystery: early thirties, slim build, average height, dark hair, wearing a blue anorak, black sweater, jeans and rubber-soled shoes. He is still alive, but comatose. Finding out who he is will be no problem once we get the run-through on his prints. In his bag were some pieces of Georgian silver, cassette recorder and gold cigar cutter, all taken from a flat in Cadogan Square. On the man himself, two cut-down screwdrivers, glass cutter and wire tickler, all fixed on tabs inside the anorak. He'd had a fair night: in the right hip pocket a bundle of notes, fives and tens, £870 in all. In the other pocket, three cheque books and a handful of credit cards taken from the glove compartment of a car stolen in Berkeley Street and abandoned in Chalfont Lane, which is nice and handy for the bus stop at the corner. An active little creeper that the Chelsea nick have been chasing for ten months, but he's always kept one jump ahead. Now we know why: in by car, but always took the gear out by bus, like a night worker. Not a bad system.

"The final passenger on the top deck was sitting in the front seat. He missed the blast from the bomb, but he got caught when the top of the shopfront ripped back the roof. Gerald Thompson, twenty-seven, unmarried, telephone linesman. He spent the evening with his girl in Dorset Street. They had been to a Chinese restaurant and had then gone back to her place. She shares a flat with three other girls, but they were out, some kind of rota system they work. Thompson was scalped and is lucky to be alive because the shopfront chopped a couple of feet off that front end. He must have ducked instinctively and got almost down to the floor, but he was still hit by the glass, and the concrete lintel caught him across the top of his head. He has a lot of lacerations on his face and forearms; one hundred and fourteen stitches. There's probably still some glass fragments to come out. He is conscious despite the sedation and has given us a preliminary statement which is no help at all. All he knows is that there was a lurch, the bus went up the pavement and the roof caved in. He can't remember any of the other passengers or who got on the bus with him. Anything immediately before the crash is a blank; he just doesn't remember and it's not likely that he ever will.

"Now, on the lower deck, we have the driver: concussion and bruises. He is already out of hospital and cannot tell us a thing; the bus went out of control, he hit the windscreen and that's all he knows. The conductor might be able to tell us something; he was on the stairs, either coming or going— we don't know which—but either way he was below the top deck and that saved him. He came down head first and the quacks have him under sedation, but there is no fracture of the skull and he should be able to answer questions sometime tonight or tomorrow. We have a team with him.

"From the rear of the bottom deck, we have Mr Charles Rudd, seventy-six, pensioner, who lives with his daughter in Purves Street. Rudd spends most of his nights riding buses to anywhere on his privilege pass. He doesn't like his daughter, her family or anyone else and he is a very lucky man because he was sitting more or less under the bomb itself, but the blast went upwards. He has given a statement, but nothing of value: he's honest enough to admit that he was more interested in the passing show than who was getting on or off.

"On the left-hand aisle seat, seventh from the rear, Miss Janet Geary, who had her twentieth birthday three days ago. She's from Edinburgh and moved down here with her parents a couple of years ago. She's a barmaid in the Wellington, the pub at the end of Ridley Road. She has no injuries from the bomb, but she was thrown about when the crash came and collected a black eye and a split lip from the handrail in front of her seat. She also fainted and was laid out when the patrolman first arrived. There's no good reason for our Janet being on the bus at all. She finished work at the pub about half eleven and she lives with her parents at the end of Ridley Road, which is in the opposite direction to the way that the bus was going. It's probably got something to do with the man sitting next to her, Thomas Benson, thirty-two, pipefitter, married with two children and star player of the Wellington's dart team. He was sitting next to the window and she was sitting next to him on the aisle. He got thumped in the crash as well, a cut above the left eye which needed three stitches. They deny being together, just coincidence that they happened to be in the same seat. Neither are of any use to us because they were probably wrapped around each other when it happened.

"Further up, near the stairs, we have Mrs Wilma de Retz, who was thrown all over the place, but came to no harm at all because she is a well-padded lady. Apart from hysterics, her main interest is who is going to pay her for her cornflakes and the stain on her skirt. She's a regular at Mario's Café and she picked out Miss Geary, Benson and the creeper on the top deck as being first-timers who got on with her.

"The last passenger on the bottom deck and in the seat immediately behind the driver's cabin was Harvey Huxton, fifty-seven, and he knows nothing either. Mr Huxton was on his way from a spiritualist meeting, where he was put in touch with his wife who died three years ago. The message he got, apparently, was that he would soon receive a dramatic sign that his wife was still concerned with his well-being, and that's what he thought he was getting when the bus took off."

Maxwell glared at the burst of laughter and cut it short with a thrust from his clipboard. He turned the next page. "The man at the site of the explosion is a real mystery and the one we need to solve pretty damn quickly. He was either touching the bomb or within inches to it when it went off and he was blown literally to pieces; his legs finished halfway up the bus, the upper part of his trunk went into the roof. The lower trunk and pelvic area were embedded into the back of the seat itself;

his arms and head were separated from the body and all were badly battered through being driven in their various directions by the force of the explosion. The face is unrecognizable and we shall have to try for an artist's impression based on the bone structure. The only good point is that the hands were both intact so we have a good set of prints, but unless he was nicked at some time, identification is going to be very difficult.

"All that the professor can tell us at the moment is that he was wearing dark clothing: black trousers, roll-necked black sweater and a good quality donkey jacket. Middle-to-late thirties, around five ten or eleven, big-framed and, according to the professor, very strongly built." Maxwell turned to his next sheet. "I have the latest here, which doesn't add much; the sweater was brand new, from Marks and Spencer's, so were his socks and underpants. The donkey jacket was blue felted wool with a wool tartan lining, first class quality. Analysis of his blood shows a heavy concentration of alcohol. Only his shoes were scuffed and down-at-heel, size ten and manufactured from a high-class plastic. In what was left of his trousers, the remnants of a flip-top pack of No. 6 cigarettes, a box of matches, three keys on a piece of string and, in a back pocket, a roll of thirty-eight five-pound notes, but no cards, licence or any kind of paper which gives us a name."

Maxwell lowered his clipboard and looked around at his listeners. "A well-built boozer in his late thirties who may possibly have some connection with building sites, almost certainly something outdoors, with that build and a donkey jacket. He might be a transient, he could just as well be local. Since we got the general description out this morning, there have been more than two hundred calls about missing husbands, fathers, brothers and lodgers; a few still to be checked out, but nothing worthwhile so far."

Maxwell turned the last page of his clipboard and glanced toward Shenton who nodded and got to his feet. He took his time in knocking out his pipe into the nearest ashtray.

"Major Bendix has made his preliminary report and confirmed the obvious: it was gelignite, a brand called Frangex which is manufactured in southern Ireland. He also found enough of the colour coding to enable it to be matched to a particular batch, and we should be hearing something about that from our friends in Dublin before too long. The major estimates that some twenty pounds were used to make up the bomb. He also found enough of the plastic tape and detonator to have no doubt that the sticks were taped together, either in one bundle or in a series. Wrapped around the bomb were between a dozen or so carriage bolts, each of them eight inches long; there were also some floorboard nails, the usual 'Belfast Confetti'. Fortunately, since most of the blast took the least line of resistance and went upwards, things were not as bad as they could have been, but certainly Mr Harvey was directly killed by one of the bolts and the bomb was obviously assembled with the idea of causing the maximum amount of damage and injury.

"Forensic have found some fragments of dark blue canvas driven into the back of the seat immediately in front of the site of the bomb, so it looks as though the bomb was being carried in a duffle bag or something of that kind. The shattered area is still being searched and analysed, but subject to any second guesses, it was a twenty-pound bomb designed to be detonated electrically, timed by a wristwatch.

"As Mr Maxwell has told you, there is the possibility that the man carrying the bomb set it off accidentally; it's possible that he was setting the timer and made a mistake. Our assumption for now is that he was either getting ready to plant it somewhere else or intended to leave it on the bus when he got off. He may have made a mistake in setting the timer, or the gelignite could have been so badly stored that it became unstable and went up when the bus lurched. Since the man carrying it is the only one who can really say what happened, it is unlikely that we shall ever know for certain, but it does make it absolute number one priority that we identify the man."

Shenton paused and let his eyes drift over the men sitting on the chairs and desk tops in the half-circle about him. "The likeliest possibility at the moment is that the man was a bomber who scored an own goal. If his fingerprints are not in our records, then . . ." he nodded towards Maxwell, "we can check with Interpol and see what they have in the Lisburn computer." His gaze moved over them and stopped at the man who sat alone on a chair beyond the first circle of desks. "Since we are dealing with the Provos, Inspector Field will give you the latest information we have on them."

Inspector Field of the Criminal Investigation Department rose to his feet with a certain diffidence and made his way through the desks to stand next to Maxwell. He opened his slim document case and cleared his throat.

"The Provisionals have a number of sleepers in the London area, but, at present, only one active service unit. Kathleen Reardon came through Liverpool four months ago and was followed into the Kilburn area; she met a number of Sinn Fein members, but made no attempt to contact anyone else. Our information is that no money has changed hands; she was under heavy surveillance and if she did deliver anything then she must have used a dead letter drop. We know from the other side that the unit has at least four members, with an outside controller who selects their targets: we do not know if they are all male. Their instructions are not to register with Social Security or any British government office: they have learned their lessons there. They are funded at around fifteen hundred a month, and since Kathleen Reardon stopped her runs we don't know how they're getting their money. They live in bed-sitters or furnished flats and their instructions are that they must not stay in any one place for more than four or five weeks at a time. The impression they give is that of construction workers who keep on the move to avoid the tax man. It's a very good cover because they can melt into the transient population without a trace.

"Another of their instructions is that in no circumstances must they contact any Sinn Fein official or anyone else sympathetic to the Republican movement. They know that we're watching most of them. They usually take a couple of rooms and stay in the same house, but sometimes split into pairs. We don't know if they pick up girls or spend much time in pubs; if they do, then it is well outside the Kilburn belt. We do know that they only ever move in at least twos, none of them goes out on his own; that's something else they've learned from when we picked up Paddy Kelly, half-cut and lonely. The likeliest place they will be is a café, cinema or strip club, and there are more of those than we can count.

"All we're really looking for are four young men in their middle twenties, maybe older but not much. They will dress like workers, but otherwise we know nothing about them. If you are suspicious, then every precaution must be taken. They're very dangerous to approach: on the job or not they're always armed, and any attempt to search any of them means that you will be in a shootout. If you do tackle one of them, he'll shoot at once, and even if he looks as if he's on his own he won't be. They also have at least one submachine gun, a Sterling; our information is that they also have an Armalite, but so far they haven't used it. The explosive they use is gelignite, and we know that when they move it in bulk they try not to use parcels or bags: their technique is to use a canvas belt holding the sticks and bound as close as possible to the body, each stick wrapped in polythene and cotton wool to insulate it from the body heat and to block off the odour. The carrier usually puts on two or three sweaters and the only giveaway is a fat outline. A man without a jacket is likely to be accepted as harmless.

"The second man carries a parcel or bag with something innocuous in it so that it passes any search. They have used this method to enter stores and other buildings where the search cannot be anything other than cursory. The jelly man takes the second man's bag into a lavatory once they are inside the store and transfers the jelly to that and sets the detonator and ignition.

"The three big ones last August were worked that way, but they moved away from that to an ounce of jelly set inside a cigarette packet or cassette case, sometimes packed around with an envelope of phosphorous. They're easy to carry, in the shoulder pads of jackets, strapped behind the calf, under the crutch. There is no way of stopping that and they can be planted anywhere: behind a shelf of books, in the pockets of display coats, under a counter, usually timed to go off after the store has shut. If they are not damped down soon after they go off, say, ten minutes, then it is likely the whole store will burn. Because they have been so successful, it is surprising that they have reverted to the big stuff; twenty pounds is a lot of jelly to use for one go."

"It makes a big bang," said Maxwell drily.

# Four

The riot had started with the stoning of a military patrol in Divis Street and then had rapidly spread along the edge of Andersonstown. The mob fought with half bricks and petrol bombs and the army fought back with CS gas and plastic bullets and it was a stalemate until the rain began. The rain turned into a downpour and the fighting slackened, finally petering out at five o'clock, leaving the roads into Andersonstown littered with half bricks and broken glass.

In the next hour the light faded and the army resumed a wary patrol of Andersonstown, sending in their teams of armoured Landrovers. The soldiers sat tensely within them, tight-lipped and narrow-eyed; no one joked or even smoked, and all kept their fingers on the triggers of their automatic rifles. They rumbled along the little streets, past the flat-blocks and deeper into the Catholic heartland, a maze of tiny terraced houses.

The girl sitting at the bedroom window of the little terraced house could have been waiting for a lover; perhaps a rough one, by the tension she displayed. The cheap curtains had been drawn to all but a slit to accommodate half an eyeball, and she was careful not to disturb them as she peered out into the street. The angle at which she sat on the wooden kitchen chair gave her a view of the road and the houses opposite, all the way to the end of the street: a drab street of identical Victorian artisans' houses that had been built sometime at the beginning of the century for the cheap labour that had flooded in from the countryside to work in the Belfast shipyards.

The girl had been at the window for more than two hours,

and her eyes were bloodshot from the strain of watching the twilight deepen into night. The only light was from the windows of the houses opposite, either through the too-thin curtains or, occasionally, from the women who defiantly drew their curtains fully back to light up the pavement so that army patrols would not have the cover of darkness. The streetlamps had been smashed with such monotonous frequency that the council workmen no longer carried out repairs. The asphalt at the end of the street was still cracked and depressed from the barricade that had been set alight in the riot of 1971; and close to the corner there was the dwarfed, blackened stump— standing like a rotted tooth—where the house of Maire O'Donnell had been burned out in the Protestant invasion of 1969.

The rumble of a heavy vehicle was coming from the main road and the girl strained her eyes to pick up the shape of the vehicle by the corner. A blaze of headlights lit up the whole street as the armoured Landrover swept up its centre. The girl shut her eye so that she would not be dazzled, and then opened it again as the headlights passed her window: she was able to pick up the silhouettes of the soldiers sitting in the rear with their automatic rifles at the firing position; then the car had reached the corner of the street and was gone. The girl shivered and picked up her cigarette, squashing the tendrils of tobacco almost flat as she put it back in her mouth.

The door behind her opened, followed by a soft footfall, and a man came across the room to stand behind her.

"All clear, Bridget?" he asked softly.

"An army patrol came through a moment ago, but it's all quiet now."

He leaned forward to peer through the slit in the curtains and then moved back again, the flap of his jacket brushing the side of her face as he did so. "You'll be able to make yourself a cup of tea in a minute or so."

He moved away from her and opened the door of the room. She glanced over her shoulder to watch him go and glimpsed, across the narrow landing and through the open door of her bedroom, the shape of a man in a leather jacket who was sitting on her bed under the back window. Then the door closed and she waited, a minute, two, three; a man was coming up the stairs—two men—soft, catlike steps confused by heavier careless ones. A murmur of voices, and then the door of her bedroom was closed. She strained her ears, but could not detect the faintest sound through the two closed doors between herself and the back bedroom.

Then she stopped trying to listen and moved her eyes back to the narrow chink in the curtains and the dark street below. The less she heard the better. Not that she was not trusted, but if she were ever interrogated she would not be able to let slip, inadvertently, who it was that had arrived. It would be a big fellow, though, a real big fellow, for the northern commander to patiently wait in her back bedroom for him to arrive. She moved herself back in her chair and stretched; her back ached and her neck was stiff. All she wanted was for it to be over.

She did not hear the door open for the second time. "I'll keep watch, Bridget; you go downstairs."

She got up from the chair and, after a glance at the man's Timex watch on her wrist, left the room. He watched her go down the steep, narrow stairs before he went across into the room and pulled the chair back from the window so that he could keep an eye on the street and on the head of the stairs at the same time.

Downstairs, the girl had moved from the short hall into the back kitchen. A man in a dirty raincoat was sitting on a kitchen chair which he had placed so that it was across the door that led into the backyard. He nodded to her.

"Hello, Bridget."

"Hello, Danny." She yawned and turned to the kettle that was already steaming on the top of the coke-burning range. "I'm making a cup of tea; you'll have one with me?"

"You're a good girl."

"I must be, everyone says so." There was a bitter note to her voice. She put the brown enamelled teapot next to the kettle to warm, and reached up automatically to the shelf above the range for the tea caddy. She had to pass the man to fetch cups from the dresser next to the door and he got up to

clear his legs out of the way. Standing, he was a tall man with
bony wrists that shot from the sleeves of his raincoat. He
smiled at her again as she passed on the way back, and as he
sat—an awkward, uncoordinated man—his coat caught on the
back of the chair and was pulled away from his shoulder. He
saw her glance at the leather holster strapped beneath his left
armpit.

She shrugged and set out the cups and saucers on the table.
A board creaked above her head and she hoped that it would
not last too long: that they would all clear off so that she could
go to bed.


In the bedroom above the kitchen, the two men were looking
at each other through a silence that had already lasted more
than three minutes. The man in the black leather jacket was
still sitting on the bed; a stocky man with thick curly hair
heavily streaked with grey. Fergus Loughran was the northern
commander of the Provisional IRA, a position he had reached
only in the previous ten months, and he was having difficulty
restraining his dislike of the man who faced him. The man
who sat on a kitchen chair with his back to the door was John
Ryder, a heavier and older man, with a cold, handsome face
under a full head of cropped hair; a full member of the Provisional Council and personal emissary of little Patrick
McGlynn, the cold-brained and cold-blooded chief of staff of
the Provisional Irish Republican Army.

It was Ryder who broke the silence. "So what do I tell Pat?"

"That it's been getting rougher all the time. The Ants and
Specials have informers everywhere. We've got enough equipment, but there's nowhere to train and we need a lot more
money."

"You know the decision on that: soldiers live off their territory; guns should be the only thing needed from the outside.
Do you really want me to tell the Council that you can't mount
a campaign?"

"We can mount it all right, Ryder, but we'll lose men and
it's always the best who go. The Ant squads are as active as
hell right now and the Specials are picking up men for jobs

that are two and three years old. They're getting the hell of a lot of information, and if we don't find that leak before we set something up, they'll take all my best men. We have to get some of this pressure off: a breakthrough on the border. This London thing hasn't helped; half of Belfast has been turned over looking for a connection."

"The London bus had nothing to do with us."

"So you say." Loughran lighted himself a cigarette and bent down to carefully place the dead match in the saucer on the floor between his feet, conscious that he was in the girl's bedroom.

Ryder waited for him to unbend so that he could look him coldly in the eye. "No active service unit was involved."

"Then what the hell happened?"

The grey-haired man shrugged. "An English gangster who didn't know what he was doing; carrying it for safe-breaking, something like that. The British police will find out sooner or later, once they identify the man."

"The description sounded like Brendan."

"I spoke to Brendan four hours ago."

"Are we making a statement?"

"It will be released tonight, round about now: the explosion was not the work of the Irish Republican Army. We are not at war with the working people of Britain; our targets are the rich and the military."

"And that's it?"

"It's not our concern. The money can be raised here; we have no objection to a special collection; use what pressure is needed. But keep a strict account, make sure of that; you know what Pat thinks of sticky fingers. There's been too much of it."

"I'd second that," said Loughran. "You know as well as I do what's happened in the past. The people are getting tired of shelling out; it's one reason for the increase in informers. You can't press these people too hard; they're sick and tired of it. They read about the American money, a lot of them get letters from New York, Chicago, Boston and they know about the collections out there. They want to know why we don't use that, why none of it comes up here."

"Do you want me to tell Pat that?"

"Doesn't he know? Isn't that why he's got a bullet for anyone who's caught at it? I know he sends the guns; the equipment's fine, great, but we need the people as well and money is as important as guns. Leaning on people isolates us: they'll give if we push it, sure, but they hate our guts for asking. It's not the way."

"I'll tell him. A better point is the leak. There must be a leak; you've had too many go, far too many for it to be luck. That's what we're concerned about."

"You think I'm not? I thought at first it was that computer of theirs; they're logging everybody now, everyone in lodgings, every move they make and they've eyes out, God knows how many. The undercover squads, the dud laundries, tally men, anyone between eighteen to forty on a door-knocker basis we've closed off. They'll have picked up a bit from watching the pattern: the bastards are organised; anyone likely has a dossier. If we knock a car off, its number and description are logged and every car, every one in the area, is checked back with the computer. We have to take cars now when it's due within minutes; take one an hour before and it's too red hot to drive round the corner. But it's not just the system . . . not in the past three months and not when they dig up guns that have been buried and take in men for jobs that were done three years ago. Some bastard is giving it to them."

"Find him."

"I will if he's here."

"You say it's coming from us?"

"Christ, Ryder, I'm saying I don't know. If I had a smell of who it was, just a whiff, I'd top them, right or wrong. It's got to be settled soon."

"Very soon," Ryder said coldly. "We need a man to go to the mainland, someone new."

"Does it have to be one of mine? I'd have thought Kathleen could do it fine."

"Not Kathleen. She's been clocked too often; they'll be ready for her. It has to be a dependable man, not important, someone we could lose in a pinch, but dependable."

Loughran sighed. "Malloy."

"Who?"

"You passed him downstairs. He hasn't been in England for three years. When he was over there he worked in a car plant in Luton. He came back when his wife fell ill. He got arrested on Orange Day and he's been with us since. They'll check him, but his story is that he hasn't worked for the past year and he's going back to find a job in the car plant."

Ryder nodded twice. "He'll do, so long as he's dependable." He looked hard at Loughran. "We don't want another miss."

"D'you think I do?"

"That's it, then."

Ryder got up and moved his chair to one side. When he pulled the door open he was facing the smooth-faced man with eyes like pebbles who had brought him up the stairs. As he turned towards the stairs, the man stepped in front of him.

"I'll bring the girl up first; the less she sees the better." He said it in a surprisingly soft voice.

Ryder gave a short nod and stepped back into the room. He glanced across to Loughran, who was still sitting on the bed. "You've a good man there."

"He is, very good."

"You'll tell Malloy tonight?"

Loughran nodded.

"And who else?"

"No one apart from Seamus. Does he go through Liverpool?"

Ryder nodded and then there came a soft tap and Seamus put his head round the door. "It's time to go."

Ryder went out and it was several minutes before Loughran got up and raised his hands above his shoulders to straighten out his back muscles. It had not gone well. The points he had made sounded weak, and Ryder's eyes had told him that they would be repeated to Little Pat without sympathy. There was no alternative now to a campaign; fire bombs in the stores behind the steel circle: they would have to use women for that. And then the more dangerous game of baiting a trap for the soldiers; they'd get one, maybe more, and, inevitably, they'd lose a couple of men themselves. He lighted yet another cigarette and then Seamus was back to stand guard while he went down the stairs.

Seamus waited until he had turned into the hall and was gone from view before he opened the second room. "We're away now, here."

She took the notes that he was holding out to her. "Thanks, Seamus, I won't say that it's not welcome."

"Sorry it's not more."

"Go safely, Seamus."

"Goodnight, Bridget."

She held her breath until he had reached the bottom of the stairs and then she turned and went into her bedroom. The light had been left switched on and the blanket was still covering the window. She bent down to pick up the saucer of cigarette ends and ash: the air was foul with smoke. There was a heavy depression in the middle of her bed which she tried to straighten, moving like an old woman, the ankles of her thick legs swollen and covered with a tracery of purple lines. There was already a thick smudge of grey at the hairline of her chestnut hair.

Bridget O'Shaughnessy was only twenty-nine years old, but older by many more in both experience and sorrow. She had seen very little of her husband, Michael O'Shaughnessy, in the four years of their marriage. Within a month of the wedding, Michael had been imprisoned in Long Kesh, and then, three months after his release, he had been out of a job when the bomb he had primed blew him and two other Provos to bloody smithereens. Since then she had lived on the social security payments of a single woman.

As the widow of an IRA man, she was given a certain respect and used as a convenience: the little cramped house, which she shared with the tiresome old woman who was Michael's mother, was one of the safe houses which the northern commander used for his meetings. Despite the double blind of moving only into rooms that had already emptied, she could have described the commander, if pressed, but had no interest in doing so. She no longer had faith in the Republican or any other cause, no longer hoped, hated or even feared. Her sole interest revolved around getting through each individual day of boredom and depression; and after the day came the Valium tablets and the fitful night through which she slept so badly.

# Five

Wesley King was propped up in the high hospital bed with the left side of his head shaved and bandaged.

Detective Sergeant Burns pressed the record button on the cassette machine and held the microphone close to King's lips. "Just as you remember it, Wesley."

The eyes flickered and dulled, but when the lips parted the voice came out with surprising strength. "It was a quiet night, the rain kept a lot of people off the street. We had a crowd when the dog track turned out earlier, but they'd gone by the end of the run. There was hardly anybody on it until we got to the stop at Odeon Corner. They're night workers and I see them most weeks I'm on that shift. I took the fares of the ones downstairs first, like always; I do that because the bus jumps a lot when it crosses the lights. Then I went up to the top deck and that's all I remember. They say I was thrown down the stairs and hit my head. I don't remember none of that; I know I was going up the stairs but that's all. I don't know if I got up the top or not; I don't remember a bang, any noise, anything. The doctors say I got concussion."

"That's right, Wesley, I understand that, but what about the passengers whose fares you took before the night workers got on? We're really interested in those who were on the bus before that, particularly upstairs."

"Two, three; three is all I remember. One at the front, he was there most of the time, then two at the back."

"Where did the two who sat at the back get on?"

"Before the Odeon, somewhere around the stadium; I don't really remember."

"Could they have got on at the stadium?"

"Maybe," the voice became uncertain, "they had a bag."

"So they got on together and one of them had a bag. Did they seem to know each other?"

"Yeah, they knew each other, because the one with the bag made like he was going to put it on the rack under the stairs and the other one looked at me and told him to keep it with him. I didn't like that."

"What sort of bag, Wesley?"

"I don't know."

"A suitcase?"

"No, more like a hold-all, you know, a grip."

"Do you remember the colour?"

"Sort of dark, black maybe. I just saw it was a bag."

"What did these men look like; were they old, tall, fat?"

"Just ordinary, average thirties, forty maybe. Big men, real heavy shoulders. They both had dark coats; I don't remember anything else."

"What about this second man, the one without the bag. The one who looked at you when you were downstairs?"

"He was just a man, but he fancied himself, like he thought he was a hard man. Something about his eyes, you know what I mean, a guy who stares when he gets your eye, like he's trying to put you down."

"Who paid the fare?"

"The guy on the aisle. I don't know which one that was, they all look alike when they're sitting down. I don't look at people much when I'm dinging tickets."

"This could be very important, Wesley, because only one of those men was on the bus when the bomb went off: the other one had already got off. We know from the other passengers that a man got off before the last traffic lights."

"Yeah, that's right; I was by the door when we got there and this guy came down the stairs and pushed by me. . . . I looked at him and he was the man. I remember now because I looked to see if the other guy was with him; sure I looked at him because they'd paid all the way to the terminus." He lay back on the pillows and closed his eyes.

"Just to get it straight, Wesley: two men got on the bus at a stop near the stadium. The man who carried the bag wanted to put it into the baggage rack under the stairs, but the second man insisted on him taking it up with him. They sat together on the top deck towards the rear, they paid their fare for the full run. The last time the bus stopped, the one without the bag pushed by you and got off the bus. Is that right?"

"Yeah, that's it. I feel tired."

"Can you remember anything else about him, his age, eyes, his hair? Did he wear a hat?"

"I don't remember a hat."

"Was he a young man?"

"Not old, not young. I don't know."

"What about his height?"

"Around mine, five-ten."

"Would you recognize him if you saw him again?"

"I don't know. I'm tired, I don't want to talk any more."

"Thank you very much."

Danny Malloy stayed in bed until he heard Mrs Rafferty leave the house on her way to the shops, then rose quickly and watched from the window as she met up with one of her cronies and then both of them moved off in a slow waddle to reach the end of the street on their way towards the middle of the town and the steel turnstiles that admitted them to the central shopping precinct. He stayed at the window and watched until the two old ladies had turned the corner before he ran down the stairs in his vest and underpants. He shot the catch of the lock on the front door and fumbled a little in a sudden surge of tension as he inserted his coins in the slot of the money box under the hall telephone. He took a deep breath and held it all the time that it took to dial the dangerous number.

The answering voice switched him through immediately when he gave the identifying code and then came the clipped voice of the duty officer. Malloy dropped his own voice into an urgent monotone. "Paddy Two. I haven't much time; there was a meeting last night at Bridget O'Shaughnessy's. I was there on guard, Loughran met a big man from the South. I was in the yard when he arrived and I didn't see his face, but I got a look at his back when he left: tall, six feet, well built, grey hair, a top man. When he left I was told I was going to the mainland. I don't know why. I'm going soon, this week. They'll tell me why later."

His hand shook as he replaced the receiver and he had to cuff away the sweat that had collected at his hairline; the old house seemed to be full of ominous creaks, each of them sounding like a pistol shot across his overstretched nerves. As he moved up the stairs, he remembered the front door and had to go back to free the catch. He was shivering when he got back to his room. He took the bottle from the bottom of the wardrobe: his stomach was in a turmoil and he went out again to cross the landing to the communal lavatory, dropped his underpants and sat on the bowl. He raised the bottle to his lips: it was the tension that was the killer.

The duty officer who had taken the call completed his cryptic entry into the log and then removed the small cassette from the telephone recorder and deposited it into a padded envelope with a red diagonal stripe. He marked the tag on the envelope with the designation of the intelligence major who controlled Paddy Two and then rang the bell for a messenger. Once the envelope had been carried away and he had lighted a small cigar, he allowed his mind to linger on the voice that had spoken to him.

Paddy Two was near the end of the line, no doubt about that; the note of hysteria in his voice was unmistakable. It was something that happened to them all in the end, especially those who could not come out. It was bad enough if you had a definite tour to do, a trick to pull off, a date to look forward to, a single target to concentrate on; but to be in the betrayal business as a way of life and to know that the odds were always shortening, was something else. He shrugged; civil wars are always the dirtiest kind.

# Six

Detective Chief Superintendent Maxwell had regarded the fingerprints of the mystery man being run through the Lisburn computer as no more than going through the motions. Since the terrorist bombing had started, none of those arrested had been on file. The most that had happened had been for the Special Branch to match a name on their surveillance list, but that had not happened too often, either. It was, therefore, with a high degree of surprise that he read the priority telex message passed on by the Special Branch informing him that the fingerprints sent from the University College Hospital had been matched by the Military Intelligence Unit.

He picked up his telephone and dialled through to the chief superintendent of the Special Branch who had distributed the message.

"I've just been talking to them," said the DCS, "and what's making them shy is that the prints don't match up with a Provo, but one of their own men; hold on, here it is: Dennis Baldry, born 1949, enlisted 1970, discharged 1986 in the rank of staff sergeant. For the last three years he was a section leader in the Special Air Service. Prior to discharge he received gunshot wounds to the upper left arm and chest; he was six months in hospital. He got those in South Armagh. That's all they've told me."

Maxwell pursed his lips in a silent whistle. "I bet they're shy; an ex-SAS man carrying a bomb into a London bus would get them hopping about like a pork chop in a synagogue. Any ideas what he's been doing since his discharge?"

"They didn't say; probably don't know. Otherwise they wouldn't have sent that telex: makes it your problem to find out."

"Yeah." Maxwell put down the receiver and stared at his desk top; his first reaction was to telephone Shenton, but then he thought again. Shenton's first thought would be to inform the assistant commissioner, if, indeed, the Special Branch super had not already covered himself by sending on a copy to the commissioner. The second thing that Shenton would want would be further information, pressing for some kind of action, so the clever thing would be to be prepared with some. Maxwell opened the second drawer of his desk, took out the thin book of unlisted telephone numbers and lifted his receiver to dial out for a direct line. He was transferred twice and then had to wait while they checked his identity. He replaced the receiver so that they could ring back through the main Yard switchboard before he was able to speak to the originator of the telex message, Colonel Black.

"The fact that the man was ex-army makes it even more urgent that we know what he was doing, Colonel. Have you any information at all about what he's been up to since he left the army?"

"Yes," came the clipped tones, "what there is I am having collated into a file which I shall send to you before the end of the morning. I have his most recent address in front of me, an obvious starting point; but the important thing is that there must be no suggestion that we are in any way involved. A straightforward civilian police investigation: you do clearly understand that, Superintendent?"

Maxwell bit back an instinctive retort. "We shall pursue our investigations, Colonel, wherever they lead. What address?"

"One twenty-nine Blandford Crescent, a rooming house in the Islington area. Baldry shared two of the rooms with a woman—Margaret Riley—known as Blonde Meg. She has a record of sorts. Since his army discharge, Baldry has had no settled employment. He was paid a termination gratuity of £8450 and he was also awarded a twenty percent disability pension; he became a very heavy drinker. Also drugs, cannabis and amphetamines. No known living relatives." The clipped voice dropped a tone. "Recent venereal infection."

Maxwell listened through a long pause. "Is that all?"

"All that's relevant."

"What was his speciality in the army?"

"He was a trained infantryman; his original regiment was the Greenjackets and he saw service in Kenya, Aden, Germany, three tours of Ulster as an infantry sergeant before he was seconded to the SAS because of his special knowledge of Armagh, and while serving there he was wounded. Upon recovery from his wounds he was discharged."

"Was he an explosives expert?"

Another pause. "He had the usual course, but he was not a trained ammunition handler. If he had a speciality, as you call it, he was at one time an instructor in small arms combat and a trained sniper. He was a first class marksman."

"A useful man for the IRA to recruit."

"Hardly." The voice was hung with icicles. "Baldry had no Irish sympathies whatsoever; he was born in Wiltshire from parents of sound farming stock on both sides. With that background and his Ulster service he would be the last man that the Provos would trust. The file will be with you within the hour." A sharp click.

Maxwell slowly replaced the receiver. But he still got blown to bits carrying a Provo-rigged bomb, Colonel sir, and unless you think it's all down to the little people, that connects him with the Provos well and truly, Wiltshire swede-basher or not. And people change, particularly heavy boozers who mix it with pot. It had the hell of a smell about it, this one, a smell not made any sweeter by the name of the woman Baldry had been living with: Margaret Riley didn't sound as if she came from Wiltshire. Colonel Black could shout hands off all he wanted, but there was just no way of keeping it quiet, no matter how many confidential memos, top secret ratings or D notices to the press. Once the investigation into Baldry started and involved the people who knew him, there was just no way of keeping it under wraps—not with a bomb blowing up a London bus. And when it did come out, the politicians would be backtracking with the speed of light, looking for a scapegoat. Don't let it be you, Maxwell.

He used the telephone again to try for Shenton. He got

through to his personal sergeant who told him that the squad commander had been called up to the commissioner for a personal interview, but, no, hold on, Mr Shenton had just returned and was going back to his office. Maxwell replaced his own telephone and almost ran.

# Seven

Detective Sergeant Arthur Milton crouched low on the dirty cement floor and grunted as he peered through the letter slit set low in the front door of the flat. He had the flap held up on the end of a ballpoint pen and was angling his head in an attempt to see beyond the tiny hall and into the living room, the door of which was tantalizingly ajar. All that he could see was one leg of a chair piled with dirty laundry. He moved his head back and gently lowered the letter flap. His left knee ached as he raised himself and he sighed as he glanced towards the thin man in spectacles and a field grey raincoat who was standing with his back against the corridor wall.

"It's all quiet and I can't see anything, Mr Gladwyn; is that good or bad?"

Mr Gladwyn hunched his narrow shoulders. "It could mean anything; he has a cyclothymic personality."

"Thanks a bunch," Milton murmured under his breath. He glanced past Gladwyn to the beat constable who was standing in front of a small group of women. Milton sighed and put his tongue to the sore point at the back of his hollow tooth. The fourteenth floor of Filbert Point was depressing with its drab-coloured doors, graffiti-covered walls and uncertain lifts. A £50 million monument to the greater glory of the GLC housing committee, and its architect had won a prize.

Its tenants would like to have awarded him their own prize of a slow castration. Milton did not live in Filbert Point, but he would not have minded helping them blunt the knife.

He caught the eye of the woman who was standing next to the beat man, a thin, long-nosed woman who had a mouth like a knife slit and a voice like an unmusical saw. "You're not going to leave him in there, are you? Bloody nut case."

"Has anyone seen the wife?" Milton asked.

A vague shaking of heads and then a younger woman appeared round the other side of the constable; she was short and plump with frizzy ginger hair and the chest of a pouter pigeon. "I saw her."

"Today?"

"Yesterday. I was coming back from the shops and she was waiting by the lift. She had a suitcase."

"Did she say anything?"

"No, didn't even nod."

"That's it, then." The thin woman folded her arms high across her flat chest. "She's left and he's done his pieces."

Milton ignored her. "What about the little boy; could he be with the mother?"

"Unless he was in the case."

Gladwyn opened his plastic document folder and came forward for a confidential word. "Last year the child stayed with Mrs Green's sister in Peterborough; the local police . . ."

"There's no time," Milton told him. "If the boy was not with the mother, we have to assume that he's still in there. Normally, I'd go straight in, but the gun makes it different, it means I have to call in the cavalry. There is no doubt in your mind that it was a gun?"

"No, none, I saw it."

"How much of it?"

"The end, the barrel when he put it through the letter flap; two or three inches."

"Was it double-barrelled or single?"

"I only saw one, but it was a barrel; I could see the hole in the end. I told you."

"I want to be absolutely sure before we bring in the heavy mob, because they're not like me, Mr Gladwyn, they break things. Do you remember the exact words that he used?"

Gladwyn cleared his throat. "He said he wanted to be left alone and then when I told him that he had to let me in, he pushed the barrel through the flap and said that if I didn't fuck off he'd blow my head off."

Milton opened up his notebook and wrote down the words. "We've no option." He nodded to the beat man and then walked away from Gladwyn and waited for the constable to come up to him. "Can you get a call out from your radio up here?"

"It's a steel-framed building; I could do it from one of the outside balconies."

"If we're going into one of the flats, we might as well use a telephone. Hold on a minute." Milton was looking beyond the constable towards the end of the corridor which led towards the lifts. A girl had come into the corridor and was hesitating, already half turned as if to go back to the lifts. Milton went up the corridor towards her, trying to recall what, if anything, Gladwyn had said about the missing wife. This one was around five foot five, but her slimness gave her the appearance of tall elegance. She was wearing a belted white raincoat of obviously good quality and her smokey-black hair flowed down to her shoulders like a fall of silk. It was difficult to see her eyes because the upper part of her face was obscured by large dark glasses. She carried a plastic shopping bag.

As Milton came closer she did not turn her head towards him and he glanced over his shoulder to see what she was looking at; Gladwyn was at the middle of the corridor, a little behind the uniformed constable, and the thin woman came forward, her mouth animated into a blur. When Milton stood in front of her, the woman turned to face him: what she saw was a middle-aged man in a crumpled brown suit and a tie that rode sideways around the collar of his blue linen shirt. He had deep-set brown eyes and thin brown hair; two deep furrows ran from either side of his nose down to the corners of his mouth. He smiled. "Do you live here, love?"

"Yes." She indicated the door next to the Green's flat. "Is there something wrong?" A low, attractive voice edged with an accent that Milton could not identify.

"How well do you know the people next door?"

"I don't know them. I don't even know their name. I've seen them occasionally, in the corridor."

"Have you seen the child, a little boy?"

"I saw him two or three days ago with his mother; we went down in the lift together. What's happened?"

"We don't know. Did you hear any noise from them, shouts, rows, any kind of argument?"

"That happens all the time in these flats."

"Have you got a telephone, love?"

"Yes."

"Could I use it?"

The woman had her key in her hand and opened the door of her flat without answering. Milton followed her into the hall and into a sparsely furnished living room: three chairs, a colour television set, a sideboard and a small table. The telephone was on top of the sideboard. He dialled the main switching number and got Newcombe at the local nick.

"I'm at this mental welfare complaint, Henry; I can't get any reaction and there seems to be no doubt that Green's still in there. Looks like the woman's left him with the kid." He waited for Newcombe's comment. "Yeah, yeah, I would, but the mental officer says Green threatened him with a gun. So would I, but the kid is likely in there with him. We'll have to do the full bit all right, SPG unit. Okay, tell them the radio's dodgey, it's a steel-framed building. That's it: Filbert Point, fourteenth floor. It could be worse; the lifts are working. Next door flat." He read off the number from the telephone and replaced the receiver.

The girl had got rid of the shopping bag somewhere, but she was still standing by the door, wearing her raincoat and with the door key in her hand. Milton tried his grin out on her. "I'm sorry about the excitement; they'll ring me back in a moment." He nodded towards the wall. "Was there a row last night?"

"I was out."

"All night?"

"Until very late, two o'clock. It was all quiet when I went out to do my shopping; that was an hour ago."

"Must have been just before a Mr Gladwyn called there; he's the man outside with the glasses and he said Green waved a gun at him. So far as I can find out, there's no way that Green could have left the flat, unless he went out through the balcony and that's not very likely is it, love? Would you mind if I had a look from yours?"

"I suppose not." She went out of the room and into the little kitchen with Milton following her. He noticed her plastic shopping bag on top of the cupboard unit set next to the stove and waited while she drew the bolt on the glass door at the end, next to the sink unit. She moved to one side as he went through the door and he caught a whiff of a subtle perfume.

He stepped onto a narrow balcony, no more than four feet wide, bordered by an iron rail, which stretched back across the window of the living room, but stopped short before it reached its end. A folded canvas chair was leaning against the middle of the iron rail and a couple of upturned plant pots were against the wall close to the door. He braced his legs against the angle of the railing and leaned as far out as he safely could.

The empty balcony of the Greens' flat was about eight feet away. The door was shut and the light reflecting back from the windows made it impossible to see into the Greens' living room. Milton relaxed his hold on the iron railing and stood for a moment looking down at the asphalt below and the road that circled the flats, crowded now with toy-like cars. It was a clear day, but at that height the wind was quite strong.

When he stepped back into the little kitchen, the girl was still standing in the precise position that he had last seen her. "There's nothing to be seen out there."

"What will happen now?"

"A special unit are on their way. He's got a gun." He had his cigarettes out and offered the packet to the girl. She shook her head as she stepped away from him. "They won't use them, unless he goes raving mad. It's the way it is now, a man waves a gun and you call in the experts. It's the kid I'm worried about. Rotten that, a mother going off without her kid."

The girl said nothing and went out of the kitchen. Milton

followed her back into the living room and the telephone rang. The girl picked up the receiver and then held it out to him without speaking. It was Newcombe. "No, I can hear you all right, Henry, sure, thanks." He turned back to the girl. "Thanks for the phone; I'll get back outside."

When he went out into the corridor again, more spectators had arrived, all women, and he helped the beat man to get them further back from the door of the flat. "There's nothing to see; why don't you get off and cook your old man's dinner." Mr Gladwyn came forward again. "I should have another try to speak to him; he could still be frightened, I mean, he could do something silly just because of the noise."

"We'll talk to him all right. I'll do it myself when the squad arrives; give him a second chance to come out on his own. But we will have to take him in, you do realise that, Mr Gladwyn. With the gun there's no other way."

"I suppose so. It's disappointing, very; I could have sworn that I was making progress."

"It's a funny world," Milton told him and moved back into the centre of the corridor to have a word with the beat constable. "When the heavy mob arrive, Charlie, just concentrate on keeping the cods' heads back. With any luck we might get it over with before any reporters arrive."

"Here they come," said the constable, looking beyond him. Milton turned around as an inspector of the Special Patrol Group led his men towards him: all were in uniform with the little silver badges on their lapels. They walked with something of a swagger, carrying their equipment in lumpy blue canvas bags, except for the long, Makrolon shield. Behind them came two ambulance men with a stretcher. Milton stepped forward.

"D.S. Milton; I made the call. What we have is a man with a history of melancholia who was discharged from Barnwood eighteen months ago. He lives here with his wife and six-year-old son. Mr Gladwyn here is the mental welfare officer supervising his case and he came here this morning and couldn't get in. When he tried, Green stuck the end of a shotgun through the letter flap. Since I've been here there's been nothing, he just doesn't answer. There's nothing to be seen on the back balcony, either. We know the wife's left, but it looks as though the child is in there with him."

The inspector nodded. "Okay, one more try and we go."

"Right." Milton got down on his knees and poked up the letter flap. The scene was the same, the inner door was still open; he put his ear to the flap and could hear nothing. He banged his fist on the door until it rattled. "Come on, Georgie, we know you're in there. This is the police and we've got to come in, you know that. If you don't open the door then we'll have to force it. Don't be silly, it's only going to frighten the boy. He must be hungry. Mr Gladwyn will help you out with your problems. You know you can trust him." He listened again. Nothing. "Now come on, Georgie, stop being stupid."

When he got up and had dusted off his knees, the inspector was already in a flak jacket and was strapping a helmet into position. Two other members of the Special Patrol Group who had also donned flak jackets were stationed on either side of the doorway. The inspector pulled on heavy leather gauntlets and finally drew his revolver.

Milton stepped away from the door and joined the beat constable standing in front of the spectators. "Heads down for a full house," a voice murmured behind him.

The man at the left of the door thrust a fireman's spike into the side of the door and threw his weight against it: a splintering sound and the side of the doorframe bulged forward as the lock tore away. The door sprang back and the inspector went in fast, smashing the inner door back with his boot, followed by the two constables. The crowd behind Milton tensed, but nothing happened—no shouts, shots, nothing. Within thirty seconds, one of the constables came out with his flak jacket hanging open. "He wants you," he said to Milton, and then beckoned the ambulance men.

Milton went through the hall and into the living room hitting his knee against the edge of the chair loaded with clothing and knocking it flying. As soon as he was inside the living room he had to turn at a sharp angle to go through another door, which led into the bathroom. It was a small bathroom and most of the space between the bath and the door was taken up by the inspector who stood, awkward in his armour, holding the drenched body of a small boy, small even for a six-year-old, who was dressed in little shorts, a shirt and sandals. Tendrils of soaked hair lay across the chalk-white face.

The bath was full of blood and water. As the inspector turned clumsily to push the boy to Milton, he glanced at a small, bald man who slumped against the far end of the bath.

Milton turned the child face down as he took him into the living room; there was almost no weight and the ribcage felt as frail as that of a young bird. The ambulance men had already set down their stretcher and Milton watched them hold the child's stomach as they started their resuscitation drill. When he went back into the bathroom, the little man had been pulled clear from the bath and was lying on his back on the floor. His wrists were heavily blooded. The inspector was standing over him with his helmet and visor in his hand. "He's had it." He nudged the skinny arm lying close to his boot. "Cut both wrists. How about the kid?"

"I couldn't see any signs of life; looks like he made a job of it."

"Yeah, he made certain before he did himself. You want any help with the photographs and stuff?"

"I'll get a scene-of-crime team down."

They went out into the living room where the ambulance men were still working on the child, but after a while the senior stood up and looked around for his cap. "He's gone some time ago."

"More than half an hour?"

"A lot more; I'd say around three. No signs of warmth."

"That's it then." Milton trod on something and stumbled so that he had to put a hand against the wall to steady himself. When he looked down he saw that it was an old .410 single-barrelled shotgun. "He sat around all yesterday and most of the night brooding about his wife; probably killed the boy when he woke up and wanted his mother or felt hungry, something like that. Then he'll have sat around again until Gladwyn called. Knocked himself off right after that."

"Funny the way nuts go." The inspector dragged off his flak jacket and Milton saw that he was drenched in sweat. "Apart from my report, you taking it from here?"

"Sure, thanks for your help."

The ambulance men wrapped the boy's body in a red blanket so that it was completely covered. Milton followed them into the corridor and scowled at the little crowd of silent spectators. "It's all over," he told them, "you're not going to see anything. Get back home. You'd better come in, Mr Gladwyn." He looked at the girl's flat, but the door was firmly closed.

"Put your boot behind them, Charlie," he told the uniformed man.

"Right, Skip."

Mr Gladwyn looked even more forlorn as he stood at the end of the stretcher. He took off his spectacles and wiped his eyes with the back of his hand, replaced his spectacles and then looked at Milton. "It is so sad, so pointless."

"He was a selfish bastard, whatever else he was. I'll need a statement from you, Mr Gladwyn, and you'll be called at the inquest, of course, but it's all a foregone conclusion. There was nothing that you could have done about it. It was his wife walking out that triggered him. I need that address now."

"Yes." Gladwyn sat down abruptly on the only upright chair and unzipped his plastic document case. "It's her sister's address, did I tell you that? She went there once before when— but she took the child that time." He handed Milton the slip of paper and then looked around the dishevelled room and slowly shook his head. "He was so passive, a timid man."

"They mostly are."

"Oh, yes, but there are signs, threats, outbursts, half-hearted attempts at suicide, cries for help of some kind. But this, and to kill his son; he idolised his son."

"Yeah." Milton walked over to the window and picked up the overturned telephone from the floor; it had been ripped away from the wall. "Hold on here a minute."

When he went out to the corridor it was clear and the beat man was coming back from the end near the lifts, having shepherded the last reluctant knot of sightseers out of the way.

"The reporters will be arriving soon, Skip."

"I know. Go back into the flat and stop anybody who's not us. If you have time, take a look round and see what you can find, any bit of paper with an address on it. I won't be a minute."

He rang the doorbell of the flat next door and there was an appreciable pause before the girl opened it. She still wore her smoked glasses, but had changed into a yellow shirt and blue linen skirt. "I'm sorry to bother you again, Mrs . . . ? but I need the telephone again. May I?"

She nodded reluctantly and moved away from the door so that he could enter the hall. He followed her into the living room. She nodded towards the telephone and sat down at the table where she had some papers spread out. There was a coffee mug and a spiral of smoke. The girl picked up the cigarette that was smouldering in a pottery ashtray and bent her head over the papers.

Milton got through to the station and found no one in the CID room; he got back to Newcombe on the desk. "I need a scene-of-crime team down here right away, Henry. It's open-and-shut murder and suicide. Yeah, that's right, don't I though. And I want the wife; the only address we've got is her sister's. Here it comes: Peachey—that's right, e-y, at 78 Althorne Road, Peterhead. The wife's name is Mrs Josephine Green and both her husband and son are dead. The locals can tell her and they don't need to wrap it up. I want to know why she left the kid when she walked out. Hold on."

The woman was stirring her coffee cup and Milton became suddenly conscious of the dryness at the back of his throat. "I need a description of Mrs Green."

The girl sucked hard on her cigarette and frowned. "Brown straight hair, shoulder length. Not tall, shorter than me, I'd say five one or two."

"Any idea of her age?"

She shrugged. "Late twenties, early thirties, with the life she's had maybe younger."

"Thanks." Milton repeated the description and replaced the telephone receiver. "You're an unusually observant girl; most

people are hopeless when you ask them to describe something." He looked longingly at the coffee cup, but she did not
take the hint. He got out his notebook. "Can I have your
name?"

"I saw nothing."

"You won't be called as a witness, but I do need your name
for the report, to confirm that there was no reason for anyone
to think that he would go the way that he did."

"I can't tell you a thing."

"Just for the report."

"Mary Wilson."

"And you live here with Mr Wilson?"

"What's that got to do with anything?"

"He might have seen or heard something, last night."

"He wasn't here."

Milton looked at her, trying to see the eyes behind those
smoked lenses. "He must have sat there all night before he
killed the little boy; one hell of a pity."

"Yes," said the woman shortly.

"It was probably just a row to start with, but it must have
turned into something else for her to walk out on him on her
own. If she wanted to leave him, well . . . " he shrugged. "But
to leave the kid behind knowing he was a nut case and . . ."

"Maybe she had no choice, nowhere she could take him."

"Even so."

"A woman on her own with a child doesn't stand much
chance, does she?"

"You have children?"

"No," very sharply.

Milton put away his notebook. "Thanks anyway; it will be
active out there for a couple of hours or so. We'll try not to
make it too noisy for you."

She did not move and he let himself out.


The girl sat for a long time after Milton left and then went
out into the little hall and slipped the chain on the outside
door. As she stood in the hall she shivered and went back into

the living room, found her raincoat and pulled it around her shoulders, lit another cigarette and went out into the kitchen to find her shopping bag. She pulled out the newspaper that she had bought and opened it out across the work top: the front-page story was about the bus explosion and she read it in full, following it through to the inside pages.

When her cigarette was finished, she went back to the living room and through to the hall. She opened the front door a couple of inches without slipping the chain; there were several people in the corridor, many with cameras. The uniformed constable whom she had seen talking with Milton came into her view, telling everyone to keep back. One of the cameramen caught her eye. She shut the door immediately, but very soon afterward her doorbell rang; she ignored it, but it went on ringing. She returned to the living room and shut the door; the bell continued to sound intermittently and she switched on the radio at full volume. Her shivering increased and she had difficulty controlling her hands.

She moved from the living room into the little kitchen and shut the door behind her. The cupboard of the sink held a plastic rubbish bin which she pulled out and then, from behind it, a dark blue canvas hold-all which she lifted up onto the draining board. It was very heavy and the end of the zipper was held against a brass ring by a padlock. The unit drawer held kitchen scissors and she used them to attack the canvas of the hold-all, but she was not able to make any impression on it; she abandoned both the bag and the scissors and returned to the living room again.

The doorbell had stopped ringing; she turned off the radio and passed back through the hall into the bedroom; her handbag lay at the foot of the unmade bed. She opened the bag and emptied its contents on the bed. An envelope fell from the bottom of the bag and she carefully took from it a six-by-four black-and-white photograph. It showed a younger version of the woman sitting on a canvas chair and looking down at a small girl who was sitting on her lap. The child had very dark hair and large serious eyes which looked directly at the lens of the camera.

The woman lay back on the bed and held the photograph in both hands directly in front of her eyes so that it was all that she could see. The doorbell started to ring again; she held the photograph tightly and concentrated fiercely upon the past until the ringing of the doorbell became a confused buzzing. She remembered many things from the past and then she wept.

# Eight

Blandford Crescent was a half-moon of high terraced houses that had been built for the merchants of Victorian London: solid red-brick fortresses of respectability with stone steps leading up to high front doors and bleak iron railings guarding basement areas. But Blandford Crescent had since passed through other times and fashions to become as down-at-heel as any other deprived area of East London. The squad Granada came into the Crescent past a house that had been gutted by vandals and a second that had been gutted by the local council who had bricked up all its doors and windows. The third had been taken over by squatters who had turned it into a commune.

Only the far end of the Crescent still had some semblance of normal urban life. The houses had not been painted for more than forty years, the guttering drooped from loose-tiled eaves and patches of stucco had fallen from the walls, but curtains were hung at the windows and as daylight faded children's bicycles were carefully lifted up the cracked stone steps and into the houses. People still tried living lives of privacy in the houses at the end of the Crescent, in one or two rooms at a time.

The squad driver pulled the Granada around the line of rusting cars and motorcycles to double-park next to an old Cadillac that had a flat tyre and had lost most of its flaring exhaust. Detective Inspector Lorimer mistrusted the cracked steps leading over the basement area and took a good grip on the iron handrail. He waited until Inspector Field and the uniformed policewoman joined him before he tried the front

# The Final Glass

door. It swung back from its worn latch and he stepped into a hallway of worn, filthy rubber tiles. A pay phone was riveted to the wall immediately inside the doorway, surrounded by years of scribbled graffiti. By the side of the bare staircase was a filled rubbish sack. A dim light shone over the first few stairs and Lorimer led the way, the others following in single file.

On the second floor he checked the three doors; it was the one furthest from the stairs. He found the bellpush and pressed it heavily. Something moved on the other side of the door, a dragging sound as if a chair were being scraped back. The door opened to reveal a fleshy woman wearing a rumpled sweater and short black skirt; her face was pasty and her eyes bloodshot. She had a lot of dyed blonde hair.

"Mrs Baldry?" Lorimer flashed his warrant card.

The eyes narrowed and she tried to shut the door.

Lorimer put his own weight against the door. "Don't be silly, we've got to come in. We've news of Dennis."

"What do you want? Why do you want him?"

"We don't want him, we know where he is. Come on, Meg, you're not in any trouble."

She backed away from the door reluctantly and stood sullenly against the wall as they went by her. Lorimer walked into the centre of the room. High-ceilinged and cold; a smell of stale food and human sweat. The pine table under the windows held an assortment of dirty dishes and milk bottles. A couple of rag mats on the linoleumed floor, a gas fire plastered into the old fireplace, next to an alcove holding a television set. In the far corner of the room beyond the edge of the dirty windows was an unmade bed, the blankets pulled back. On the floor beside the bed was a vodka bottle with a few dregs, an empty can of supermarket orange juice and a chipped beer mug; a saucer filled with mouldering cigarette butts.

"How many more of you bastards?"

"Sit down, Meg." Field pulled a chair away from the table and turned it round for her. "You'll want to be sitting for this."

She plumped herself down, full breasts riding high before bouncing low under the grubby sweater. "Come on then."

"When did you last see Dennis?"

"No bloody questions, no flannel. What do you want him for?"

"He's dead, Meg; he died in that bus explosion."

She sat silently for a full minute before her face crumpled. "What—how!"

"I said he was on that bus, close to where the bomb went off, on the top deck. We've only just identified him. Where was he going, Meg?"

"You're lying."

"Why should we? Here." Lorimer nodded to the police-woman who moved to the side of the chair. He went over to the bed and picked up the vodka bottle, pouring what there was of the liquor into the beer mug. He came back to the table and gave it to her. She drank it in a single gulp and turned to move her hands aimlessly around the debris on the table, picked up a cigarette packet, found it empty and threw it down again. Lorimer produced his own cigarettes and gave her one. He pulled a second chair away from the table and turned it so that he could sit facing her squarely. "I'm not here to give you a bad time, Meg, but I've got to know. You're not really his wife and that means that whatever he left could go else-where. I'd like to help you, but I can't even start until I know what he was doing on that bus."

"But he couldn't—wasn't . . . "

"He was."

"I read about that, two days ago and . . . "

"It's taken us this long to find out who he was. Come on, Meg, I know you've had the hell of a shock, but try to help us. Is there someone you know, someone you want us to bring around?"

"I don't know anybody."

"When was Dennis here; was he here last Monday?"

"He went out, he had to see a man."

"What man?"

"I don't know, I never saw him."

"What did Dennis call him, this man? Where did he go to meet him?"

"He went out, he wanted money, change for a phone call.

That was Sunday, he went out to make a phone call. He came back and we went to the pub, he said he had to meet a man, a different man. The one on the phone had told him where to go. I asked him if it was something bent. I didn't want any trouble. He said he might be away a few days." Her voice changed. "It's a trick, you bastard, you're tricking me, telling lies. He's not dead."

"He is dead."

She got up from the chair, jerking away from the hand of the policewoman. "I want to see him, I don't believe you, I want to see him."

"You can't see him, Meg. Take it easy." Lorimer held her arms. "He was too close to the bomb."

"You bastards, bloody lying bastards!"

Lorimer took the list from his pocket. "Listen, he was wearing a black sweater and a brand new donkey jacket, with a tartan wool lining. He could only have just bought it. There were no papers on him; we only found out who he was from his fingerprints. He couldn't be identified, but his prints were with army intelligence." Lorimer took out the keys. "These were in his pocket."

She looked at the keys and put out her hand to touch the long front door key that had been bent at the shank, but abruptly withdrew her hand and almost fell back in the chair. "Oh Christ, what'll happen to me now."

"Come on, Meg." Lorimer nodded to the policewoman and between them they got her to her feet. They found a cheap cloth coat on a hook behind the door and hung it around her shoulders before they took her out. Field exchanged a glance with the rest of his squad as they jollied Meg out of the room and down the passageway to the stairs. The inspector closed the door behind them and then, viewing the room with deep distaste, crossed to the bed to commence the search.

Meg Riley was taken back to the squad room for her interrogation and, once her suspicion and dislike of all policemen had faded, she became very cooperative. Lorimer used a combination of cajolery and patience to get her to talk, but it was

not really necessary. Meg was badly shocked. She clung pathetically to the hope that Baldry had somehow left money to
which she was entitled as the woman who had been living
with him.

Lorimer spent six hours with her, during which he gave her
cup after cup of canteen tea, endless cigarettes and a half bottle
of vodka, authorised by Maxwell. Three floors above the interrogation room, Maxwell himself received the report from
the team searching Baldry's room that nothing worthwhile was
to be found on the first-run search; he ordered a full forensic
turn-out. It was only a thin chance that Baldry's room was
under observation by anyone else. Maxwell decided against
an evacuation of the other inhabitants of the house or a search
of any of the other rooms. It would create a fuss and too much
public comment. The note sent up by Lorimer left little doubt
that Baldry had no connection with anyone else in that slum.

Meg's story had a staightforward ring of truth about it and
she was obviously neither bright enough to tell complicated
lies nor a good enough actress to be anything more than she
appeared, which was just plain scared. She had met Baldry
two years before in a pub called the Iron Duke when she had
just lost her last job as a waitress. Before that she had worked
as a cleaner and at other odd jobs since she came to London
in the early seventies as an eighteen-year-old colleen from
Carrickfergus. She freely admitted to Lorimer that she had two
convictions for soliciting in 1978, having been put on the
streets by her Maltese husband who left her abruptly the following year. She had not seen him since.

Baldry had been a regular in the Iron Duke, where he was
known as a quarrelsome drunk. That lunchtime he had bought
her drinks and taken her back to his room. They had spent
the afternoon in bed together and then out drinking again in
the evening. The following day she moved in with him and
they had been living together ever since. She had left him
twice because of his bad temper, but had gone back each time,
mostly because she had nowhere else to go. He was at least
more dependable than her vanished husband.

She had been with him more than a year before she discovered that he had been in the British army and only then

because of an argument when he was more drunk than usual. She had been brought up in the Republican tradition, but she no longer cared about anything like that and she never told anyone else about Baldry's army service, especially not that he had served in Ulster. Baldry himself was embittered by his treatment by both the British government and the military authorities: he had been shot and when he was no more use had been dumped on the rubbish heap. They would have been married except that she was still officially married to the Maltese, and Baldry had told her that he had a wife somewhere that he had not seen for years—she had gone off at the time he was shot. Lorimer did not tell her that Baldry had never been married.

Any available money—sometimes the odd job, but mainly Baldry's disability pension and whatever they could get from the Social Services—went on drink and cigarettes. Sometimes they lived for a week on baked beans, but somehow always scraped up enough money for vodka or red wine if times were bad.

She took some time to come to anything worthwhile, but Lorimer allowed her to ramble and only nodded to his DC to commence note-taking when she talked about the events of the previous week. Baldry had received a letter more than two weeks ago, which made it at least ten days before the bus explosion. He had been very surprised to get the letter, but she did not know what it said because all he would tell her was that someone wanted to see him, someone who knew that he had been in the SAS. He did not tell her he was going away and, in fact, during the next two days he hardly spoke to her at all. He was simply not there one morning when she woke up, not that that meant much because she rarely came out of her stupor until midday. He had taken his razor and most of his clothes. She thought he had left her for good.

He was away all night, but when he came back the following evening he had money, a roll of notes, four or five hundred pounds, and he said he was going to get a lot more. He told her that if anyone asked, she was to say that he had been with her all the time. She thought that he had been involved with some kind of gang and that he was going to rob a bank. He had just laughed and they went out and got drunk.

For the first time since she had known him he bought himself some new clothes, a donkey jacket and black sweater. He also gave her fifty pounds to spend on herself and bought himself a wristwatch. On the Monday, he told her that he was going out to see a man, but that she was to stay in all evening until he got back so that if anyone asked, she could say that he had been with her. She thought he was involved in some kind of robbery. That was the last time she had seen him.

Lorimer went through his repertoire of interrogation techniques, but each time it came out the same. He had no doubt that she was telling the truth, but it didn't take them any further. Meg cried a lot towards the end and seemed more frightened of going back to her room than she was of anything else. She wanted to stay where she was, and eventually Lorimer arranged for her to spend the night in the room usually put aside for accommodating juvenile runaways. He made his final report to Maxwell verbally and was sent home.


Maxwell waited into the small hours of the morning to receive a copy of the forensic report on Baldry's room. It had been very thorough and had included the removal of all floorboards, light switches and fascia surrounding the gas fire. Scrapings were taken from the cupboards, shelves, the wardrobe and battered suitcase, tested and found to be negative. Not the slightest trace of any explosive was found, nor any hand tools, electrical wiring, batteries or even any clocks or watches. It was a proven fact that Baldry had not stored or handled explosives in that room.

Baldry's hidey hole was found in one of the hollow legs of the bed and its contents were delivered to Maxwell in a forensic bag. A wad of sixty five-pound notes, an envelope with a dozen obscene photographs, a small amount of cannabis in an oilskin pouch and a Commando dagger. From the rest of the room a few scraps of paper, one headed "Leicester" and a lot of figures—train departure times, Maxwell thought. Another was a list of some kind, "suit" it started out and then "T. Test"—what the hell was that? The only piece of paper that brought any gleam to Maxwell's eye was a visiting card, found stuck in the middle of a paperback book. It was an old visiting card, yellowing and scuffed at the edges, which simply stated in black type:

MARK ROBERTS

with an address in Hampstead and a telephone number.

Maxwell put his hand out to his telephone and then realised that it was almost three a.m. If Mr Roberts was still in Hampstead, it could wait until morning. He assembled his notes into chronological order so that he would be ready for Shenton in the morning.

It was progress of a kind, but all it told them was that Baldry had probably made a trip to Leicester and three days later had gone out on a very cold and wet Monday night to meet an unknown man. Two-and-a-half hours after that he had been sitting on the top deck of a London bus with a twenty-pound bomb which had blown him and four innocent people to Kingdom Come. The woman he had lived with had no idea of who that man was. It made no more sense than it had before. He yawned heavily and for the second time in that very long day he was glad that he was not the squad commander.

Shenton listened to the report in silence. Mark Roberts' Hampstead telephone number was no longer valid; he had left the address seven years before. He would have to be traced the hard way.

At the end of Maxwell's recital, Shenton lay back in his chair and looked at the ceiling of his office. "We're jumping through hoops."

"Sir?"

"Someone is setting up hoops for us to jump through. We need a short cut to the man that Baldry went to see in Leicester."

"It could be anyone, sir."

"Not anyone. It was someone who knew Baldry or knew a lot about him, including where he lived. Until he got that letter, Baldry never even told the woman he was living with that he had been in the SAS. That was what shook Baldry, that someone knew about him; he brooded on it all day."

"The IRA wouldn't write him a letter, sir."

"Whoever did write it wanted something from Baldry himself, either information or something they wanted him to do; he came back with money and the promise of more. When he went to get it, something went wrong. It's all tied in to his visit to Leicester. If someone had just wanted Baldry dead, they wouldn't have asked him to Leicester and back. Why Leicester of all places? Who would know about Baldry's army service? He was very close-mouthed about it himself."

"Someone who served with him? Another squaddie, but they wouldn't be likely to know where he lived, would they?"

Shenton spread Maxwell's notes across the top of his desk and tapped a pencil from one sheet to the other. "What we need is a talk with your Colonel Black; that's the one man who definitely knows all about Baldry. A lot more than he's told us and it's time he shared it."

"He's not going to like that, sir."

"No," said Shenton, "I'll make sure he doesn't. I'm seeing the commissioner in half an hour. In the meantime try the Leicester police; I'll speak to them if you like; see what they have on their watch list. No, on second thought, do it through the Special Branch: their man up there will know who's interested in ex-army men, particularly ex-SAS."

"We might get something worthwhile from army records," Maxwell said. "We'll have a full run-down of the men he served with later today."

"What about that card he had hidden, Mark Roberts?"

"Roberts lived there with his wife up until '82, but he was often away. He is or was then a writer of some kind, a journalist; he's worked for some well-known papers. But he left that address when he split with his wife. If he's still around he won't be hard to find; I've had a word with the press officer and he's putting out some feelers. We've also logged his NHS number and we've got the Income Tax boys onto it. Something should break soon. I'll get onto this Leicester thing right away."

"But Colonel Black," said Shenton, "first of all."

# Nine

Despite the piercing east wind, Danny Malloy was sweating by the time he reached the long shabby street. He had stopped several times since leaving Willesden Green underground station, in order to check the paper that he carried in his jacket pocket. He had been instructed to memorize the directions and then destroy the paper they were written on, but he had not trusted himself to remember the twists and turns in their correct order. He had not been given the name of the street, only a number.

He came to the final turn and walked slowly down the street, glancing at all the cars parked in the roadway. He could not see anyone in them, but was suspicious of a new-looking van that was on the other side of the road: no one was in the driving seat, but he could not see beyond the driver's cab into the interior of the van itself.

The house with the number he wanted looked run down, and as he paused at the gate there seemed to be a slight movement at one of the upper windows. He walked past the house and then hesitated, and came back again. The only other person in the street was an elderly coloured man, leaning heavily on a walking stick as he made his painful way some fifty yards further up the street. Malloy went through the token front garden and pushed the bell at the side of the battered front door. Heavy shoes thudded on bare boards before the door was opened by a short, wiry man wearing jeans and an open-necked shirt, the sleeves of which had been rolled up to veined biceps. He looked at Malloy with eyes as hard as marbles.

"Is Pat living here?"

"Who wants him?"

"His brother Danny."

The man pulled the door back and looked beyond him into the street; he jerked his head and Malloy stepped through the door. The man shut it behind him. It was a wide hall with a door to the right and a flight of stairs to the left.

"Up," said the man and Malloy started up the stairs with the man a few paces behind him. At the top of the stairs, a small landing turned into another flight and on the second floor this was repeated, but then the stairs ended in a short corridor with three doors. The middle of the three doors was slightly ajar and the man stood back to allow Malloy to enter.

The room was about twenty by fifteen, with two windows looking down into the street. Two camp beds were at opposite ends of the room, with sleeping bags on them. A table and some wooden chairs were in the centre of the room; in the far corner was an old gas stove and, on a shelf by the door, a colour television set. There was no one else in the room and Malloy turned back to the man who had remained in the doorway.

"What's going on?"

"We haven't seen you before."

"But you'll know I was coming. You were told what I look like."

"Down there." The man indicated a chair with a jerk of his head.

Malloy sat down at the table facing the door and the man came forward from the doorway and stood on the other side of the table from him. "Who told you to come?"

"You know who, the commander."

"How did you come?"

"By boat to Liverpool. I got the train down and then straight here; I haven't slept all night."

"You should have been here an hour ago."

"I got here as soon as I could. I had to wait for the train at Liverpool. I came straight through on the underground. I got here as soon as I could."

"Where's your bag?"

"I left it at the station, in the luggage store. What the hell is this; I came to see the team. Who are you?" Malloy got up from the chair and stood six inches taller than the man with the hard eyes.

"You'll sit down," said the man quietly.

The door was pushed open and two more men came quietly into the room. The first was a thick-set man with a ruddy complexion, somewhere in his late twenties; the second a slim, dark boy who looked like some kind of student. They both wore anoraks over their jeans, as if they had just come in from the street. They remained by the door, blocking the only exit.

Malloy slowly sat down again. "Which one of you is Brendan?"

It was the man in shirtsleeves who spoke. "You'll see Brendan if you're the right man."

"How do I do that? I've told you I was sent; what else do you want me to do?"

"Have you no word for us?"

Malloy moistened his lips and spoke very carefully. "I was told to come straight here. I was instructed directly by Fergus, the northern commander. I came over on the boat through Liverpool. I took the train to London and it got in about an hour ago. I dumped my case and came out by underground. I followed the directions to this road. I made sure no one was trailing after me. When I saw the number I had a look around and rang the bell. I was told to ask for Pat: I did that. You let me in." Malloy swallowed on a dry throat. The man in the shirtsleeves turned away from Malloy in contempt and stood at the window to make an abrupt sign with his left hand, then turned away and left the room. Malloy looked after him in some bewilderment. The other two men came over to him. The young dark one smiled shyly and offered his hand. "I'm David." He indicated the second man, "Liam."

"Hello," said Malloy and shook hands with both of them. "And who was that?"

"Sean," said Liam simply.

Other footsteps, heavy and careless, sounded on the stairs. Sean came back into the room, followed by a big man, wide-shouldered and bull-necked, with abundant black curly hair. He made straight for Malloy, holding out his hand. "You're welcome, Danny."

"You must be Brendan."

"We'll sit down." Brendan pulled the chairs out from the table and Malloy sat down opposite him. The stocky man, Liam, also came to sit with them at the table, bringing with him a bottle of Powers whisky and a handful of glasses. The dark boy, David, and the morose Sean settled themselves on the beds. David took a paperback book from the pocket of his anorak and raised his knees so he could rest the book on them; with a lock of hair falling across his forehead he looked like a schoolboy.

"I'm Brendan, all right," said the big man as he poured the whisky, "and you'll have already met our little team, Liam, David and Sean. It's about time we had a visitor; we've been feeling neglected."

Malloy searched through the lining of his jacket until he found the letter—taking his whisky glass in the other hand—and passed it to Brendan. He also brought out his packet of cigarettes and offered them.

Brendan took one and smiled. "Afton's, by God." He ripped open the envelope and read quickly, tossing the sheet to Liam when he had finished with it.

"So, Danny, you've brought us a couple of thousand and want to check our store because Loughran doesn't believe us."

"It's just orders, Brendan, from the South. It didn't come from Fergus. It's the bus thing that's got them puzzled; they can't understand it."

"And me, and the reason you had to be sure to meet me as well as the others was to prove I'm alive, isn't that it?" Brendan smiled easily. "Sure, it's obvious. I read the description of that man on the bus. I can hear Little Pat now: 'sounds like our Brendan off on a lark of his own and after scoring an own goal. So check and double check no matter what they say and this time we'll send our own man.' "

"I didn't hear what was said. I was just told." Malloy tossed off the whisky and looked around the room with curiosity.

"You don't keep it up here?"

"It's within reach; you'll see it all right. We haven't used any since we had a go at the railway." He poured another whisky into Malloy's glass. "We were already to go for the rich bastards around Jermyn Street when the bus went up, so we haven't done a thing for four weeks, just sat around and spent money." He grinned again.

Malloy stood up and took off his jacket, pulling the sweater over his head and then the tee shirt. He peeled the plaster from under his armpit and unwound the strip of cheesecloth from around his chest and stomach. As each spiral came away the money showered down to the floor around him. Liam got up and bent down to collect the handfuls of bank notes. Brendan remained, grinning, at the table.

"Like a bloody cabaret act. Kathleen just dumps it out of her old carrier bag, but maybe next time she'll put on a show and give it to us out of her knickers."

Liam put the bank notes on the table and Brendan patted them into a neat pile before dealing them out, like a round of cards, into four little sub-piles.

"One thing," said Malloy, and became self-conscious under Brendan's sardonic eye. "I was asked to check—to see if you knew anything—"

"About the bus? It wasn't us so we wouldn't know and I can't see it being another unit. Buses with ordinary people aren't our kind of target. And we don't cart sticks around primed. It was an amateur because if it went off without ignition then some idiot's been storing it wrong. All we know is what we've seen in the papers. I thought maybe you were coming over to tell us all about it."

Malloy shook his head. "No one knows; the Army has put out an official denial. The people on that bus were just ordinary working people. Fergus says it wasn't a unit, but whoever it was, the English police will be trying harder than ever."

Brendan nodded. He had finished his distribution of the money, and the first pile he picked up and shoved into an inside pocket of his leather jacket. He nodded towards Liam who took the pile nearest to him. Brendan got up from the table. "We'll show you the stuff."

He went across to the door and waited for Malloy to follow. The only other man to move was Sean, who was off his bed like a cat and came behind Malloy as they all went through the door. Brendan led the way to the stairs and then down to the landing below; he opened the door at the end of the landing and looked in before swinging the door back. It was a bathroom, and with all three of them inside it was very crowded. Sean put the catch on the door and then stood with his back leaning against it.

"You'd better sit while I get to it." Brendan indicated the lavatory seat as he got down on the floor next to the bath. He took a penny from his trouser pocket and used its edge on the top screw of the aluminium trim on the corner of the bath's fascia board. The screw came out very easily, bringing with it the whole of the aluminium strip. Brendan put his thumb under the edge of the board facing the front of the bath and eased it away from its framework. There was a space of some eight inches wide along the side of the bath and lying within it was a long canvas-wrapped parcel which Brendan pulled free and laid on the bathroom floor. He then flattened himself on the floor to reach beneath the bath itself and pulled out a box heavily swathed in sheets of clear plastic.

He unwrapped the plastic sheeting with cautious slowness before unclipping the hinged lid of the box itself. Malloy leaned forward from his seat on the toilet to peer into the box and saw the two neat rolls of brown oiled paper cylinders. "Forty-two sticks." Brendan glanced up at him. "Do you want to count them?"

"You don't keep the detonators with them?"

"Are you kidding? They're down the other end. You want to check them as well?"

"No, of course not. Are the guns here?"

"Right here." Brendan pulled open the canvas wrappings of the first parcel, revealing the body of a Sterling submachine gun and two magazines. "This is the one we use on the toff's restaurants," said Brendan casually. "We haven't used the

Armalite at all so far. We don't want them to know we've got it for sure until we hit them with it, and that means a special target. We've got around two hundred rounds of 9mm and about fifty for the pistols, except me. I'm down to twenty for the magnum."

Malloy cleared his throat. "I'll tell them."

"Yes." Brendan got up from the floor and he was no longer smiling. "That's just what you do, tell them." He nodded to Sean who unbolted the door and looked out onto the landing before signalling that it was clear. "Come on." Brendan took Malloy out to the landing and indicated the stairs.

"Is that it?" Malloy said.

"Why, have you something else?"

"Well . . ." Malloy spread his hands and then let them fall again.

Brendan took him down the stairs and saw him out of the front door before going back up to the first landing to tap on the bathroom door. Sean opened it; the canvas parcel of guns and the box wrapped in plastic were still on the bathroom floor.

"So that's the man," said Sean.

"It's Loughran's man; he picked him. We'll soon know if he's the one."

"It'll be him, the scumbag." Sean spat savagely into the toilet bowl. "He's got the look on him, scared shitless."

Brendan laughed. "He don't look like a hero, but it doesn't mean he's a traitor." He stopped laughing. "We'll know one way or the other very soon." He looked down at the floor. "Take the guns."

"You using all of it?"

Brendan put his hand on Sean's arm. "There's no shortage; the guns are a different matter and besides there's no safe way to store it in the other place. I don't want any accidents. If Malloy's clean we can always lift it later."

Sean thought about it. "All right."

"I'll do it now. You get the guns to the van and make sure the boys wipe their prints off that room."

Brendan let Sean out of the bathroom and locked the door.

Skirting the gelignite on the floor, he reached into the cavity at the far end of the bath and found the second box. Taking out the contents he arranged them in order along the floor: pliers, metal secateurs, insulating tape, batteries, time switches, mercury balance and spring fuses. A flat tin box held the detonators, packed between layers of rock wool. Brendan sat astride the equipment, his back pressed against the door, and deftly wired the sticks into a continuous relay. He used three detonators, wiring them to a single battery, after carefully separating the open leads with clothes pegs. A final check and then plastic sheeting around the whole assembly. He slit the plastic with a razor blade to bring the leads through and pushed the bundle back under the bath. He paused to wipe the sweat from his hands and neck before selecting one of the trembler fuses and fed the leads into its terminals. He clipped home the wires and got down on his belly to gently push the fuse through the plastic sheet so that it angled itself beneath the gelignite. Taking infinite care, he moved it a millimetre at a time until it vanished completely.

He felt round the plastic, checked that the whole bundle had lodged itself under the bottom of the bathtub and took the final step. Hardly daring to breathe, he gently withdrew the locking pin from the fuse and released its spring. Nothing.

Brendan got to his knees and gently repacked the tools and remaining detonators into their box, moved the bath trim back into place and twisted home the chromium screw. Two clipped ends of wire remained on the floor and he put them in his pocket. A final look round, he picked up the box, tucked it under his arm and unlocked the door.

Sean stood on the landing holding his duffle bag. Liam and David were waiting at the head of the stairs.

"All clear?" Brendan asked in an unnecessarily loud voice.

Sean nodded and moved towards the stairs. Brendan followed them down and in the hall he gave Sean the ignition key and stood on the porch and watched them cross the road to the van. He looked up the road and waited for a car to pass before he shut the front door behind him. When he got to the van, Sean was in the driving seat and the other two were already settled into the back. Brendan got into the passenger seat next to Sean and waited until the van moved off before he turned to sit sideways and look over the back of the seat.

"What did you boys think of our friend?"

"Nervous," said Liam. David said nothing.

Brendan turned back with a glance at Sean, who sat poker-faced, and no one else spoke until they had driven the half mile or so through back streets to draw up before a house similar to the one that they had just left. Sean got out and went across the pavement to the door of the house, which he opened with a key. He disappeared inside for a few minutes and then emerged to cross back to the van and put his head through the side window. "The old biddy's out shopping, but it's two rooms up top."

Brendan stayed where he was as the other two clambered from the back of the van past the driver's seat, carrying their luggage with them. "I'll see you Thursday," said Brendan in farewell. "I'll have everything sorted by then."

He moved over into the driving seat, fired the engine and drove off, checking both mirrors as he turned the corner into another side street. He drove for half an hour, moving mostly through minor residential streets and only crossing main roads when it was absolutely necessary. Finally satisfied, he drove into the centre of London, emerging into heavy traffic as he came up the Edgware Road.

An hour after he had dropped Sean and the others, he was moving along Piccadilly, taking Green Park on his right as he approached Piccadilly Circus. He glanced at the Ritz as he came level with it and toyed briefly with a thought which he dismissed almost as soon as it formulated itself in his mind. The one golden rule: always concentrate on the matter in hand.

The traffic was jammed at the Circus and he pulled left at Regent Street; as he came level with Air Street, a car signalled that it was pulling out from one of the meter spaces. Brendan cut the van into the kerb behind it and got out. There was still twenty minutes on the parking meter and he did not bother to feed it. He walked back the way he had driven until he reached the subway entrance into the underground concourse of Piccadilly Station.

He waited impatiently at the rank of telephone boxes and moved in after a couple of giggling teenage girls had finished a shared call. He lit a cigarette to kill the smell of cheap perfume and then stacked tenpenny pieces on the ledge of the coin box as he dialled the number. He glanced at his watch as he did so and blew a smoke ring in satisfaction; his call was falling exactly halfway in the hour that it was timed for. The telephone at the other end rang four times before the receiver was picked up.

"7821." It was Ryder's voice.

Brendan pressed home the first of the coins. "The man called," he said briefly.

"How did it go?"

"He'll do. Made to measure."

"What about the others?" Ryder's voice overrode his.

"They're out of the house; that went all right, but they're getting restless, need putting to work. I'll sort something for them."

"Good," Ryder cut in again, sharply. "Report when it's over." A click and Brendan was left holding a dead receiver. He regained the call tone and dialled his second number; when he was answered he gave his message with deliberate precision and immediately replaced the receiver.

In the small suburban house off the South Circular Road in Dublin, John Ryder was already moving through the hall, car keys in hand. It was unlikely that the Irish Special Branch had known of this particular number and even less likely that they had tapped the call, and even if they had, they would not be able to make much sense of it. But the trouble with Brendan Casey was that he could not stop himself from saying more than he should. If you didn't step on the bastard he'd end up telling you where the team was likely to hit. But enough of that—get the report to Patrick McGlynn that the visit had been made and that the carrier was Loughran's man, picked by Fergus himself; no possible connection with Ryder or any of his team. It was Loughran's man who had gone to London.

# Ten

Shenton sat in the chair at the end of his conference table and watched, without expression, as the men arranged themselves on either side of the table to face him. A muscle twitched in his cheek as the Special Branch chief inspector waited deferentially for his companion, the mysterious Colonel Black, to seat himself first. Colonel Black was difficult to place: the complexion of a man who spent most of his time out of doors—the tweed suit emphasized the impression of a country gentleman—someone who spent his time shooting on an estate in Scotland. But his thin grey hair and trimmed moustache, together with a voice that carried the clipped vowels of an army staff college, gave him the unmistakable air of a man intolerant of argument or dissent.

Shenton shifted slightly in his chair so that he faced him directly and made sure that he caught his eye: an eye so palely grey that it was almost colourless.

"This discussion is confidential and unminuted," Shenton began formally. "It will not be discussed or referred to in any way outside of this room and must be regarded as if it never happened. Its purpose is to clear the air and to enable us to formulate policy; we are treading a thin line here between straightforward police work and security strategy. Colonel?"

"Yes." Black raised his jaw and looked at Shenton down the length of his nose. "I would add that all the information that I have to impart or anything else stated here is covered by the Official Secrets Act and that its disclosure elsewhere could be regarded as treasonable."

Shenton glanced first at the ceiling and then at Detective

Chief Superintendent Maxwell who was staring at Black with a completely blank face. "We know that Baldry was ex-SAS, Colonel."

"He was a sergeant in the Special Air Service, but there is no question of his having any connection with army intelligence or any department of the Secret Intelligence Service. He was a low-ranking soldier, efficient enough at the level he attained, but that is all. He left the army three years ago and, as you presumably know, he became an extremely heavy drinker and generally shiftless. Ten days before he died he paid a visit to Leicester, and I can tell you that he went there at the invitation of a man called Castle. Castle also served in the British army, but earlier than Baldry."

"Do you mean the Castle who recruits mercenaries?"

"I do. Castle is under surveillance, naturally, although none of his activities in this country are in any way illegal. He is meticulous about that; he knows that we would be down on him like a ton of bricks, otherwise. What he engages in abroad is not our affair. Castle contacts discharged soldiers as a matter of routine, a fishing expedition; he needs to know who is available, what sort of shape they are in, whether they would be open to offers: it's the stock-in-trade of his business. Baldry's record, particularly his SAS experience, would have made him of interest to Castle."

I bet, thought Shenton. "Tell me, Colonel, does your information extend to what was discussed between Baldry and Castle?"

"It was a preliminary discussion. Castle confirmed that Baldry's record was first class, but also saw what he had become. He gave Baldry a drink and sounded him out about the possibility of becoming a training officer in an overseas post. Baldry wanted to know if he could take his wife with him; I suppose he meant the Riley woman. Castle told him it depended on where the contract was; it was obvious to him that Baldry was a drunk and he had made up his mind that Baldry was unemployable in any position. He told him that he wanted more up-to-date information on what was available and would get in touch with him again. That is all."

"Did he give Baldry money or explosives?"

"Absolutely not." The clipped tone became biting. "There is no question of Castle supplying Baldry with anything. He gave him fifty pounds to cover his fare and time, but he gave him nothing else, nothing whatsoever. Castle has no place in this enquiry."

Shenton sighed and felt Maxwell's eyes upon him. "I can appreciate that Castle is of value to you, Colonel, and that you are bending over backwards to protect him. I have no wish to fish in muddy waters, but I must have more information. Baldry went to Leicester broke and looking for a job, any kind of job as long as it was a way of cashing in on his military experience. He came back with money and he told Riley that he was going to make a lot more. He went out to complete that deal, and two hours later the bomb he was carrying blew him and four other poor devils to Kingdom Come. I accept that he did not bring that gelignite back with him from Leicester. He was given it here, in London, but he was involved in whatever it was because he went to Leicester. The deal was made there, the connection, the man he saw."

"It was not Castle; I am not going into details, but it was absolutely not Castle."

"His office is bugged?" asked Maxwell drily.

Before Black could reply, Shenton cut back in. "We're not interested in Castle being one of your agents, a valuable one if he keeps you informed of mercenary recruitment and the foreign connections. I accept that the deal was not with Castle; for him to deal personally with guns or explosives would be stupid. But we both know, Colonel, that Baldry made his connection at Leicester, and if it wasn't with Castle then it was with someone else who was up there and who does deal in them. And Castle would know who that was, wouldn't he? So who else would he see, Colonel?"

"I am not at liberty to say."

"That's a pity," said Maxwell.

"I have no further information."

"You have certain privileges, Colonel, and I respect them, but I am conducting a major enquiry into the deaths of five people, the maiming of three others and the likelihood of a terrorist bomber squad about to let loose at any moment. In the course of this unrecorded and privileged conversation we have established that Baldry connected with a man or a group who deal in explosives. Baldry was either carrying for them or was set up by them and I need to know how or why."

"I have nothing to tell you, Commander, and I must remind—"

"A great pity, because, Colonel, if you really have nothing to tell me, then Castle has. I have already spoken to the Leicester police; they know about Castle as well, they keep a file on him. They would have great pleasure in pulling Castle."

"This is a matter of state security, Commander Shenton."

"And I am following a major criminal enquiry, Colonel Black."

A slow exhalation and Black's mouth became a bitter line as he brought his document case up to the table and removed a single file. "Castle had two other visitors that day: Charles Bennett, ex-REME, cashiered for fraud, two other convictions, '62. A drunk and a coward, he left the same day for South Africa; he was going anyway, one jump ahead of a warrant for non-payment of alimony. He wanted Castle to give him an introduction to the South African recruitment office. He was unlucky. Bennett knows nothing about explosives or any kind of fighting."

"And the second man?"

"He has even less connection; no military experience whatsoever, no relevance at all to Castle's mercenary activities."

"But you do have his name?"

"It can be of no possible use to you."

"Surely you can see, Colonel, that if he is a man who has no connection at all, then there can be no harm in allowing me to know who it is. Otherwise, I am sure to wonder, aren't I?"

Black threw Shenton a look that was as friendly as a flame-thrower. "Hans Van Hoeck, a Dutch businessman, import and export. Castle has a completely separate business supplying consumer goods to various parts of Africa. Van Hoeck left for the Continent the same day; he visits this country half a dozen times a year. He is a very respected businessman and has absolutely nothing to do with your enquiry."

Shenton smiled pleasantly. "Thank you very much for your cooperation, Colonel. If anything comes to light during our investigations that is of interest to your office, we shall, of course, keep you fully informed."

Black rose abruptly and left, followed by the Special Branch man who threw them a final glance as he shut the door.

"He could be having us on."

Shenton shook his head. "I don't think so." He opened his own file and pushed a long sheet of concertinaed telex paper along the table, moving his finger down to the chinopencilled paragraphs. "Castle's first visitor was tall, around six feet two or three, long grey hair, about fifty years of age, arrived by taxi. That was Bennett. He was with Castle less than twenty minutes. The next came at eleven forty-five, a slim man of middle height, dark hair, greying at the temples, very well dressed, arrived by hired car. He was in Castle's office around half an hour, came out with Castle who saw him into the pub next door. Castle went back into his office and the third man came over the road. His description is of a man in his forties, slightly under six feet, five eleven or so, very heavily built, dark hair, dressed as a workman. That could only be Baldry."

"Where did all this come from?"

"It isn't only Black who wants to know what Castle is getting up to. The locals keep a sighting log and the head of the CID up there doesn't like secret units any more than I do."

"You didn't need to screw Black at all."

"Baldry was with Castle fifteen minutes; then they both came out again and went into the pub. Castle went back to his office at one-fifty."

"What about Baldry?"

Shenton shook his head. "They were watching Castle. There wouldn't be enough manpower to check everyone who called in."

"Photographs?"

"A bit difficult; they smudge everyone going anywhere near

Castle as a matter of course, but they go straight to the Special Branch."

Maxwell shrugged. "It would only tell us what we know; it must have been Baldry. Nice to have it in black-and-white, though."

"What about the other visitors?"

Maxwell looked startled. "Bennett?"

"The Dutchman." Shenton tapped the third marked paragraph on the telex roll. "Castle took Baldry into the pub and left him there; the Dutchman was there already, right? When Castle went back to his office the other two were still in the pub."

"They arrived separately, it means Castle connected them. Do you think that Black . . ."

"I don't think anything. All we've got is that Baldry connected in Leicester. He went into a pub with Castle and stayed there. All we know is that the Dutchman was in the same pub; a Dutchman the colonel insists has nothing to do with this case. I don't like being told what to think, so we'll leave the James Bonds out of it. This is a police enquiry and that means that we check everyone Baldry met or could have met in Leicester."

"Do we pull Castle?"

"We go through channels; the Leicester boys know their job. They've got the number of that hire car and before long they'll know if the Dutchman left Leicester and if so, when. We'll have a CRO on Bennett; he'll be easy to run down."

"But what about Castle?"

"You fancy him?"

"More and more I like him; he's in the market for gunmen and bombers, bloody psychopaths most of them; he's probably one himself."

"Let's see what we get on the others first."

"I'll run out Bennett." Maxwell moved towards the door and then back again. "Black didn't like any of it, did he?"

"Neither did I," said Shenton, and returned to studying the telex message.

# Eleven

The men who approached Malloy in the buffet bar in Liverpool Street Station gave him a moment's panic. The elder, by ten years or so, was a heavy-jowled man with a thick head of grey hair and a massive body on short legs. The second was over six feet tall, with small eyes and a hooked nose; both wore black raincoats.

They stood close to Malloy at the far end of the bar, where it adjoined the back wall. "Mr Malloy?" asked the older man.

The taller man had pushed himself against Malloy on the open side of the bar. When Malloy tried to move away, a bony elbow caught him hard under the ribs.

"It is Danny Malloy?"

"And who the hell are you?"

"Police officers." The older man looked around the rest of the bar before negligently flashing a small folder in front of Malloy's face. "Detective Sergeant Smith." He smiled. "Relax, Mr Malloy, we're your contact." A nod to hook-nose. "Get the drinks in, John; I'll have a gin." The elbow was removed from Malloy's side and the tall man went up to the bar.

"Let's sit down, Danny." Smith indicated a small table at the back wall and Malloy allowed himself to be led over to it. Smith put himself facing the rest of the bar. Malloy sat down on the opposite side of a plastic table littered with crumbs, wrappers, beer slops and a filthy ashtray. "Paddy Two, isn't that right? I'm your control in London, Danny. Time for a chat."

"Here?"

"Why not? It's better than the shop. You could well be seen

there, son; we have to be careful. Here it's just a couple of blokes having a drink. You got off the boat this morning."

Malloy nodded.

"You were clocked through Liverpool, Danny, and on to the train, so we'll leave all that for the time being. What happened when you reached London?"

"I went straight to the house. I saw three men and then another one came in, the boss; he said his name was Brendan. I gave them the money and then I was taken down to see the equipment, on the floor below, in the bathroom. They had it behind the bath panel, a Sterling and an Armalite. They said they'd never used the Sterling. Then there was gelignite, forty-two sticks. Then they told me that was it. I came back; all I've done since then is walk around. My bag is still at Euston."

"You've done very well, Danny." Smith drained his glass of gin and tonic and then hooked out the slice of lemon and sucked it reflectively. "What did they look like?"

"The boss, Brendan, was a big man with black hair. The others were younger, their names were Sean and Liam; Liam didn't say much, a fat man. The fourth one, David, didn't say anything at all. He's the youngest, with long hair, very dark; he can't be more than twenty. All he did was read a book."

"Now you said Brendan came in after the others; does he live there with the team?"

"I don't know. There were a couple of beds in the room. Brendan came from outside the house after I arrived. The other one, Sean, went down to the street door to let him in."

"When do you go back?"

"I don't. I was to help out if they wanted me to, but they told me to go back, to leave. I've got no way of making contact with them now."

"You can go back to the house."

"I can't do that. They'd know there was something up if I went back."

"This doesn't make much sense, Danny Boy; they wouldn't fetch you all across the water just to hand over some money, not just for that."

"I know, it's funny, like some kind of test. I walked around after I left them in case they were following me."

"Maybe they're just keeping you on ice, waiting for the big one. They'll contact you when they're ready."

"They don't know where I am."

"Who do you report to, Danny?"

"Back in Ulster I'd report to any of Loughran's men. Most times it's just go back to the room and wait."

"So the thing to do is to see what turns up. Get down to Kilburn and put yourself around the pubs; you've got a great entry there. Make contact with the right people and ask them to send the message for you, that you've delivered and are waiting for orders. That should get you in big with the locals. No matter how they check you out, you'll come up smelling of roses."

"I don't want to do any more. I've kept my part of the bargain. I came over and made contact. I was told by Major Flint that when the time came I could come over here, I'd be given a new identity . . ."

"You'll be looked after, Danny; once you're our agent you're on the right side. You can't go wrong, son. But you haven't delivered anything, have you? I mean, all we've got so far is four blokes in a room in Willesden. They could be bombers, but it could be a take on, couldn't it? If we pick them up we have to take a chance on what they've got . . ."

"You can't pick them up. If you do that they'll know it was me."

"So we need to take them on the job, when they're all tooled up, but that could take a long time, Danny; far better that you should be on the inside telling us when. That makes it a lot more certain. We could get the lot if you were on the inside: Brendan the boss, all the contacts. You could do a great job for us, Danny, and it wouldn't be forgotten."

"I can't go back there."

"You think about it, son . . . here . . ." Smith put his hand into his breast pocket and slid a thin sheaf of notes across the table. "You fix yourself a room and wait for a contact. It won't be long in coming; they'll not have told you half of it yet.

You've got the paper with the instructions for getting to the house?"

"You can't go there."

"Of course not, but I'll need it for the report, won't I? We've got to keep an eye on it. It's the only thing we're getting that proves any of this, isn't that right?"

Malloy produced the paper reluctantly. "So long as you promise . . . if they're raided . . ."

"Relax, son, relax, we're not amateurs." Smith glanced at the paper and shoved it into his side pocket. "You're a bit nervy, very understandable; I know what the beer boat run's like. You need a bit of kip; get yourself a room round Kilburn and wait for a contact. Give me a call tonight if anything's up; otherwise in the morning round about ten." He took out his notecase and produced a card. "Bell me on that number; if I'm not there then leave a time and number where I can contact you. Don't go near the shop. Just keep your head on, son, you'll be all right."

Malloy got up and for a moment towered over the littered table. "Major Flint . . ."

Smith flipped a negligent hand. "I'll make sure a copy of my report gets through to the brown stuff. You go pick up your bag."

Malloy looked as though he wanted to say something else, but after a moment he turned and walked out. Smith watched him out of sight before he took the piece of paper out of his pocket and spread it flat on the table. "This could do us a bit of good. What about our friend, John?"

"A lot of nothing."

Smith pushed his glass across the table and produced a five-pound note. "Get me a gin."

"How much did you give him?"

"Twenty-five. You can countersign me."

"Oh yeah."

"And then we'll put it to the heavy mob; can't be bad, taking a real group of bombers. Be a good one that."

John got up, taking the five-pound note.

# Twelve

Brendan drove his car through the heaviest of the traffic moving out of the City, making good time since he was going against the stream of commuters. The traffic clogged up most of the roundabouts, but the closer he came to East London the better time he made until, at last, he reached the clearway and moved easily, pulling the car onto the ramp that led up to the forecourt of the flats. He parked on the end of the line, closest to the road, backing the car into its space so that if he needed it in a hurry he could make the road in a matter of seconds.

A light rain sprang up as he crossed to the entrance hall of the flats. A few other men were moving across the car park, working men in anoraks and duffle coats, some with cement on their boots, one or two with tool bags. The lift smelt of urine; no one spoke to anyone else and all the others had left the lift so that Brendan was the only passenger by the time it got to the fourteenth floor. The corridor was empty, but he stopped short when he saw the battered door of the Greens' flat: the splintered door-jamb hung forward and several planks had been nailed across the door. Although he had his key in his hand, he put it back in his pocket and then pressed the bellpush of his flat, holding his hand inside his leather jacket as he did so.

The girl opened the front door on the security chain. When she saw who it was she slipped the chain.

"What's been going on?" he asked.

She shut the front door behind him and led the way through to the living room. He noticed that she had changed into a denim skirt and yellow sweater.

"As well that you didn't get here earlier; the place has been crawling with police."

"What's happened?"

"Next door." She sat at a chair by the table and picked up a smouldering cigarette from the full ashtray. "That little man killed himself this morning; he killed his little boy and then himself. The police smashed the door in: a Special Patrol Group, CID, the lot. A real circus."

Brendan relaxed. "Did he do his wife?"

"She'd left him. They thought that was why he did it."

"Who thought?"

"The police . . . the sergeant said so, while he was using the phone."

"This phone?"

"He wanted a phone, so he asked me. I couldn't do anything about it."

"I don't like that."

"Nor did I. What did Ryder say, Brendan?"

"Nothing." He moved to the sideboard and opened one of the cupboards to take out a bottle of Jamesons.

"He must have said something."

"Well, then, maybe he did." He opened the whisky bottle and put it to his mouth to take a small swallow, put the bottle on the table and slipped off his leather jacket. The pale blue shirt was held tight across the heavy shoulders by the cross strap of his shoulder holster. The holster itself hung low under his left armpit, sagging under the weight of his revolver. He unclipped the cross strap and allowed the revolver to swing from his shoulder. "What did the police say, exactly?"

"He asked to look out from the back balcony, to see if he could see into the next flat. Then he telephoned a police station for help. They arrived and smashed the door in. Then he came back for the telephone again. It was a couple of hours before they all cleared off. Only the one came in here, a sergeant, he said, just the ordinary police."

"Twice he came." Brendan got himself a glass from the sideboard and sat down at the table to pour himself a whisky.

He looked at her reflectively as he sipped it. "He'll really know what you look like."

"If he needs to."

"Yes," he said, and poured another whisky. "We had our visit; not Kathleen, an old friend of yours, it was; Malloy."

"Who?"

"You haven't forgotten Danny Malloy. Don't lie to me now."

"I remember the Malloy who came to Holland," she said. "I saw him twice: tall, stupid. There was nothing special about him. What was he doing over here? I thought he went back south, something about his wife."

"Wrong in the head; he left her with her mother. Danny Malloy." He grinned suddenly and the whisky caught at the back of his throat; he coughed, choked and then scowled. "He was sent by Loughran to check up on us, to see the article."

"If he was sent to check your explosives it looks like they're still wondering about that bus, doesn't it?"

"Does it? They won't be now then, will they? He counted the sticks and all. So it's all right then, isn't it?"

"Is it?"

"What does that mean?"

"Malloy isn't the man to send on a check-up; he'd believe anything he was told," she said. "Now Kathleen . . . whose idea was it for Malloy to come on this trip, Brendan?"

"He's Loughran's man."

"Loughran doesn't run you; there's something you're not telling me. I don't like being taken for a fool, Brendan. It's a mistake to do that to me. I'm going back."

"You'll go when I say."

"This isn't my work. I'm doing nothing here. Less than nothing, intelligence work . . . you tell me less than you tell that unit of yours. If I'm the intelligence officer, why is it that I never speak to Ryder? What information do you ever give me to evaluate? It's time to go back."

He poured more whisky. "Where to?"

"Anywhere—what do you care?"

"Maybe I care a lot." He reached across the table and grasped her wrist. "We're on the same side; we've got enough battles to fight without fighting each other. You're a fine woman, Maureen."

"Take your hand off me." She looked him in the eye. "I'm not some poor bitch out of the Bogside ready to fall on my back because the big bully boy's arrived."

He withdrew his hand and threw off the whisky, picked up the bottle and poured some more into his glass, carelessly, slopping whisky over the rim. His mouth had set and the eyes became vicious; only his voice retained an easy note. "Aren't you the sharp-tongued bitch. Maybe it's your time of the month; takes people funny old ways. Where is it you want to be off to, Maureen?"

"God knows—I haven't seen my family for two years, but what good am I doing here? I was sent to be the intelligence officer, choose targets, coordinate the service units, assess reaction . . . and what the hell have I done? I don't even get to speak to Ryder. I don't see the units; all I see is you. Just tell me what the point is of my being here, Brendan."

He sipped his whisky while she spoke, and after it, until his glass was again empty. His eyes were becoming cloudy and red-rimmed. The liquor was having its usual effect, flushing his cheeks and untying the knot in his stomach. "I didn't send you, Ryder did, and you're under orders like all of us. When you're needed you'll be needed in a hurry; in the meantime you cover. How many men do you think are clocked? A man with his wife, now, that's different; and wasn't it you yourself who worked that out? When you were in Amsterdam working the supply line with Long John. Wasn't it a good idea then to go along as cover?"

"He was my husband and I did a sight more than give him cover. Anybody can do that. Don't tell me you're hard up for company."

The phone rang and they sat in silence, counting its rings: three times and then cut off. They sat without speaking, both heads turned towards the telephone and then almost immediately it started again. Brendan got up from the table and picked up the telephone on its fourth ring. He turned away from the woman and she watched his back stiffen. She could not hear what he mumbled into the receiver and then he put the telephone back on its rest and turned to look at her. He looked at her all the time it took him to come back to the table and get back on his chair; as he did so, his left hip hit the table edge and almost upset the whisky bottle, but he caught it before it spilled and automatically refilled his glass.

# Thirteen

The Special Branch inspector who rang the bell of 275 Prentice Street held a clipboard, and the sergeant behind him carried a surveyor's tape measure. The door was opened by a squat man with enormous shoulders and a large bald head. His eyes were small in proportion to his head and he was still chewing on a mouthful of food.

The inspector looked as deferential as he could and flashed the photostated copy of a building inspection notice. "Mr Kycinczi? We are carrying out a general survey of all boarding houses where current regulations apply, all small hotels and registered guest houses. We have to compile a list in case of fire."

"Vot fire?" Kycinczi swallowed whatever he had in his mouth and rubbed the back of his hand across his lips.

"In case there is a fire; the number of people in each house so that the Fire Brigade will know how many there should be. Perhaps you could go through the names with me while my colleague checks the egress—escape points." He manoeuvred Kycinczi around in the hallway and the sergeant slipped behind him and had reached the stairs before he could be intercepted by the fat woman with startling yellow hair who had now emerged into the hall.

"What is it, Bula?"

"Madam," the inspector included her in the conversation with a flip of his clipboard, "it's a building regulation matter."

The sergeant had already reached the second landing, moving quietly and very fast, pausing briefly before each door before passing on. The third flight of stairs he took with extra care, using the outside edge of the treads to avoid the possibility of a warning creak. The two doors on the top landing were both shut, and after listening outside each, he took a sonic pad from his pocket, placing it in turn on each door frame. Not only no sound of occupancy, but not the minutest vibration: nothing at all, negative.

He returned swiftly to the second floor. The information said that the middle door led to the communal bathroom. He tried the door handle. The room was empty; he found the light switch, shut the door behind him and slipped the catch. Grubby walls, worn enamel bath, stained toilet. He ran his eyes along the bath trim and at once saw the scratches around the head of the corner chromium screw. He knelt down, took the Minox camera from inside his jacket; two general shots of the bath, close-up of the trim. The screw came loose under finger pressure.

He pulled away the fascia board and crouched down on all fours. The plastic-wrapped bundle was obvious, but the guns must have been moved, probably out on a job. He used the Minox to photograph the box from three different angles and then glanced at his watch. They had been in the house for five minutes and he had been in the bathroom a little more than two. The important message to get back was that the guns were on the streets now and maybe they had taken some of the explosives as well.

He put the Minox completely to hand and touched the lid of the box with his left forefinger. It would not move because of the lack of clearance under the bath. He pulled it forward a few inches and in the microsecond between the tremble-spring operating and the detonation, knew that he had made a terrible mistake.

The inspector who had come up the stairs to tell him that according to the landlord the top floor was clear of tenants, saw the explosion blow out the bathroom door. Large chunks of plaster cracked and fell from the wall as most of the ceiling came down. The inspector made an instinctive movement backwards on the top step, tried to recover, but his balance had gone at the same moment as his eardrums ruptured. He went head first into the wall bordering the staircase and then down onto the first landing.

It was Mrs Kycinczi who called the Fire Brigade.

# Fourteen

"Has something happened?"

He raised the glass and looked at her over its rim. "The house got raided."

She stared at him. "They caught them?"

He held the glass between his hands and stared hard and long at her. "The boys were away. I moved them as soon as your friend Malloy left."

"He's not my friend . . . how many times do I have to . . ."

"It was Malloy, all right. As soon as he leaves the house he informs. I bet he ran all the way."

"Well, so long as the boys got away. Did they get anything else, did they . . . ?"

"The guns were away; they got the explosives . . ."

"Are you sure, how . . . ?"

"I'm sure. Sean saw it go up from the end of the road. All the windows came out of the house, police everywhere, a few ambulances as well. They must have gone in heavy-footed."

She lit a cigarette and looked back at him across the table. "You set it up? Oh, very good, Brendan, that solves all your problems in one. No one can count the sticks now, can they?"

"Malloy counted them."

"He wouldn't know what he was looking at."

"He must have done; they went up after the police went in."

"You're playing games, Brendan. I don't know how or why, but I know it's going on, and I know it's got nothing to do with what I'm supposed to be here for. It looks as if Malloy's the leak, the police come the same day as he goes to the house—what else could it be?—too much of a coincidence. He'll run, of course, and either be taken or live the rest of his time shivering, waiting for it. You're still playing some game and I don't like not knowing what's going on, but I'm glad the boys got away."

He laughed. "And you being glad makes it all right, does it, you tricky bitch."

"Look, Brendan, if there's something to say, then for Christ's sake come out and say it, because I'm not wasting any more time. I want to speak to Ryder direct. I either want to be attached to another unit or go back."

"I'm the link with Ryder. You know the rules. One cell, one contact. One man whose word can be relied on."

"Who the hell do you think you're talking to? My husband . . ."

"Oh, sure now, I thought we'd get around to him. The holy streak of bog piss himself . . ."

"Keep your filthy tongue to yourself. He was a better . . ."

"Man? Was he now—a hero maybe—the great speechmaker who came down from his fine university and condescended to do our thinking for us."

"He was an idealist, you pig!" Pushing herself forward, she spat in his face and jumped up from the table to run past him. But too slowly, for his right hand caught the side of her face and knocked her against the sideboard. When she tried to get to her feet he held her down easily with his knee, and then he caught her wrists and pulled her to her feet, slamming her against the wall. She tried to bite him, but he knocked the breath from her body with a savage knee into her stomach and then inexorably forced her arms up past her body and held her wrists flat against the wall on either side of her head.

His head came close and his breath was horrible. She ducked her head and tried to wriggle free, but he pushed his bulky body hard against her and she was completely helpless.

"A hero? You lying, treacherous bitch. He was a traitor, he died a traitor, like a dog, shot down by the men he betrayed. I've been laughing every time you've come out with that crap.

He wasn't shot by the Brits, he was shot by us. He fooled a lot of people, but never Little Pat."

"Pat?" It came out as a croak.

He put his total weight against her, crushing her ribcage hard into her chest until she felt she would faint. The cramps in her arms were crippling.

"We took him from the car as soon as it cleared the border and gave him a court-martial. He talked at us, Jesus, did he talk, but it didn't make a fart's difference. He was guilty and we shot him and now he lies with all the other canting bastards. The Brits didn't come until we shot him and they didn't hit fuck all. Oh, sure, we said it was them. He was a hero all right; it was our bullets that made him a hero."

Agonising though the pain was, she was engraving into her memory the words and the tone and the depth of his voice. She did not question what he said, she instinctively knew he was telling her the truth. She should have guessed it before. They had shot him all right, but instead of burying him in that field with the others—the money men, the embezzlers and the northern commander accused of treason; the deaths kept secret rather than bring a further slur on the Provo image—his death had been used for propaganda. A paper hero. Of course it was true, there had been so many signs. But brave as he had been and as perceptive as she knew herself to be, she had accepted their story. Why? Because she had wanted to. She had fooled herself, she had done it herself, had never, ever allowed herself to believe what the British said was true, even a remote possibility.

She looked up into his blood-gorged eyes and suddenly he jerked her away from the wall and pulled her with him back to the table. Releasing her left wrist, he used his own left hand to pick up the whisky bottle to refill his glass. He forced her right wrist down to the edge of the table as he picked up the glass. Her knees gave way and she was forced down, half kneeling, half crouching at the side of the table. He turned his face towards her and grinned. She raised her left hand from his forearm, where it was pushing uselessly in an effort to release her right wrist, and thrust it over his shoulder to jerk the glass upwards, throwing the whisky up into his face. He released her and jumped to his feet, sending his chair onto its back; the table lifted on his thighs, rising eight inches from the floor before it dropped down again. The whisky bottle fell over and rolled off the table onto the floor.

Maureen was already out of the room and into the hall, snatching her raincoat from a peg; at the door she pulled the latch, but the chain was on. The door only opened six inches and then a fist hit her hard in the centre of the back, sending her hard into the door. She was on the floor, pulling her head down as far as she could to her knees, terrified that he would kick her, but instead he stooped to pick her up, his fingers digging hard into the flesh of her upper arms. Lifting her clear of the floor, he swung her down the hall, raised his right foot to flick down the handle of the bedroom door and then man-handled her through it. She became less inert when they went across the bedroom threshold, twisting her neck to get her teeth down to his hands and kicking wildly backwards. But she was swinging in mid-air again, and for the first time she had the sickening, staring realisation of his exceptional phys-ical strength.

He flung her at the bed with a force that sent her across it and beyond to collide with the wall, and she fell to the floor. The upper part of her arms were numbed. She got to her hands and knees and managed to pull herself to the edge of the bed. Brendan had switched on the light and was in the act of slip-ping the strap of his shoulder holster down his left arm. His hair was loose across his forehead and there was a film of sweat across his cheeks and nose. The whites of his eyes were bloodshot and he looked mad.

"Brendan," she said, "look . . ."

"Get up." He came round the bed and caught the back of her yellow sweater, pulling it half over her face.

She got up and nearly fell down again; her legs had no strength in them and when she put out her hands in weak protest, she could not control their shaking. A shove: the side of the bed hit her legs and she was falling again, sideways across the bed. He came to the head of the bed and slipped the straps of the shoulder holster over the corner of the bedhead. Her eyes were half-closed as she pulled herself painfully to a sitting position. He was standing level with her and she watched his hands as they moved to the belt of his trousers. Now, she thought, now! As he pulled the buckle of his trouser belt free, she twisted round and threw herself towards the revolver swinging in its holster at the bedhead. Her fingers brushed the saddle stitching at the edge of the holster opening before she was pulled backwards, the front of her yellow sweater biting into her windpipe as he wrenched the back of its neck. Deliberately, he pulled the top part of her body erect with his left hand, hunched his shoulders and punched her hard in the left side of the face.

The pain was excruciating and she fell back on the bed. This could not be happening to her, it just could not be happening. She tried to open her eyes; something went wrong with the left one and the right one was clouded with tears. Rolling a little to the left, she decided to simulate unconsciousness, screwed her eye to clear its moisture and hooded its lid. He was up by the head of the bed and out of her view. She glanced towards the door, which was open: the light was still on in the hall, the hall carpet scuffed. The left side of her face was stiffening and she had an almost irresistible impulse to put her hands up to her head to nurse her injuries. A wave of nausea came chokingly up from the back of her throat.

He was moving again, along the side of the bed; her eye was level with the upper part of his thighs, and as he came into view she saw that he was naked from the waist down, his penis arcing away from his scrotum. The thought came into her head that it was precisely the shape of the old lead water pipe that had stood over the rainbarrel in the back of her grandmother's cottage in Wicklow.

He was bending over her now and she closed her eyes, letting her mouth slacken. His hands were upon her, moving her head—she let it loll—and then across her face; moving down her body, fumbling across her breasts. She moaned as if in her sleep and moved slightly.

"Open your eyes." His hands were moving down her legs

to the hem of her skirt. "You're not out, you lying bitch; open your eyes or I will."

When she looked he was still standing over her, and then he bent down and slapped her heavily across the face. "Move," he said.

She did not move and he bunched the front of her sweater to pull her over, her head forward, and that hurt so much that she could not play dumb any longer. "Please, Brendan, for Christ's sake. I can't move."

"You'll move." He was pulling her sweater over her head now and it was half smothering her; her arms, caught in the sleeves, were wrenched above her head, then they were free and she fell back.

"Let me up, Brendan, I can't see. I've got my contact lenses in, the left one is . . ."

"Shut up." His fingers were poking at her again, and she shuddered.

"I'll do it myself."

"Yeah."

She had difficulty in finding the catch of her bra behind her back, but then it was gone and she fought the impulse to put her hands across her breasts.

"And the rest."

She forced herself upright again, against the pain in her arms and her head. It's not real, she told herself, it isn't really happening. Ignore it, survive, just concentrate on surviving. He had moved to the foot of the bed with his knee against its edge. Too far to kick; no good to kick, he would kill her the next time. Too big and too heavy. She unzipped the crumpled denim skirt and worked it down her legs, too slowly for him: when it was at her knees he pulled it out from under her and tossed it on the floor. She rolled down the top pair of panties and then the tights which he again tore away when they were at her ankles.

She took a deep breath and closed her eyes as she put her hands on the bikini briefs that she wore next to her skin. She felt him come onto the bed and then his hands were on her thighs, forcing her legs upwards. He tore the briefs off as he forced his body between her legs.

She felt herself blacking out and then heard the whimper—was that her? She felt a surge of self-hatred. Give the bastard nothing, nothing at all. Be like a stone: hate him, hate him. Concentrate on hating him; hate will get you through.

She did not know how long he was on her, his hands on her shoulders forcing her down, his body flattening her, crushing her ribs so that she could not breathe except in shallow gasps. He was grunting and sweating, using her savagely; she felt as though she was being split in two. He stopped but still lay on her; then he moved down her body. Oh God, he hadn't finished; she screwed her eyes tightly shut as his teeth sank into her breast. Jesus, oh sweet Jesus, the tears came despite her resolve.

He rolled off her and sat on the edge of the bed. She opened her eye and could see only the rounded bulk of his back as he bent forward to search for something on the floor. The pale flesh covered by its film of sweat, the pale blue shirt rucked to the shoulders and the line of repellent hair down the curve of the spine. He was between her and the head of the bed; then he moved sideways and she saw that he had picked up his trousers and was taking his packet of cigarettes from the pocket.

Slowly, painfully, she moved to the side of the bed away from him, had to use her hands to position her legs over the edge and onto the floor. It took considerable effort for her to stand upright and she would have fallen if she had not been able to support herself against the wall. She was unable to see anything from her left eye, and she put her fingers to the eyelid in an effort to move the contact lens that was caught so painfully on the inner lid. She heard Brendan moving on the bed, and when she got to the end of the wall, by the door, she turned her head completely round to look at him. He was lying full length on the bed, watching her, one elbow supporting the hand that was propped to the side of his head. The other hand held a cigarette and he blew the smoke at her.

"Bring the drink back with you."

"I . . . I . . ." Even her vocal chords would not work properly.

"You heard, unless you want to run again. You're not dressed for it."

". . . bathroom . . ." She held on to the edge of the door for support.

"You'd better have that bottle when you come back, Maureen."

# Fifteen

Shenton was in the process of putting on his topcoat at the end of a very long day when Maxwell knocked and entered in one smooth manoeuvre.

"I'm sorry, sir, I . . ."

"What is it?"

"Bennett took the plane to South Africa, at quarter past ten, on the twenty-first, just about at the same time as his wife was making an application for his arrest for non-payment at the High Court. He landed in Jo'burg around midnight their time. The South Africans have confirmed that he is still out there, being interviewed by immigration control, they say; BOSS, probably. The only other thing about him is that he has a lump of money with him, in English currency, God knows where from; sold up everything here, I suppose. That's all on him."

"The Dutchman?" Shenton asked.

"Nothing much. Interpol have confirmed that there is a Hans Van Hoeck, aged forty-two, executive director of—can't pronounce it—import/export firm with offices in Amsterdam; travels frequently in Western Europe, the Middle East and Africa. He is also in the transportation and procurement business—funny word that; all it means here is that if a customer wants a particular commodity, then Van Hoeck's company finds a supplier and arranges its purchase as well as transportation. Complete service. He's a Dutch national who went to America when he was twenty-one and returned eight years ago to set up the firm. It's a private company; its accounts are not published."

Shenton sat on the edge of his desk. "Get a message to the

Dutch direct. Say 'Have reason to believe Van Hoeck engaged in illegal arms shipments, destination unknown. Appreciate confidential evaluation.' "

Maxwell had wide eyes. "Do we?"

"I do."

"What signature shall I put on it?"

"Mine, as Anti-Terrorist Squad Commander; ought to look good in Dutch."

# Sixteen

Maureen had to hold her hands against the walls of the hallway to keep herself erect as she made her painful way to the bathroom. The contact lens in her left eye had caught on the edge of the upper lid. She groped her way to the bathroom and carefully filled the handbasin with cold water; when it was full she turned off the tap and lowered her head into the water. She brought her face clear of the water again and carefully lifted the lid of her left eye with the second finger of her right hand: the lens came out and immediately the knifelike pain ceased, but she still could not see because of the streaming tears.

She remained bent over the handbasin, dabbing cold water into her face with the ends of her fingers and her vision returned. She looked into the water and saw the little disc showing greyly in the bottom of the handbasin. Opening up the medicine cabinet, she took out the bottle of cleansing fluid and her lens case. She swirled the water in the handbasin to lift the lens away from the bottom by its current and then cupped her hand to fish it out. She cleansed it thoroughly by rubbing the fluid lightly between the pads on the tips of her thumb and forefinger. Then she put it into the lens container and, bending again over the handbasin, used her left hand to pop the lens from her right eye, put that through the cleansing ritual and again into the lens container, finally filling the whole container with cleansing fluid and clipping shut the cover.

She leaned over the handbasin and splashed the water up again into her face and then her breasts, pressing her hands hard into her flesh to wipe away the sensation of Brendan's hands and teeth. She wiped the rest of her body with a towel from the side of the bath and then the clouded mirror of the cabinet to examine her face. The punch she had taken at the left side of her face had raised the flesh above the cheekbone, and the inflammation was turning purple. Her dark hair was sweat-soaked across the whole of the hairline.

She dropped the wet towel onto the bathroom floor and opened up the airing cupboard to take out a clean one. She became conscious of the pain between her legs; bruised finger marks were raised on the soft flesh of her inner thighs. She wrapped the dry towel around her middle and went out into the corridor in a cold fury. Brendan was leaning against the side of the bedroom door frame.

"Where's that drink?"

"I'm just getting it."

"You'd better." He went back into the bedroom.

She stood looking after him and then went back into the bathroom and opened up the cabinet. His razor was on the lower shelf in a clear plastic case: a black-handled twist razor with a blade dispenser. She opened up the dispenser and took the first blade, unwrapping the waxed paper; it was double-edged and awkward to hold, but she took it with her. She went out again into the hall as quietly as she could, and then through the sitting room and into the kitchen. She opened up the drawer next to the cooker: knives, but round-edged and not very sharp. She tried the vegetable knife, a steak knife with a serrated edge; the steak fork with its three sharp prongs was better.

The thought came to her suddenly, and she knew she was a stupid bitch not to have thought of it before: she opened the drawer under the sink and pulled out the heavy canvas bag. She shivered on the plastic-tiled floor and the razor blade cut through the first fibres easily enough, but then stuck. She pulled it away and made the angle more acute so that only the corner was cutting into the canvas. The blade bent sideways, her fingers ached, but then she had a hold and it was easier. She sawed away until she had a line some ten inches long before the blade broke. She tore at the canvas, oiled paper and a tin box.

She managed to get the box clear; it was sealed with Scotch tape. She almost wept with frustration and then her hand felt the package: odd-shaped, heavy and wrapped in cloth. She pulled it through the opening, bending her wrist double in the process. It was wound around with twine, which she cut with the broken edge of the razor blade. Her fingers were trembling, not only with the effort that she had put into cutting the bag open. Inside the cloth was an automatic pistol. She angled it up to the light: Sturm Ruger .22. At the bottom of the bag was a smaller parcel, two empty magazines and two cardboard boxes of cartridges.

She got up from the floor, leaving the bag where it was and ducked her head into the living room. No sound. Her fingers trembled as she opened one of the cardboard boxes and spilled loose the tightly packed little cartridges. They were greasy and she dropped several. It had been a long time since she had handled a gun, and she forced herself to take things slowly: in under the magazine lip, push down on the spring. It was a long magazine, but she stopped after the fifth cartridge; some memory from the past . . . what was it? An overloaded magazine can jam the slide.

She pushed home the magazine into the butt of the pistol and heard the click as the catch engaged. She pulled the toggles at the end of the sliding jacket: nothing . . . hell, take it easy, take it easy. She pressed down the safety and the jacket shot home, half-pulled the slide back again and saw that the first cartridge was seated in the chamber; check again that the safety had not ridden up. Now, you bastard!

On her way back through the living room she saw the half-full whisky bottle on the floor and picked it up. In the hallway she hesitated and then unloosed the towel that was around her waist. She put it over her right arm, draping down over her hand and the pistol. I might shake . . . I have to get close . . . as close as possible. She held the whisky bottle in her left hand. Her right she brought back again across her body.

Brendan looked up at her as she came into the bedroom and

then grinned sardonically. He was on the bed, lying on his back, with his hands cupping the back of his head. He had not bothered to pull down the shirt that had ridden above the thick pelt of hair across his chest. He was still naked apart from his shirt and socks. She watched his eyes move down to the centre of her body.

"You're learning," he said.

She came closer to the bed and took her arm away from her body; he sat up and reached out for the bottle. She moved back a little.

"Does Ryder know, Brendan?"

His grin turned to a scowl. "Shut your fucking face. You think Ryder cares? He doesn't. You're mine . . . whether you live or die is up to me, get that. Whatever I say, you do." He moved surprisingly quickly and grabbed the whisky bottle; she held onto it a fraction too long before she let it go and the towel fell from her arm. For a frozen moment Brendan stared at the pistol before he threw himself at her. She fired instinctively as he hit her, the butt of the pistol coming back hard into her stomach. The pistol fired again without her consciously pulling the trigger; the pistol was twisted sideways and the ejected case hit the side of her face.

The impetus of his dive had taken him over the edge of the bed; his hands were on her again, scrabbling at her waist, trying to get hold of her arm. His head was buried in her groin. The pistol had twisted in her hand and then he had her wrist and was biting at her stomach. He was a heavy man and she could feel her legs buckling. She made a supreme effort to get the pistol back again as she fell; it fired a third time as she hit the floor and then it was gone.

She lay pinned to the floor by the whole weight of his body, his hard head flattening her breasts. She pushed at him, wriggled, desperate to get clear. When her hearing returned, Brendan was making a whistling noise. She twisted sideways and managed to get her knees up against his body to push herself clear; the threadbare carpet took the top layer of skin from her right thigh, and then she was free. Brendan fell face down onto the carpet with only his feet left on the bed.

She moved away from him as far as she could, still on the floor and then in a sitting position, moving cautiously until her back touched against the wall by the door. Brendan had not moved, but she was terrified by the noises that came from him, and it seemed an eternity before they stopped. She tried to rise, but could not, and eventually got on all fours and held onto the door frame for support. She staggered out into the hall and, without really knowing how, found herself in the bathroom again.

She looked in the mirror and was surprised to see the blood that had smeared across her neck and breasts. She touched it and watched it come away on her hand. She was bewildered by the blood, and it took several seconds for her to realise that the blood was not hers. She shivered and her hands went into convulsions; she could not stop shivering. I'm shocked, she said to herself, I am suffering from shock, she repeated aloud in the voice of a child. In the jumble of her thoughts she remembered that the classic remedy for shock was warmth and turned on the hot tap of the bath. She knelt at the side of the bath, lost in a cloud of steam, for a long time before she managed to summon up enough control to put in the bath plug. It was a complicated manoeuvre to drop the plug into its hole without scalding her arm, but it never occurred to her to turn off the flow of hot water.

A moment of terror as she heard Brendan coming for her along the hallway . . . she forced herself to her feet and got to the doorway—the hall was full of steam. Pressing herself against the wall, she got to the bedroom door and peered round the opening: Brendan still lay on the floor . . . he looked smaller somehow. The barrel of the pistol lay beside his head; she must have dragged herself over it as she fought to get free. She stood at the end of the bed. Timidly—expecting any moment that he would regain consciousness—she leaned on the bed and reached down for the pistol. It seemed terriby heavy, and as she tugged, his head turned. She jumped back and dropped the pistol, but he did not move again. She left the gun where it was and went back to the bathroom.

The bath was half-full of water, much too hot; she ran the

cold tap. She was in control now, apart from the tremor in her hands. Just concentrate, one thing at a time, don't think about it now, fill the bath, check the temperature, put in the salts . . . where are they? God, I'm cold. When she got into the bath the water came across her body like a warm velvet glove, but once she was in the bath she started shivering again and then she cried. She felt absolutely helpless and the tears streamed down her face into the water.

She stayed in the tub until the water lost its warmth and then she got out and wrapped herself in her bathrobe, but she was sweating so much that no matter how much she wiped herself she became sticky again. She used a whole tin of talc and left white footprints as she moved about the bathroom.

She took clean underclothes from the airing cupboard and put them on in the hall; to get to her outdoor clothes she had to return to the bedroom. Brendan's body still lay face down, but seemed to have moved further along the floor. The wardrobe was built into the wall beyond the bed and she had to step over his head to reach it; once she had the wardrobe door open she took all her clothes from it and then her suitcase from the shelf at the top. She bundled her clothes haphazardly into the case and then took all her shoes from the bottom of the wardrobe and pitched them past Brendan into the hall.

She took the suitcase, worked her way past his body again, and went up the hall to the living room, taking her time deciding what to wear, finally settling on jeans, a high-necked sweater and her suede jacket. Once dressed she began to shiver again; she needed a drink, any kind of drink. She tried the sideboard and found a flat pocket flask of Jamesons and she took a water glass from the top of the sideboard. It burned the back of her throat and made her cough, but it did take some of the nausea away and slowly thawed a little of the ice in her stomach. She opened the suitcase on one of the chairs and repacked her clothes neatly, fetching the remainder of her clean underclothes from the airing cupboard in the bathroom.

When she had finished, she used the telephone to find out the time: 1.20 a.m. The room was very cold. She switched on the electric fire and drew up one of the chairs very close to it. She badly needed a cigarette and she tried Brendan's leather jacket which was still hanging over the back of the chair close to the door. There was an unopened packet of Rothman's King-size in one of the side pockets, but no matches. She brought the jacket with her to her chair and lit one of the cigarettes by holding it against the radiant bar of the fire. The jacket was heavy, and she went through the rest of the pockets to find that most of the weight was caused by a cardboard box packed with large calibre pistol rounds; she put them on the floor by her chair. In an inside pocket was a wad of ten- and twenty-pound notes, around four hundred pounds in all, held by an elastic band. In the outside top pocket, two twenty-pound notes were folded individually along with a piece of paper folded lengthwise; the folds were grubby, as if the paper had been handled several times.

Despite the electric fire her feet were cold and she wrapped Brendan's jacket around them. She lit another cigarette and tried to marshal her thoughts into some kind of constructive sequence, but they kept slipping back into the past. Her next thoughts were that she was choking and she came abruptly awake. The jacket was blackened and there was some smoke and a smell of burning: the leather collar of the jacket had fallen against the bars of the fire. She found it difficult to move, her arms and thighs ached as if she had been carrying heavy weights. The lights were still burning. She pulled the coat away from the fire and used the telephone to dial the speaking clock: 4.20.

Her throat was burning and she moved aimlessly out of the living room into the kitchen. The canvas grip was still on the floor with the tin box and broken razor blade. The jar of Nescafé was still standing on the draining board with its cap off, where she had put it down a century ago. She filled the electric kettle from the sink tap and looked blankly at the wall until it had boiled; she mixed some of the powdered coffee and drank it without milk or sugar, glad of its searing heat against the phlegm lining the back of her throat.

# Seventeen

Inspector Field had been given the responsibility, among other things, of checking out all known military contacts of Dennis Baldry. He, in turn, had delegated the chore to Sergeant McGillivray who was waiting to see him when Field passed through the main office at eight forty-five a.m. Field's main interest at the moment was to get some genuine coffee, not the diluted carpet dye that dribbled out of the vending machine, but Blue Mountain filtered through the metal drip arrangement that he had stolen from the French Railway Service.

He glanced at his watch before perching himself on the edge of McGillivray's desk to look at the list. Several of Baldry's comrades were still in the army: eight stationed in Germany; two—both privates in Baldry's time—were in Northern Ireland with another unit; one was now a sergeant and the other a corporal. The rest of Baldry's unit had become civilians. Three had been traced: a bus driver in South Wales; a rigger who had an address in Norfolk, but who was presently working on a rig in the North Sea. The third was a self-employed plumber and heating engineer who lived in Fulham; the address had been circled in heavy black chinograph: 83 Menlove Gardens East. Field pursed his lips; William Coburn's house was about three miles from Baldry's room.

He looked up into the expectant face of Sergeant McGillivray. "You've checked?"

"I rang the local nick, but they don't know him; there's nothing in subversives, he's never been a member of any fringe group, nor his family. He had a good army career, eleven years in all: Aden, Germany, Ulster, class one small arms instructor,

SAS for his last four years, ended up as corporal, invalided out five years ago, wounded in the left leg by a sniper. Rated as excellent by every officer he served under. Married, no children; his wife's a primary teacher. He owns a Ford transit van and a Rover 3500."

"You've been busy."

"I've put out fliers to the Inland Revenue and asked the locals to do a check on his business, employees. We should have the lot by midday, if the bureaucrats get their finger out."

"Excellent. Get a copy for Mr Shenton."

"I have, sir, it is on his desk now."

"Get anything else on Coburn up to him as well. He's the sort of man the governor will likely want himself."

"I thought so too, sir. What about this balls-up at Willesden last night; anything for us there?"

"It looks like them; pity about the bloke who copped it, but they ought to know better than go poking around without a bomb man."

"Mr Maxwell was out all night. His sergeant isn't in yet."

Field nodded, crossed the room and unlocked the metal cupboard to remove his personal kettle and half pint mug. He opened up the plastic box of ground coffee and savoured the aroma that rose from the tightly wrapped packet wedged inside. He set up his metal dripper on the mug and carefully spooned in two and a half measures. Then he went out to fill the kettle at the drinking tap in the toilets. Back in his office, he plugged the kettle into the power socket behind his desk.

Only then did he light his first cigarette of the morning and settle down to flip through his overnight messages. Most were routine, but one flimsy was of interest: Mark Roberts, the man whose visiting card had been found in Baldry's room, had been traced to a bedsit in Westbourne Terrace. The information had come, of all places, from the Yard press office—who the hell had told them that Roberts . . . ? Never mind, a couple of drinks or whatever around Fleet Street and there was Mark Roberts, nailed to the wall.

# Eighteen

At eight o'clock, Maureen turned her transistor radio to LBC and listened to the morning news broadcast; the main item was the explosion on Prentice Street. When the newsreader said that the three men lodging in the house had left earlier and were now being sought, she turned off the radio and got to her feet. She had come to a decision and immediately became emotionally calmer and more efficient.

She went into the kitchen, opened the refrigerator and took out six eggs and eight rashers of bacon; she cut the bacon into strips and tossed it into the heating pan, cracked the eggs into a bowl and beat them into a froth. Then she hooked out the bacon and poured the beaten eggs into the pan and made herself a huge omelet. After a couple of minutes she turned off the cooker and ate straight from the pan, forcing herself to eat it all. It was more than twenty hours since she had last eaten and it could be a long time before she would eat again.

She put the pan into the sink and carried a big mug of black coffee back into the living room along with the canvas bag. Clearing the table, she opened up the bag and carefully took out everything it contained. Besides a wooden box, coils of wire, cord, a slim metal case, there was a canvas bundle which, when unrolled, had pliers and other small hand tools arranged in leather loops. There was a thick metal tube, a sealed oilskin pouch, a mapcase, a cleaning rod, oil and a spare magazine for the pistol.

The wooden box had obviously been made by a cabinet-maker in what looked like dark mahogany, about fourteen inches long and six inches deep, its hinged lid held both by brass clips and masking tape. She slit the tape with the point of her scissors and cautiously pushed back the clips. Beneath the lid was an inch-thick layer of rock wool heavy with grease, and under this the box had been neatly partitioned into compartments about two inches across, each again padded with its individual wool nest. Gingerly, she raised the contents of one compartment and drew out a squat glass cylinder with a rubber stopper. She put it back and then carried the whole box into the kitchen and deposited it carefully on the draining board. The metal case held what she recognized as pencil fuses; the mapcase was empty. The oilskin pouch had a number of black-and-white photographs, some of buildings—Buckingham Palace, Law Courts, Westminster Abbey, several imposing office blocks, the Ritz Hotel, the BBC at Portland Place. She flipped them onto the table as she looked at them: the last three had also been taken outside, but it was impossible to say where. They were not very good, but two appeared to be of the same man; in the first, his back was nearly turned to the camera and all that could be seen of his profile was the curve of his cheekbone. The second was better, but had been taken at a greater distance: the man was bending forward on a kerb in order to speak to the driver of a large car. He looked to be around forty, with dark hair greying at the sides; an even-featured, rather good-looking man. She knew she had seen this man somewhere, the name, the place was tantalizingly on the edge of her consciousness. The third was a photograph of John Ryder, in profile, scowling in fierce concentration at something off camera.

She looked at the photographs a long time, trying to will herself into Brendan's mind. He had taken and kept pictures of this man for a reason; why, it was impossible to know. She smoked a cigarette and took the piece of paper that she had found in Brendan's pocket; it had been folded lengthwise several times and all it had on it was a ten-digit number. It made no sense, of course, could have been anything, a code of some kind maybe, only operative if you reversed the figures.

She lingered with the end of her second cigarette and stubbed it out with reluctance because she had struck a bargain with herself that when it was finished she had to return to the bedroom. She went up the hall reluctantly and stood at the doorway to look at him dispassionately: in some indefinable way he looked sad, head down on the floor, his feet still caught on the edge of the bed, his skin pale and slightly wrinkled. She stepped over him without a qualm and bent to pick up his crumpled trousers. In the back pocket, a thick roll of notes, tens and fives. In the right hip pocket, his car keys on a ring with a leather tab, some small change. In the left pocket, some keys on a piece of string, the key to the door of the flat, a small padlock key which probably fitted the lock on the canvas bag; another small, flat key and then a brass fluted key about six inches long with a number stamped into the shank.

In his side of the wardrobe were two jackets, a raincoat and several shirts: nothing in any of the pockets nor of the three pairs of trousers and jeans; a few handkerchiefs, gaudily striped underpants, one tie. In the cupboard above the wardrobe, two suitcases and a spare blanket. The first suitcase was empty, the second rattled as she pulled it clear on the shelf; it was locked, but the small key on the string opened it and inside was a zippered document case and a camera case. She stepped back over Brendan's body and took the document case to the foot of the bed to unzip it: a bank deposit book in Brendan's name showing an account at a Dublin branch of the Irish Free Bank: balance £4,724; several passbooks on Building Societies in other names, but the signatures were all in Brendan's handwriting. She added up the amounts in her head: together with the Irish book they came to £26,000 odd.

Also in the case, half a dozen Scandinavian pornographic magazines, and beneath those a British passport issued at Petty France in the name of Brian Chambers. The photograph showed Brendan with a shorter haircut and full mustache. "You bastard," she said aloud. The camera case held a Pentax fitted with a long-range lens. She looked at the settings; the counter showed that the spool had been half shot, but she had lost interest and tossed the camera back on the bed and returned to the living room.

She took her leather bag from the sideboard. She checked

the contents, her driving licence and passport in the name of Mary Wilson, the pistol which she removed and laid on the table, the wad of notes that she had taken from Brendan's jacket, cosmetics, comb, mirror and two tampons. She added the roll of notes from Brendan's trouser pocket to the rest of her money and checked the total: she had £848 in cash. In the compartment at the back of the bag, she put the photographs of the man with Ryder and the paper with the mysterious number. Then she stripped and oiled the .22 pistol and loaded both magazines with cartridges from the cardboard box. The box itself she left on the table with the remainder of the equipment from the canvas bag. She put the pistol itself into the side pocket of her suede jacket; the butt protruded and dragged the pocket away from the coat. She put the pistol into her leather bag, setting the strap so that it hung from her right shoulder. The weight was still dragging, but no longer noticeable.

She carried the case and her shoulder bag into the hall and placed them carefully by the front door. She put on her raincoat, and then, on a thought, went back into the bedroom, stepping over Brendan, and stood on the dressing table stool so that she could reach to the very back of the wardrobe cupboard. From it she took a plastic bag which she shook free from dust before she opened it: inside were two wigs, a short medium-brown with lighter flecks, and a longer, black-haired one. She rolled them over and stuffed them into the two pockets of her raincoat.

When she was back in the hall and reaching down to pick up her bags, the telephone rang. She stood hesitantly with her hand on the latch while it rang four times; then she returned again to the living room and picked up the receiver.

A man's voice: "Mrs Wilson?"

"Yes."

"Milton."

"Who?"

Sergeant Milton, I used your phone when . . ."

"Yes, I'm sorry, I wasn't . . ." She let her voice trail away into a small silence.

"I forgot to ask if Mary Wilson is your full name; I'm getting the paperwork wrapped up and they're sticklers for details like that."

"Oh. . . ." Laughter was building up and she had to put her hand over the receiver while she brought herself under control. "No other names."

"That's all right then; I tried the voter's list, but I suppose you haven't been there that long." He paused, but there was no answer to that. "You won't be called to the inquest. That's why I called, really, in case you were still worried. We've got more than we need from the wife. So, you'll be spared the unpleasantness."

"Thank you," she managed to say before she replaced the receiver and exploded into laughter. She laughed all the way into the hall and put her hand to her mouth as she felt it mount into hysteria. She wiped her eyes and took the cosmetic bag from her handbag and repaired her makeup. Then she replaced the cosmetics, checked the position of the pistol and swung the bag onto her shoulder.

She gave a final glance into the door of the bedroom. "No unpleasantness," she murmured in the direction of Brendan's right shoulder. Then she picked up the suitcase and opened the front door, to step into the corridor.

As she waited at the lifts, a man came up from the corridor to stand beside her: a short man with a long nose; she had never seen him before. He dropped a canvas toolbag on the floor beside him while he hand-rolled a shag cigarette. When the lift arrived from the floor above it was already half-full of people with soured faces. The air in the lift was thick with halitosis and the smoke from cheap cigarettes: no one spoke to her, but she was conscious of their eyes.

At the ground floor, most of the others walked directly from the battered entrance hall to the edge of the roadway and then onto the pavement. The man with the toolbag unlocked a dirty transit van parked close to the entrance doors. He had some trouble starting the engine and she waited in front of the buildings until the van had driven away in a cloud of oily blue exhaust fumes. Then she looked at the vehicles left in the car park. Brendan changed cars frequently, but never the colour, sometimes only the plates, and the only thing she knew about his current car was that it was green. She forced herself to think rationally: Brendan had once said that he always left a car so that he could get it moving in a hurry. She walked slowly around the cars and could see only two possibles, a dark green Cortina at the end of the second line, close to the slipway into the main road; a second had been backed against the perimeter fence. She carried her case over to the second Cortina and tried the key; it did not work and she panicked, stabbing with the key and straining against the handle. Someone walking the other side of the perimeter fence was looking at her and she stepped away from the car, picked up her case and walked towards the Cortina by the slipway. There were more people about now, both workers making their way past the car park to the industrial estate on the other side of the main road, and women escorting their children to primary school in the opposite direction.

The key operated the driver's door and she almost collapsed with relief. She put the suitcase on the back seat and forced herself to take enough time to consider the layout of the car and particularly the controls of the gearbox. She switched on the ignition and moved the gear knob into drive. The car moved off immediately, and she took it to the edge of the parking apron and relaxed as she waited for a break in the traffic; it came and she moved smoothly out ahead of a double-decked bus, going west.

# Nineteen

When Field tapped at the door it was opened almost immediately by a small man who peered up at him through large tinted spectacles.

"Mr Mark Roberts?"

The little man nodded abruptly. "Who are you?"

Field showed him his warrant card. "Can we come in?"

"What do you want?"

"Some questions; it would be better inside."

Roberts stood back from the door and pushed the spectacles up on his nose. "If it's about . . ."

"About what?"

"You tell me."

He stood aside to allow Field and McGillivray to enter the room and then shut the door behind them. The room was narrow, with the door at one end and a window at the other. The only table had been pushed under the window and there was a litter of papers and paperback books around an Olivetti typewriter. In front of the table was an ordinary kitchen chair which Roberts turned around before he sat on it. Field glanced around the room. To the left, a single mattress on a divan frame with a couple of rugs thrown over it; against the wall on the right, running up to the corner next to the table, was a counter with a tiny sink and Baby Belling cooker plugged into a wall socket. An empty Johnny Walker bottle stood next to a half-empty bottle of milk, two chipped mugs, an electric kettle and a tarnished teapot. Between the door and the bed were a couple of wooden armchairs with torn cushions and stained carpet worn down to the cords. The air in the room was still.

Roberts blinked up at them. "I've got a deadline."

"Can we sit down?"

"Help yourself." Roberts screwed himself around on his chair and scrabbled around amongst the papers to emerge with a paper packet of cigarettes. He lit a Gauloise with a kitchen match and then turned back to face them again, rubbing a nervous finger up the side of his nose.

Field turned one of the armchairs round to face down the room and something twanged under him as he put his weight on the seat; he leaned forward to sit gingerly on the edge. He waited until McGillivray had settled himself on the bed.

"You were a reporter in Belfast, Mr Roberts."

Roberts sat erect and blinked rapidly. "What about it?"

"When were you there last?"

"Jesus, I don't know, early eighties."

"While you were there you made a number of contacts on the Republican side, isn't that right—you interviewed IRA leaders?"

"Everybody did."

"Do you still have those contacts?"

"I haven't been in Ireland since . . . I want to know what the hell all this is about."

Field nodded. "You're entitled." He took the polythene envelope out of his pocket. "Is that your card?"

"Yeah, I've used cards like that."

"It was in the possession of a man that we want to know a lot more about."

"What man?"

"A dead man. This card was among his possessions; he must have kept it for a reason."

"Bloody hell." Roberts got up and looked down at Field. "I haven't used those cards for years; the telephone number goes back to when I was with my wife. You'll know that if you've tracked me all the way here. I used to give those cards to all sorts of contacts, editors, people who might be useful, a job, a tip, anything. I must have handed out dozens of them, but never in Ireland; one thing I guarantee is that I never handed any of them out in Belfast. Who the hell would I give my home address to over there? Any contacts I had over there rang me at the hotel or the paper."

"But this man had your card."

"I didn't give it to him. There was no way I would give my London card to a Provo."

"He wasn't a Provo."

"But you said. . . . You're playing games."

Field looked hard at him for half a minute. "Your card was in the possession of a man killed in the bus bomb. This is how he used to look."

Roberts took the photograph. "Could be a lot of people . . . looks like a right bastard; I've met a few of those."

"He had your card for a reason."

Roberts still had the photograph and he turned with it towards the window to get a better light. "Could be . . . all I can think of is a British soldier, he looked a bit like this."

"What was his name?"

"All I know is he was a bastard. He was in a patrol that was in a shoot-out, leading it, I think. An ordinary four-man army patrol which didn't make sense. I mean, the Provos had a machine gun; they'd set up an ambush and wait for the patrol to walk into it, then gun them down and run for the border. Except that they got the worst of it. Six of them, a machine gun, Armalites and shooting from cover and they got done: three Provos shot dead, two wounded and one, just one, who got taken with a whole skin. An ordinary patrol is twenty-year-olds who've joined up because the local shipyard's closed. This was heavies dressed up in the local uniform; they used to do that."

"Who did?"

"The SAS. Jesus, don't get me wrong, I'm not complaining. With bastards like Provo killers about, who else do you send in? A bloke in a red coat and a busby? They went looking for the ones who were looking for them, that's all. I never could understand why the Whitehall craphounds made such a mystery of it."

—119

"You're saying that the man in that photograph was an SAS man?"

Roberts giggled. "I can't, can I? Like when I asked, I was told they were all in the Durham Lights or whatever the straight regiment out there was at the time. But yeah, of course he was SAS; he wore sergeant stripes, so I suppose he was one, but they wear any uniform or none—civvies, anything."

"Just what was your relationship to this man?"

"I'm not certain that it was the same man. There's a resemblance, that's all, something about the eyes. The bloke I'm talking about was a hard case. I was trying to write an inside view on the SAS at the time; no one really knew much about them, part of the mystique. There were only around a hundred or so in Ulster all told. They worked in groups of four, rarely more. Real tough bastards, sometimes in uniform, sometimes civilian clothes and ordinary cars, but there is a look about them that you can't really mistake. Like who the hell is going to take four hard-nosed herberts trolling around the border in a Granada for a bunch of tourists? And when they come in they come in with both feet, no hanging about because of regulations written on a little yellow card; they come in like Batman with shotguns, Sterlings, Uzis, Ingrams, shock grenades."

"You know a lot about them, Mr Roberts."

"A bit, but I never wrote that article. I tried enough times but it never came out right. I could never hit the right note . . ." He shrugged. "They either came out like the Gestapo or Gung Ho, like an Errol Flynn movie. That's the trouble with writing anything about Ireland, you can only get the stuff over if it is biased one way or the other."

Field tapped the photograph. "Let's get back to this man."

"Dead, you said."

"Very dead. Blown to pieces by a bomb that was practically in his lap."

"Then they got him after all."

"Who got him?"

"The Provos." Roberts leaned forward to take the photograph again and closed one eye against the smoke rising from the cigarette hanging from the corner of his mouth. "I'm more or less sure, I think his name was Balling, Dan, Dan Balling, something like that. The idea was that I would slip him a few quid for the inside line. I wasn't trying to suborn him or anything; I didn't want to know anything in advance. All I wanted was the inside track on what had really happened."

Roberts twisted around in his chair to grind the cigarette into a saucer that was already overflowing with dead ends and mouldering ash. He shook another cigarette from the pack and struck a match. "If some poor bastard got dumped in a ditch, the Provos would make an announcement, but not usually right away. Or they might issue a statement saying it was the British army. The British army only gave statements through the press officer at Lisburn, but you had to wait for him as well. Sometimes you got a blank from both. That usually meant that the Provos had made a balls and got the wrong man or that the UVF had offed one. Time's important to a stringer; if I could know for certain that it was an IRA caper, then I could save up to a day on the stuff that I filed. You know, 'I understand from a reliable source' stuff. If you can keep that up and be proved right, then people remember, and being known as quick and accurate in that game puts you in the big league.

"Where was I? Oh, yes, Balling. I told him what I've told you; just a word, a nod: he wanted twenty quid. That was when I gave him that card. He didn't want to call me in Belfast so I gave him my home number. I was still with my wife then and anything important she'd ring me back. He did ring once and wanted a hundred for a hot tip about a load of guns coming up from the South. A right load of horseshit that turned out to be. I saw him once more, in a bar when he was wearing civvies; he made out he didn't know me and I didn't press it. But when I went into the yard to my car he clobbered me. I can't prove it was him, but I know he thumped me and took my wallet. He didn't have any call to do that. All I am is a poor bastard trying to make it as a writer, doing my best to be honest, accurate and give value. He'd already cheated me out of twenty quid; I knew it, he knew it and he knew I couldn't do a thing about it. To thump my teeth in and drop me in the dirt without a penny, just because he knew he could get away with it. Bastard."

"Did you see him again?"

"No."

"Never?"

"Never. I avoided any place that he was likely to be, to tell you the truth."

"Did you keep up your connections with the IRA?"

Roberts looked down at his cigarette which had dwindled to a tiny butt between the fingers of his left hand. He dropped it into the saucer and then took off his spectacles and massaged the skin at either side of his nose. "I never had any IRA connections." His voice dropped to a monotone. "I interviewed the leaders of both factions; we all did, journalists, television people, like it was a fashion. We all went down to the Bogside and got blindfolded, met up in little rooms and then came back and wrote them up. I got a few pieces into the *Guardian* and sold quite a bit to the *Boston Herald*. The American stuff was sympathetic to the IRA, but I didn't tell any lies. The leaders I met were violent, sure, but they were idealists as well, romantics really. I sympathized with their aims; in the early days it was an extension of the civil rights movement."

Roberts started another cigarette and inhaled deeply while his fingers played with the earpieces of his spectacles. "It changed, though. The idealists all went, imprisoned or exiled or murdered and then the gangsters took over, thieves and killers, all the psychopaths out on the streets acting out their fantasies. You ever thought what a vested interest they have in having things stay the way they are? No one pays you for writing about things like that. So I came back to London and my wife decided that she preferred this Neville she'd been sort of living with while I was over the water. A great homecoming that was, and I went to South Africa. That'll be in your little file as well. Another piss up the tubes. It's all the bloody same; you can angle it from one side or the other."

He sat up straight in his chair, and Field noticed that without his spectacles Roberts' eyes were long-lashed and startlingly blue. Field looked at McGillivray and got up from the edge of the chair. "Thank you very much," he said to Roberts, "you've been extremely helpful. I hope you meet your deadline."

Roberts just looked at him. McGillivray opened the door and as Field gave a final glance before he went through it, he saw that Roberts was still in his chair; the spectacles were back on his nose and the cigarette ash was falling into a small grey pyramid on the thighs of his crumpled jeans.

# Twenty

Danny reached the meeting place almost an hour early and tried to make himself as inconspicuous as his size permitted by sitting close to the wall and holding a newspaper up in front of his face. He had spent a miserable night and worse morning when, unable to stand the narrow, strange bed any longer, he had walked the streets at the back of Paddington Station.

He had bought a cup of terrible tea and a bun and taken them, with a copy of the *Daily Mirror*, to a shelf built along the wall of the café. The headline of the paper had shocked him into pouring the tea down the front of his jacket. He had read the story three times, and it had taken nearly an hour before he had dared to walk out again into the street. He had walked across the west end of London, always close to the wall, blundering up streets he had vaguely heard of but did not know. He had tried to hide himself on the underground system, travelling out and then back again. He did not dare to look anyone in the eye.

He forced himself to buy cigarettes and chain-smoked them, his second packet of the day.

He rang the number three times that Smith had given him; the first two times Smith was not there, but Danny would not leave a message. The third time Smith answered but was reluctant to arrange a meeting; he wanted to know what Danny had to report. Eventually he agreed and told Malloy to sit on a bench at the edge of Martinshaw's Recreation Field, second bench from the gate.

It was cold on the bench and Malloy could not keep still;

he paced the path under the trees, pulled his anorak up to his ears and smoked.

When Smith came he got out of the passenger side of a car that drew into the kerb by the park railings. Malloy saw him say something to the driver before he strolled towards the gate; he saw Danny through the railings, but made no sign of recognition. He was wearing a finely checked black-and-white suit under a fawn sheepskin coat, and as he walked towards the gate he arranged its collar behind his ears.

"Jesus," he said by way of greeting, "you look rough. On the batter last night?"

"You've blown me, you went to the bloody house. I asked you not to, you promised . . ."

"Steady up, brace it." Smith looked him in the eye and then gave a reflective nod. "Keep your voice down. We'll take a stroll up by the trees; just a stroll, no need to go galloping about. Now, look, Danny, no one's dropped you in it; I told you I wasn't going to do anything about the house except report and that is all I did do. The two who went to the house are another unit entirely. Listen, I'm giving you the full strength. A tip came in from a different source, a call that there was a unit in that house with guns and explosives. It cross-referenced with what you'd told me, but that's all. When we get a call like that it has to be actioned."

"What call, who called?"

"I didn't take it. Anonymous. Most of them are; people don't want to get involved, probably an ordinary bloke who'd noticed something, lives in the street maybe. He wouldn't want his name in the paper about a thing like that, would he? So relax, take it easy; you've got nothing to worry about."

"But they'll think it was me. Christ, the first visit I make and the law arrives; I can't go back now. Major Flint promised me I'd be looked after, as soon as I was blown . . ."

"That's absolutely right, you will be looked after; but listen, Danny, you haven't been blown, your important work is still to be done. But you've got to get in touch, you haven't done anything wrong, you did exactly what you were told to do. You took the money to the house, handed it over; if you were going to lumber them you'd have hung on to the money, wouldn't you? So you passed the test; all you've got to do is stick with your story."

"You don't know them, don't know. For Christ's sake, they don't have to prove anything, they'd top me just for being in the wrong place at the wrong time. I've got to be put somewhere safe."

"No, son," said Smith firmly, "you're just not thinking straight. What you do is make contact and ask for orders and whatever they are you do what they say. Even if it's criminal, so long as it's not a killing. If you're arrested, we'll sort it out. You've got it all wrong, Danny, this thing has made you fireproof. A boyo who got away. The only mistake would be to lose your nerve now. It's if you don't go back that'll make you a marked man."

"But it was a test, don't you see, sending me over. It was testing me and I was the last man in that house before the police came!"

"Use your head. Whoever phoned in that tip is still out there, and he'll be phoning again; now if you're with them, maybe even being questioned, when the next squeal comes in you'll be in clover. Maybe it was a test, but it can work in your favour, the one thing that can put you in really solid. You think it over, son, and you'll see I'm right. Bell me when you've got something worthwhile."

He left Malloy slumped against one of the silver birches, the whole of his long angular body slumped in defeat.

When he got into the car, Smith settled his backside comfortably in the passenger seat and took his flat tin of little cigars from the pocket of his sheepskin jacket. John turned the ignition key and then glanced sideways at Smith. "You think you sold him?"

Smith flicked his lighter, put the spear of flame to his cigar and then shrugged. "Who knows with these bastards? One minute they act like James Bond and go crying for their mothers next. It's all that crap they put on the telly."

"Is it straight up about that call on the house?"

"Yeah, a couple of case officers went glory-hunting and made a right cock-up."

"He's still up by the tree; look at him. You really want him to go back? He'll cough the lot the first time they shake a fist at him. He'll cough."

"He's sure as fuck no good to us over here. He'll go back all right; what else can he do?"

"Yeah."

# Twenty-One

Maureen Driscoll drove slowly, constantly crowded and passed by other drivers who knew more definitely where they were going and were impatient to be there. The fuel gauge showed an almost full tank, more than enough to take her anywhere she wanted to go; if only she could think of somewhere that it was safe to go.

The traffic became much heavier and she looked at the other drivers, all remote in their little tin boxes. Beyond the turnpike she lost her way; there was a sudden proliferation of traffic signs and diversions; everyone else seemed absolutely sure of where they were going and she followed them in fitful left- and right-hand turns. She lost her sense of direction and soon did not know if she was heading north or west. Other drivers cut in front of her, braked and then as abruptly moved away to cut in front of someone else. She glimpsed the people on the pavements as she moved anonymously onwards. Men and women who moved along the pavements as though they were sleepwalking, shoulders hunched, mean pinched mouths, or standing blank-eyed at traffic lights or bus stops. Poor sad bastards, slouching their way to dirty, uncomfortable and grindingly pointless jobs.

It was these people she was fighting for, had dedicated her life to them back in Trinity College—how long ago, more than nine years, in another age—when she had been a girl and had had ideals. In a world in which John Driscoll had been a live and vital presence, the most magnetic and physically beautiful human being that she had ever seen, with his dark blue eyes, long eyelashes and fine black hair that was like a handful of silk. But most of all, his superb mind and incandescent spirit. It was no sacrifice to join him in his dedication to the betterment of the people, people whom she could see on the pavements, going their grubby way while he was no more than a handful of grave-maggots and rotting bones, under a stone with lying words. Pontificated over in the name of a religion in which he had not believed. A black farce.

And as another act of that farce, she was passing these indifferent people who did not even know his name. The same old people in whose name every atrocity and cynical swindle was perpetrated. They had not the slightest interest in her or in revolution, and she admitted to herself at last that she had no interest in them. All that her praised intelligence and wit and idealism had led her to was degradation and the shooting down of Brendan Casey. Her fellow revolutionary, a bully and the destroyer of the only noble human being that she had ever known.

She flicked away the tears. Where could she go? She had to think clearly. She had an analytical mind, a mind that was as capable of logical and constructive thought as any Trinity lecturer. John had always told her that. The trouble was that all her intelligence had told her so far was that there was nowhere she could go, that sooner or later either the police or Ryder's men would find her.

She had never been more alone. After John's death she had allowed that vaunted intelligence of hers to be swamped. She should have known that his enemies had been within; he had known, had said that if anything happened to him she was to run, change her name, lose herself, trust no one. He had known and so had she and yet, when it happened she had refused to believe it. He had told her what to do, had made her promise, but instead she had believed Ryder. Of all people, she had believed Ryder, had believed that John had been killed by the British, that all the denials were a cover-up.

She knew that Ryder was a liar, had seen so many proofs and yet she had accepted this, the most obvious, blatant lie of all. She had allowed him to manipulate her, to put her in the power of the man who had killed her husband. The bastard had fooled her, but no, face it, even that was not true; she had gone against her own intelligence, had refused to see what was right in front of her face, had refused to look because the truth was too painful. She had fooled herself.

# Twenty-Two

Shortly after seven o'clock, Shenton packed his document case with the reports that he had selected for his evening's study. He included the telex message from the Amsterdam police and would have been unable to explain precisely why he did so, but he had long ago ceased to bother to identify the reasons for the choices that he made. His subconscious had a twenty-year track record that he trusted completely.

He used the interphone to order up his car and then went into the outer office to pick up his personal sergeant, a very tall, dark-skinned young man. Detective Sergeant John Morgan had, among other things, graduated from Swansea University with a degree in computer studies and, despite the vast gulf in their respective ranks, often made Shenton feel as though he was being examined under a microscope. Morgan's father was still serving as a uniformed sergeant in the Glamorgan force.

Menlove Gardens East turned out to be a pre-war street of red brick houses with very small front gardens. Number 83 was at the very end of the street with more ground to its side on which stood a transit van; its rear doors were open and a ladder protruded, held in position by ropes. Shenton rang the bell and the door was opened by a dark-haired, very pretty, plump young woman with an infectious smile.

"Go on through, Billy's in the back room."

William Coburn got up from the settee when they came in, a tall, lean man who gave an impression of laconic strength. He had been watching the television set and his wife crossed the room to switch off *The Morecambe and Wise Show.*

## The Final Glass

Coburn resumed his seat on the settee and puffed on a long brown cheroot, his shirtsleeves rolled high over his biceps, wearing faded denims and battered suede shoes; he sat relaxed, but his eyes were wary. His wife sat at the other end of the settee, leaning forward, bright-eyed and curious to know what it was all about.

Shenton took the armchair on the other side of the television set and waited for Morgan to settle himself by the door. "As I explained on the telephone, it is absolutely essential that we find out everything we can about Baldry, particularly what he has been doing or who he has been seeing recently."

Coburn carefully broke the ash from the end of his cheroot against the side of a blue glass ashtray. "Like I said, I can't help you. I've had nothing to do with him."

"He lived only three miles from here."

"That's news to me."

"Have you seen him at all since the army?"

"About two years ago when I was doing a job over at Glendale. I went into a pub around lunchtime and Baldry was in there with a woman, both half cut. The woman was Irish; she didn't sound it, but Baldry made a point of telling me."

"Did you talk about Ireland?"

"I didn't. He talked about a lot of things, whining about the army, the government. He said he didn't have any money. I didn't give him any."

"You don't like him?"

"I don't like piss artists in general and Baldry was never a friend of mine. He was all right in a bundle, quick, plenty of guts and all that, but he liked putting the boot in. Fancied himself as a hard case, put the frighteners on people; there's two micks at least he planted stuff on."

"Do you blame him in any way for what happened to you?"

Coburn tapped his left thigh. "You mean this? Baldry wasn't even there; the only one responsible is the kid who did it."

"Kid?"

Coburn shrugged and flicked the end of his cheroot in the ashtray. "Seventeen, sixteen, maybe younger. We were going up this street where a house had been burned out, front man watching, second man covering, third man at the garden wall: I won that raffle. I got to the wall all right, got behind it so I could cover the rest of the street. I don't know why the hell I looked behind me, instinct I suppose. There was nothing left of the house; what hadn't been burned had been knocked down, just a few bricks and general rubbish lying around. This kid must have been laying flat when I went over the wall; by the time I saw him he already had his rifle up, an Armalite, you can't miss that triangular sight. It's funny what you have time to see at a moment like that, your mind speeds up or something; when I looked at him he nodded like he'd caught my eye and was letting me know. There was nothing much I could do, my rifle was in my right hand pointing down the road. I drew my legs up, like a baby, and he put it through the leg, through the thigh and into my arse. If he'd got the knee I'd have been a cripple."

"You were lucky," said Shenton.

Coburn looked up as if he had just noticed that he had an audience. "Lucky would have been not being there at all."

"What happened to the boy?"

Coburn shrugged. "The others had him. He went through the garden and got into the lane at the back; it's like a rabbit warren round the back of those houses. McBain said he got him, and if Jock reckons he got a hit then he did. They found some blood in the lane so the women probably carried him off somewhere. Jock reckoned he got him square between the shoulder blades and that means a broken spine; he wouldn't have lived more than a couple of days."

Shenton glanced towards the other end of the settee where Coburn's wife beamed happily at him. "If he died, then his body . . ."

"They'll have buried him somewhere, maybe took him across the border and made a do of it, a priest and all that."

Shenton felt the interview slipping away from him. He looked away and then down at the blank page of his notebook in order to break the spell of Coburn's personality. "From what you know of Baldry, would you say that there could be someone who had it in for him personally, a grudge to settle?"

"Anyone who had anything to do with him."

Shenton closed his notebook. "Could Baldry have sold out to the IRA? I know you have no way of knowing, just an opinion."

Coburn took his time, putting his elbow up on the arm of the settee and leaning his chin on his fist. "I wouldn't put it past him, especially the way he was that last time. He'd take money off the Provos if it was an offer, no question, but what deal would that be? He'd been an SAS man and that makes him number one on their shit list."

"If they knew where he lived, traced him in some way, perhaps through that woman he lived with. . .it needn't have been money, they could have frightened him."

"That's balls; you've got the wrong idea about Baldry. He was a grade one bastard all right, but there wasn't a man alive or dead who could put the frighteners on him."

"People change."

"He hadn't when I saw him."

"They could have threatened the woman."

"That wouldn't make any difference to him."

"All men are frightened of something; a man who feels no fear is a madman."

"Maybe that's what he was then."

# Twenty-Three

Maureen Driscoll sat in the Cortina on the second tier of the multi-story car park and tried to keep her thoughts in sequence. Her suitcase was in the luggage office at the bus station and in her handbag was the telephone number and address of the Airways Hotel in Gloucester Road, who were holding a one-night telephone reservation for her. They would be used to casual callers, more or less complete turnover every day, big, anonymous; it was not perfect, but it would have to do. The big problems were still to be solved.

The raincoat was the same she had worn when she had left the flat, but that could not be helped. If the people in the lift remembered, they would describe a woman in a white raincoat with short hair. She put on the long dark wig. It came down low on her forehead, and with the contact lenses instead of the tinted spectacles, she did not look much like the woman who had walked out of Filbert Point.

Now was the time to leave the car. There was no point in trying to wipe the car clean of fingerprints; she had left enough in the flat. Her prints were not on file, she had never been arrested, so they would have to take them from her physically to match them, and if they ever got that close to her she was finished anyway. She put on the interior light and opened the glove compartment. In it was a flat bottle of Hennessey brandy with a few dregs; she put the bottle back.

On the rear seat a piece of plastic and several old newspapers mixed up with discarded pyrofoam cups. On the seat next to her was her shoulder bag, bulkily heavy; the flap was back, showing that most of the space was taken up by the wad of banknotes and the .22 pistol. A car came up the ramp into the tier and she immediately switched off the interior light. The car's headlights turned away and she watched in the rear mirror as its brake lights came on. The car lights were switched off, then came fast steps and voices; two couples went across the cement floor to the stairs at the centre of the tier.

She switched on the interior light again and picked up the wad of notes from her handbag. She pulled up her sweater and poked the end of the notes between the cups of her bra, but the wad of notes was too thick and the straps cut into her shoulders. Unsafe, uncomfortable and too noticeable. She un-zipped the fly of her jeans and took a handful of the notes, about a third of the wad, and pushed them under the waist-band of her panties, then a third to the left hard against the thighbone, the rest she put to the right. She held her breath as she pulled up the zip of her jeans: it stuck halfway. She got out of the car and was able to pull the zip to a close. She tried a couple of steps and was very conscious of the bulk across her waist, but it was comforting rather than awkward.

She took her bag from the car, and the keys from the ignition. She slammed the door shut and listened: no sound, dark, except for the single meagre light by the stairs. On an impulse, she took the pistol from the handbag and held it in her hand, checked with her thumb that the safety catch had not ridden up and put it in the outside pocket of her raincoat; the butt protruded, but was completely hidden if she held it in her hand. The abandonment of the car made her feel vulnerable. She closed the catch on the handbag and swung it from her shoulder. She put her hand back on the butt of the pistol and walked to the stairs.

The first few concrete steps were lit by a low-wattage bulb in its wire mesh cage bolted to the ceiling, but then she was in darkness and had to feel her way cautiously to the next landing and then the next. The stairs ended and she walked through the narrow opening into the walkway that had been built next to the entrance ramp. She orientated herself to the main road and saw the sign marking the alleyway which linked up with the main shopping precinct. She walked to the end of the alleyway without incident and emerged into a large paved area, some benches, and concrete steps with a handrail which led up to the shopping levels.

She could sense that she was not completely alone, but she could see no one. On either side of the alleyway the light level faded, the streetlamp at the alleyway entrance was unlit; smashed probably. She reached the stairs and paused. Nothing. She went up the stairs onto the catwalk and as she went along it she sensed an indeterminate shape at the far end. As she hesitated, she heard someone coming up the stairs behind her; she turned and there were two of them, both young, wearing leather jackets and basketball boots. She backed away as they came towards her, moving softly on rubber soles: quick, healthy, strong and malicious.

She withdrew her hand from her pocket, holding the pistol against her coat. Her hand trembled a little as they came closer, fists clenched, bouncing on the balls of their feet. Then, suddenly, there was a third one, stealthy as a rat, pulling from behind at the strap of her shoulder bag and, at the same time, punching her shoulder hard. Hands groped at her breasts. A face in front of her was grinning with a show of even white teeth framed by a cluster of black, tightly curled hair. As he punched her in the face, she ducked, avoiding the full force of the blow; but something on his hand stung her lower lip. She raised her right hand; someone caught her elbow and she fired before she meant to. The face showed stunned incredulity and she spun round, unwinding herself from the shoulder strap.

The one behind her still held onto the strap: tall, straddle-legged, a black PVC jacket, red silk shirt and some kind of chain around his neck. His hulking size and the cunning of the trap made her coldly angry. She fired again and he dropped the bag, falling back against the handrail. She glanced over her shoulder for the first two; the man she had shot was almost at the end of the catwalk, nearly falling when he had to leave the support of the handrail, moving fast, but lurching. The other one had disappeared.

When she turned back, the tall man had dropped to his

knees, both hands pressed into his stomach. She kept the pistol up as she recovered her bag and then went past him, her bag in one hand and the pistol in the other. When she reached the end of the catwalk the paved area leading to the centre of the shopping precinct was empty. She kept to the centre of the flagstones, ready for the onrush of whatever might be lurking in the darkened doorways, but there was nothing.

When she entered the main concourse of the shopping precinct the lighting became brilliant, all the shop windows blazed with light. She slipped the strap of the bag over her left shoulder and touched the wetness on her lip; it was blood and she sucked it from the edge of her lip, tasting salt. She found her handkerchief and dabbed at her bottom lip; it was slightly swollen. Then she put the pistol into the right-hand pocket of her raincoat, kept her hand over the butt and walked across the shopping precinct.

On the far side, past the fountain with its blank-faced sculpture of a broad-hipped earth mother, there was a wide flag-stoned broadwalk, flanked by more shops and then the main road. When she reached the main road she fell into step behind a couple who were walking towards the cinema at the cross-roads: *Love in Sweden* double-billed with *The Monster*. A taxi pulled across the traffic lights in front of the cinema and she hailed it, and not until the taxi had pulled out into the mainstream of the traffic did she fully relax back into her seat.

She put the handbag on her lap; the side had been scuffed where it had been dragged along the ground. Watching the back of the taxi driver's head, she slipped the pistol from the pocket of her raincoat and put it into her handbag, thought a moment, and opened the bag again and searched for the small slip of paper from the back compartment and put that into the pocket of her raincoat.

She left the taxi at Victoria Station and the driver looked at her with curiosity as she got out a note from the pocket of her raincoat.

"You been in an accident?"

"Yes, a silly one." She paid him and went across the concourse to the women's lavatories. Again she felt people looking at her, but she avoided their eyes. Inside, the attendant ran water into one of the handbasins for her.

"Had some trouble, love?"

"I fell over."

She looked a mess, her wig was slightly off centre, makeup that she had used to disguise the bruise from Brendan's blow had streaked and run. The area of the bruise had increased and had raised the flesh in a bump about an inch across. There was a streak of blood coming from the lip split by the first mugger; he had been wearing a ring, probably with a filed edge. Blood had smeared the bottom of her chin.

She washed her face, which made it a little better, but the hot water stung and the lip was already beginning to fatten. She combed her hair and made herself look as presentable as she could, but it did not do a lot; there was no way of disguising her damaged face. Wigs and changes of makeup, a differently coloured coat, none of that was going to be any good now; whatever she did she had an unusual feature that people would remember. She applied a light foundation cream and a little lipstick and put on some eyeshadow; it was an improvement, but she was still obviously a woman with a bashed face. It would be particularly noticed in a hotel; her first idea of using overnight hotels each night, changing her name and appearance each time, was no longer feasible.

She left the toilets and walked across the concourse to the luggage store; there was a small queue, and while she was standing in it a uniformed policewoman walked by: she forced herself to look casually at her as she came level. The policewoman glanced at her, eyes flickering as she took in the bruises, hesitated; Maureen looked ahead and the policewoman passed on. Once she had collected her case and recrossed the concourse she felt very depressed. Take it easy, she said to herself, you are in the worst possible mental state to make decisions. Emotional shock, pressure, anxiety, sudden stress: the old textbook stuff from Trinity College. She was passing the women's waiting room and turned in, choosing a bench far from the door. She put the case next to her and fished in her handbag cautiously, holding the flap high to conceal the pistol, while she found her cigarettes. She fished further for her lighter; it was not there.

She looked around the waiting room. A sleek teenager in tight jeans and jacket. A woman, little more than a girl, was sitting on the furthest possible seat, surrounded by bags and shawls, with a small baby at her breast. By the door, two middle-aged women, wearing identical hats of plastic basket-weave, were in animated conversation. A sad, thin, woman, shabbily dressed, sat with her elbows on her knees while she stared at the floor, a cigarette hanging from the centre of her mouth.

Maureen went over to the woman who jerked erect and looked up with fear in her eyes. Then she nodded and fumbled in her handbag to produce a box of matches. Maureen lit up, thanked her and went back to her bench. Her brain refused to work; she wanted, needed, had to find a place to stay, for what, ten days, two weeks, perhaps a little more. A place where she would be safe, unnoticeable, or at least unremarked, and where the hell would that be? Come on, you're supposed to be intelligent, since you were ten years old, a very clever girl our Maureen, the bright one, the one who would go far. So bloody far that you end up sitting in a draughty railway station, your child three thousand miles away, and hunted; hunted by both sides now, by Ryder—the bastard, he really did have a reason to put you down now. And as soon as they got into that flat, the British police. A very good police force, particularly on murder. Oh, yes, they really could catch their murderers, and transients. They could drag out bed-sitter land and the cheap hotels like shaking out a cider apple tree.

She drew on the fag end of her cigarette and looked blankly at the discoloured posters on the opposite wall. *Join the Woman's Army Service; Be a Traffic Warden; Good Opportunities in Catering; Samaritans, Ring This Number. Are You in Trouble?* (Am I in trouble!) *VD Clinic: Complete Discretion.*

She was still staring at the small final notice when the cigarette burned her fingers.

# Twenty-Four

Shenton's car had left the South Circular Road and was within two streets of his house when the car radio bleeped and he leaned forward to take up the receiver. He watched the back of the heads of his driver and sergeant who were sitting in the front passenger seat.

"Purple One."

"Stand by, Purple One, message from Mr Maxwell for Commander Shenton."

"Shenton speaking."

"Mr Shenton to contact Mr Maxwell by landline soonest. Message ends."

Shenton watched the backs of the two men in the front seats stiffen with interest.

The telephone kiosk stank of cheap wine and Shenton's shoe crunched on broken glass. He dialled the Yard's number and asked for the Operations Room. It was Maxwell who answered.

"It's a murder enquiry, sir; Filbert Point, the tower block. There's a bomber's kit in the flat, no explosives so far, but it looks as though the place could have been used as a bomb factory. The dead man was shot, that's what the doc says as a first impression, and there was a gun in the flat as well, heavy stuff, .357 Magnum; they would have heard that if it had gone off. The whole thing's weird; the body was found by gas board men, someone reckoned they could smell gas."

Shenton sighed. "Do we have any idea who the man is?"

"Bernard Wilson on the tenants' roll, but a second passport was found in the flat; it could be a straight gang murder. We should have the run on his prints before the night's out. The body was found an hour ago so the murder squad are still out there. I thought you ought to know."

"Of course. I'll proceed home, but keep me advised. Who have you sent?"

"Field took a full squad in. The murder team is headed by Jimmy James."

"He's all right. Do we know who lived in the flat?"

"Married couple, Bernard and Mary Wilson. The woman's gone. The murder boys are doing the doorstep bit of course."

"Of course."

A cough came over the wire. "Another telex came in from Amsterdam, signed Jo-Ho . . ."

"Hojean. What does it say?"

" 'Van Hoeck, travels widely, no criminal activity known. Subject enquiry on arms shipments, documents in order, business connections West German arms manufacturers, also British and American companies under licence. Travels Middle East, believed visitor to Libya. No known connection terrorist organizations, frequent visitor to UK. Please advise reason for enquiry.' Sounds like he's interested."

"I'll deal with that tomorrow, but if there's anything on this man, Wilson, let me have it at home."

Shenton put down the telephone and stepped out of the kiosk, standing on the pavement to breathe deeply some of the wet fresh air and to clear his head of the fetid fumes of the telephone kiosk. He took his pipe out of his pocket and tapped it out against the heel of his shoe, then produced his pouch and slowly filled the pipe with fresh tobacco. A man found shot dead in a high-rise flat surrounded by a bomb maker's kit, and at least one active unit out somewhere with the bombs themselves, perhaps setting them at this very moment. Things were certainly hotting up, ten times more active than they had ever been before, always tempting to butterfly your mind on the latest incident, the latest thing that happened. But an easy mistake to make. The bastard to concentrate on was the one who had set the bomb on that bus.

# Twenty-Five

The driver of the mini-cab that Maureen Driscoll had hired was so unsure of the street that he had checked his city guide before plunging into the back streets behind the Goldhawk Road. Maureen felt a little uneasy herself as they moved further away from the lighted shopping areas and deeper into the mean littered streets. This was a heavily deprived area, more depressing than any she had yet seen in an English city. Some houses were little more than shells, with roofs gone; others had boarded windows. Squatter land, derelict, despairing and vicious.

The cab moved into slightly better territory, less rubbish in the roads and lights in the windows, even curtains. The house, when they came to it, was detached and ablaze with light; the garden was crammed with bicycles, a child's swing and old car tyres. There were no curtains at any of the downstairs windows and Maureen could see several people about. She paid off the driver and carried her case up the garden path. The front door was solid and there was a light high up in the porch over a scuffed street door.

She put the suitcase down and hammered on the door before she saw the bellpush. There was a great deal of noise going on in the hall, and then the door was opened by a woman of gypsy good looks, backed up by a woman with the build of a heavyweight wrestler. The first woman leaned forward to look beyond her and then back again, her eyes going immediately to the lump at the side of her face and the black eye she had emphasised with eye makeup.

"I telephoned earlier and . . ."

"Yes, come in."

The tall woman led the way across the short hall into a tiny room on the right. Most of the space was taken up by a kitchen table and two wooden chairs. On the table were a telephone and a mess of papers, an electric kettle, jar of instant coffee and a large tray of drinking mugs.

"Put your case down by the door, it'll be all right. Sit down." The woman switched on the kettle and sat down at the table. "It was Jenny you spoke to on the telephone and she told you we're full up and bursting at the seams. There are thirty-six women here right now and fifty-four children. We're already in trouble with the local council for overcrowding. I can see you've been hit by something, but you don't look in bad shape."

"I was hit three times."

"How did you get away?"

"I laid him out."

The woman laughed and picked up a cigarette packet. "You don't need our help, love."

"I have to get away from him, somewhere I'd be safe."

"How much money have you got?"

"Enough to pay my way, for a few weeks anyway. That's not my problem. He's a bastard and he's got a lot of friends. If I stay in a hotel he could trace me. He's dangerous, he knows a lot of criminals. I've got to get away from him; I must be on my own for a few days. I've got to get myself sorted out."

"Mm." The woman looked at her speculatively and then rose to attend to the boiling kettle. She spooned coffee granules into a couple of the mugs and then stirred in the water. She passed one across the table to Maureen and pushed across a mug full of sugar with a spoon sticking up in it. Then she pushed by Maureen's chair and went out into the hall, leaving the door open.

Maureen ignored the sugar bowl and sipped at the scalding coffee. There had been a look in the woman's eyes that was unexpected, a hardness, suspicion. She held her handbag tightly on her lap and, shielding it from the open door behind her, cautiously opened the flap and got out her packet of cigarettes and matches. She lit a cigarette and put the dead match carefully in the tray. Behind her came a sudden eruption of noise, women's voices and shouting children.

When the gypsy woman came back she was with a tiny woman, somewhere in her late forties, little more than five feet high and with magnificent clear grey eyes. "I'm Jenny; we spoke on the telephone."

Maureen half rose from her chair, but the woman put her hand on her shoulder to keep her seated. She bent her head slightly so that she was looking directly into Maureen's eyes, and then she made a thorough examination of the rest of her face; it was a studied look of cool appraisal.

"Come down here; bring your case if you must." Maureen followed her out into the hall and down a passageway; the room to the left of the passage had no door and Maureen followed the woman, picking her way between mattresses that covered most of the floor. There was an overwhelming smell of urine and badly cooked food. Most of the mattresses had sleeping bags: children seemed to be everywhere, the very youngest sharing sometimes three to a mattress. About six women were also in the room, either kneeling or sitting amongst the children. One was changing a baby's napkin.

Although none of the windows fronting the house was curtained, the panes of glass were so heavy with condensation that nothing could be seen of the garden beyond. A right turn through another doorless opening and then they were in what was once the kitchen. Two washing machines were jammed next to the sink and on the floor stood a huge pile of soiled clothing.

Two women were sitting at the kitchen table scraping vegetables. Jenny darted like a bird through all the obstacles, but Maureen almost fell when her foot caught the edge of a sack of potatoes.

"Sit down." Jenny pulled a chair out from the table and put it close to the washing machines, directly beneath the strip light. A towel appeared from somewhere and was tucked into the neck of Maureen's sweater. "Put your head back."

A tap ran and then the little woman was back dabbing cotton

wool into a bowl. "Turn your head to the right." The fingers were practised; the pungent smell of an antiseptic. She winced as the fingers probed the swelling over her left cheekbone.

"That's a very bad bruise; did it knock you out?"

"No."

"It could have cracked the bone, but I don't think so. Have you had any treatment?"

"No."

"It didn't happen today; the cut on your lip is more recent."

"Yes."

"Lean forward."

It was very soothing to be treated like a child; the hands moved skilfully over her face. A pad held by a strip of plaster was placed over the cheekbone, a salve applied to the split lip.

"The swelling will increase over the next day or so and then it will go down, vanish in a week or so; there won't be any scarring. Is it painful?"

"It aches, but not too bad."

"It could stop you sleeping." The hands and bowl were gone and the sharp, clear grey eyes were looking directly into hers again. "Where else do you hurt? You've got something wrong downstairs, haven't you? It's the way you walk."

"I . . . it's . . ."

"We do have a doctor who's willing to come out, or we can take you there. Did he use his fist, a stick or something?"

"No, just . . . himself."

"Any question of VD?"

"No, I don't—no, I'm certain."

"So long as you are." The eyes no longer probed, the woman stepped back and then aside to allow one of the women who had got up from the kitchen table to get to the sink. "Let's go back to the office."

Maureen touched her face gingerly as they retraced the obstacle course of the main downstairs rooms. As they passed through the hall, the big woman was helping the gypsy-looking woman to lay yet more sleeping bags in the space before the front door.

The little woman sat down at the table and took a cigarette from the packet before offering one to Maureen. When she struck a match she suddenly looked weary. "Rosita thought you might be a council spy; we've got a court injunction against us for overcrowding." A mirthless smile: "But those bruises of yours are real enough."

"I didn't know where to go. I was sitting in the railway waiting room when I saw your notice."

"Most of the girls who come here are scared out of their skulls, really at the end of their endurance. You're not that desperate, are you: you're articulate, well-dressed, and Rosita said you had money. You could employ a solicitor, go the middle-class route."

"All I wanted to do was get a breathing space, just to get away and think what to do. It's complicated and. . ."

"You don't have to tell us anything at all. Everyone has to work it out for themselves. All we do here is put some kind of roof over the heads of poor cows that have no one or nowhere else to go. It isn't much."

"I can afford a room; it was this feeling of being safe. I can't take up any room here, you've more than you can manage. What I was hoping was that you would know of somewhere safe, just a room that I could stay in for a week or so."

"Hold on." The little woman stood up and searched among the piles of papers to emerge with a child's exercise book; she turned the pages quickly. "Let's see." She pulled the telephone towards her and quickly dialled a number. "Hello, dear, it's Jenny." A quick glance at her wristwatch. "I'm sorry, I know it's late, but I've got a girl here who wants a room for a week or so . . . no children, no . . . no charity, she's willing to pay. That's right." She turned her back and Maureen could no longer make out what she was saying. Then she put down the telephone. "Mrs Meadows is an old friend of ours; you can have a room for as long as you need. Sort out the rent with her when you get there. It's a few miles from here." A quick smile. "Different area entirely."

"Thank you," said Maureen, "I'm very grateful. Would a cab come out here?"

Another quick smile. "We can get one we know. I'll ring; he'll be here in ten minutes."

"Thank you," said Maureen again and searched in the pocket of her raincoat to find some loose pound notes. "I'd like to . . . I don't mean it as . . ."

"Charity?" said the small woman briskly as she took the money, "but that is exactly what we are, dear."

# Twenty-Six

Danny Malloy peered from red-rimmed eyes at the ruck of heaving shoulders between him and the bar. Great clouds of tobacco smoke pressed down from the cellar roof and stung his eyeballs. A small group were thumping out traditional jazz on a small stage at the other end of the cellar. The place was called the Swinging Coconut and he had come across it by chance after leaving the late show of a sex film in an alleyway cinema off Berwick Street.

His head was thumping in time to the music and the brandy he had drunk, and hot and sweaty as he was in his thick, oiled jersey and blue serge donkey jacket, he knew that the inhospitable streets outside were both wet and freezing cold. Endlessly his mind circled the insoluble problem. He had nowhere to go; the police, the lousy, rotten, stinking Special Branch, were sending him down. His final hopes had gone when he had looked into the hard eyes of Detective Sergeant Smith. How could he go back?

A screeching laugh came from the group in front of him, and one of them lurched back heavily into his shoulder, a tall, thin youth wearing a sheepskin jacket, hair as long as a carthorse's tail. The group was standing around a woman with a long neck and heavy green eye makeup. She had her head back and was puffing a very badly made cigarette; then the group moved back together again. Malloy realised that the smell of burning leaves must be marijuana. So what? If only some of these people could know who he was. There must be a way, must be somewhere. He fingered the money in his pocket; the small roll of notes was pathetically thin, twenty,

twenty-five pounds at the most, and everything was so bloody expensive in this lousy, rotten, stinking city.

One thing he knew, just one thing: he would never give any information, never lift a finger or do any damn thing that would help a policeman again. He had to get back somewhere, find a place, surely there was a hole somewhere he could crawl into, where he could do no one any harm. Jesus, why had he been so scared of going to jail? Long Kesh would have made him a hero. He would give one of his arms to be in a cell somewhere, to be treated like a real man.

His mind briefly touched on his wife, poor bitch; he had been no good to her, either, half daft since the girl had been born. Sitting on the earth floor of her mother's cottage, watching the fire, waiting for the magic letter to come from over the water. The house he was supposed to be buying for her to come to, that palace with a carpet and a real bathroom. Sure, she was better where she was.

He was being jammed even closer to the wall now as the crush in front of him moved back to permit the musicians to move up to the bar. Like a piece of flotsam, he was being moved along to the bottom of the steps that led up to the street. He made a small effort to keep his place, but it did not matter, he had no will to stay where he was.

Luton: the word floated into his mind. The one place in England that he actually knew, had lived in. Maybe he could find someone there, someone in the Irish pub, could hint that he'd come over to find a job; someone would sort him out. Of course, hadn't he put a few bob into a hat on the Friday night to help out some poor sod who was down on his uppers? Get a job, any job, however stinking; they always needed people on the line, night shift, get a room, lay low, change his name. Just give me a chance, Jesus Christ, a chance.

It was suddenly of vital importance to breathe fresh air, but the stairs were cluttered with people who were going neither up nor down. When he finally got to the top, he found a heavy rain was falling so that those who had been on their way out had stayed and blocked the door. The air coming in from the street was wet and chilling. The man standing next to the door was wearing a yellow-and-black striped shirt with a bow tie and black bowler hat: one of the musicians. Malloy slipped and almost fell on him.

"Easy, squire, easy." A broad good-natured face with wary eyes, but a mature man, easily fifty years old.

"What would you do . . ."

"What's that, Jock? I don't understand you."

Was his accent really that thick. Malloy tried again. "Ah, where do people sleep around here?"

"In their beds, mate."

"I mean, I mean . . ."

"You sound pissed, squire, and a long way from home. No place to kip out there, the winos fill up the dry corners. Try the Sally Army."

Malloy lurched out into the rain.

"Or the Arches," said the voice behind him.

# Twenty-Seven

Commander Shenton stood at the window of his fifth-floor office in New Scotland Yard and looked out onto Victoria Street. Rain, so fine that it was little more than mist, had dampened the road so that it gleamed like the eye of a startled bat. A crocodile of schoolchildren was being shepherded towards Westminster Abbey. Even at that height he could see small blobs of upturned faces, little boys who were far more curious about the headquarters of the Metropolitan Police than they were about any thousand-year-old abbey.

He moved away from the window and allowed the net curtain to drop behind him. It would have been pleasant to have walked in the autumn rain, through to the other side of the square and then past Big Ben and down to the Embankment. A quiet walk in the rain to sort out his thoughts; how long since he had done that? Probably not since he came in from the beat and swore that he would never walk a rainy street again. But it would be pleasant to breathe something other than this machine-controlled hygienic air that tasted as if it had been exhaled by a robot. He sat down at his desk, feeling empty, stale and remote. He opened the centre drawer of his desk and took out the little packet of bismuth tablets, selected one and put it on the end of his tongue. He sucked at it resignedly and then stood up again and took his pipe from the heavy glass ashtray, banged out its dottle, and put it in the side pocket of his jacket. Glancing at his watch, he swallowed the final chalky fragment of the bismuth tablet and, collecting the file from the corner of his desk, went out into the corridor.

The conference room was on the other side of the corridor

and only slightly larger than his own office. The officers present sat in a semi-circle facing Detective Chief Superintendent Maxwell. A large pinboard covered most of the left-hand wall of the conference room.

Everyone stood up as Shenton came in; he nodded to the tall, grey-haired man who stepped forward.

"Hello, sir."

Shenton put out his free hand and smiled. "Good to see you, Jimmy, it's been too long."

Superintendent James nodded. "Six years, sir. A pleasure to be working with you again."

"For coordination of enquiries, there's no question of the murder enquiry being run by anyone but you. Anything that the squad comes up with on that is yours."

"Thank you, sir."

Shenton dropped his file on the seat next to Maxwell's and waved them back to their seats. "This morning the commissioner impressed upon me that the tracking down of the bombers is of absolute priority. The one at the house in Prentice Street was around twenty pounds. We have no way of knowing the extent of supply, but as they are using such large amounts, they must have plenty in reserve."

Shenton turned towards his file and took out some foolscap sheets. "The Special Branch report that their agent went to the flat to deliver money. He reports four men, the descriptions are vague except for one possible, the leader, Casey, and we should have a photograph of him soon. But before we get into that we will hear from Superintendent James."

James got to his feet as Shenton sat down. "Well, sir, if it wasn't for the bomb kit, this one would add up to a straight family killing. The couple who lived in the flat as Bernard and Mary Wilson had been there nine months and that's about all we know at the moment. They lived quietly, went out for most of the day and had no visitors that anyone can remember. The man had a car, a Cortina, and we know its registration since the log book was in the flat. It was bought six months ago for cash, again in the name of Wilson. Both keys and car are missing, so we have to assume that the woman ran off with it. We have it out on the red list. We know the woman left the flat yesterday morning carrying a suitcase; a neighbour who knew her by sight saw her on the forecourt."

"Description?"

"Five foot four or five, medium build, dark hair worn short, wearing glasses with wide frames, tinted lenses, jeans and a white raincoat. Wilson was dead when she left, the Professor reckons at least six hours, shot by a .22 automatic at very close range. He was on the floor of the bedroom, face down and naked except for his socks and a shirt pulled up around his shoulders. Part of the bed quilt was under his feet, and I'd say he was on the bed when he was shot and then fell off."

He paused and Shenton caught his eye. "Did anyone hear the shots?"

"They live like zombies in that block. The woman in the adjoining flat swears she heard nothing except television. An old couple two flats away on the other side said they heard a row, voices and then thumps, not uncommon in that block, and no one ever interfered. Once home, they shut their doors and stay there and couldn't care less if their neighbors were cutting each other up with buzz saws. It's the second murder on that floor in as many days."

Shenton came sharply erect. "What?"

"The adjoining flat, a family called Green; the wife walked out and the husband killed their son and then topped himself."

"The local CID." James looked down at his notebook. "A Sergeant Milton made the report. Green was a Ramsden mental patient discharged under supervision. His case officer could not gain entry and was threatened by Green with a shotgun; he called the police and Milton called in the local SPG because of the gun. They found the child drowned in the bath and Green with his wrists slashed."

"Any possible connection?"

"Absolutely none that I see, sir."

"Has anyone spoken to Milton?"

"Not so far, sir."

"If he did his job even middling well he would have

knocked up the neighbours and seen this couple. Sorry James, please go on."

"Yes, sir. As I've said, it looked like a routine murder. A row of some kind, bit of bullying and the woman going over the top, except for a gun being used and the bomb kit. There was another gun in the flat, a Star .357 Magnum, unfired, fully loaded, in a holster, hanging on the bed headboard. The bomb kit was in the kitchen, a real craftsman's outfit; the boffins will be able to say more on that. The other stuff was also unusual: a silencer, about ten inches long; ballistics say it was made for a .22 weapon, but they also say it was unused. Then there was the passport in the name of Bernard Shaw with the picture of the dead man, and bank passbooks, building society deposit books, quite a bit of money in them, twenty-six thousand in all. I have a team in the flat, they're still printing everything; the dead man's prints aren't on CRO, but I've farmed them out in every direction. The other prints—lots in the bathroom—look as though they belong to the woman; again, nothing so far. There was a camera in the bedroom, actually on the bed itself. I've had the roll developed and we've put them up on the board."

Shenton turned in his chair and then got up to look at the photographs more closely. Maxwell and James stood on either side of Shenton, who had perched his spectacles on the end of his nose. Most were simply of buildings: Westminster City Hall, exterior shot of Victoria Station, the entrance to a block of offices, a bus terminus, one of a bridge crossing a railway.

"I thought . . ." James was hesitant, "they could be bomb targets?"

Shenton nodded and moved to the final three photographs. The first taken at an acute angle in what looked like a long, drab street; a tall man, half turned from the camera, was standing in front of a high terraced house, the lower part of his body obscured by a parked car. A poor photograph, the whole print spotted and blotched. Maxwell aimed a blunt finger at the apparent staining. "Dirt streaks; that was taken through a windscreen or side window."

Shenton was already looking at the final photograph, a much

cleaner print, in crisp focus. Two men were standing in apparent conversation beside a parked car; a tall, heavily built man was half turned from the camera, looking down at a second man who was shown full face. A strikingly handsome man with a mass of white or grey hair that had blown slightly to one side. Shenton put his age around forty.

"We have no idea who these men are?"

"No sir; neither is Wilson."

"He was probably the photographer. Do we know the order in which these photographs were taken?"

"I don't, sir, but it will be easily checked from the roll."

Shenton nodded. "What would you say that car was?"

"A Granada; we can't see the plates."

"Then this man is about six one."

"Maybe an inch more, sir."

Shenton stepped back and took off his spectacles. "Were there any photographs of the woman in the flat?"

"None. Nor papers, letters, anything that related to her at all."

"Sir."

Shenton turned to find Inspector Field, the squad collator, standing behind him.

"What is it?"

Field pointed to the stained print of the man standing before the house. "The bay window on the ground floor of that house, at the top, some kind of patterned cornice. It's on a lot of Victorian houses, but that particular style is on the bombers' house in Prentice Street. I'd say that that is an actual photograph of the house or one exactly like it."

Shenton glanced at the photograph of the gaunt shell of the bombed house that was in the centre of the pinboard, unfastened the stained photograph and held the two against each other. He nodded once, twice. "You're absolutely right, it is the same house."

"If I'm right," said Maxwell, "about those streaks being on a windscreen, it looks like whoever took it was in a car photographing anyone who went into the house."

"Yes." Shenton took the photograph back with him and

handed it to the Special Branch superintendent who was sitting in his chair at the end of the row.

"We know one man who went to that house; can you confirm whether or not the man in that photograph is your informer?"

The Special Branch man shifted uneasily. "I never met him. It was a low-level contact; the man was simply delivering money and we did not know the rendezvous. Once he had reported the address a check was made and as you know . . ."

"But since then."

"He was instructed to return to his contacts, re-establish his position. When he makes his next report . . ."

"You have no contact with him?"

"He has been instructed . . ."

"Do you have his description?"

The SB man dived into his document case: "Six feet two, medium build, brown eyes, dark brown hair worn moderately long . . . wearing jeans, dark sweater and reefer jacket. I would say, sir, that that photograph could well be him. His controlling officer would be able to make a definite identification."

"Thank you, Inspector Field will arrange a copy." Shenton handed the photograph to Field and walked back to his chair; he sat down and took out his pipe and tobacco pouch. "The reason for that photograph being taken we can't begin to guess at any more than we can about the man shot at Filbert Point. If he was the bomb maker then it should mean that we have a breathing space, but there are no guarantees; no explosives were found in the flat so there could be a stockpile of bombs already in existence. In any case, the rest of the active service unit are at large and, bombs or not, we know that they are well-armed. The woman who lived at Filbert Point has at least one gun, the murder weapon itself. Our first priority is to find the rest of that unit and that woman. It's possible that they are all in it together, but even if they are they will have split up by now. Which means that it's back to routine: the boarding house, bed and breakfast, cheap hotels. The woman could be either on her own or with one of the men. The run now is on new registrations in the last twenty-four hours."

Maxwell nodded to Field. "That's already in hand, sir. We're getting a printout of all new registrations within the last forty-eight hours."

"Good." Shenton turned his attention back to the SB man. "As I understand it, your informer visited the house in Prentice Street, handed over the money and only then made his report. The same day, two of your agents went to the house, searched and found explosives in the bathroom."

"Yes, Commander, but that house check was a completely separate enquiry to the informer's report. He reported at a low level; if there had been any suggestion of an arrest you would have, of course, been informed immediately. But before his report was evaluated, information had already come in about the house. Unfortunately, the two enquiries were not coordinated."

Maxwell breathed heavily, or perhaps snorted; Shenton looked pensive. "A second informer?"

The SB man glanced at his file of papers. "An anonymous phone call, received at twelve-twenty p.m. The caller was male, mature, slight Ulster accent. He asked for the Special Branch specifically and gave the Prentice Street address, stated that the house was a bomb factory and that the men on the top floor were armed terrorists. The call had to be taken seriously for obvious reasons."

"When did your informant report?"

"At two-twenty p.m., by personal contact; his controlling officer made his written report at four thirty-seven p.m., but it was not, unfortunately, actioned by his superior until two hours later."

"By which time the first team had already been briefed and were at the house."

"On their way certainly."

Maxwell stirred. "Has this second informer been heard from before?"

"No."

"It looks," said Maxwell flatly, "as if it was made to get your man into that house just so they could trip that bomb."

Before the SB man could say anything, Shenton turned to Inspector Field. "Let us have the details."

Field produced his report. "The explosive was gelignite, Frangex, colour-coded to the same batch as the bus bomb; the charge was about twenty pounds, detonation by immediate fuse on a trembler switch. It was contained inside a metal box. The investigating officer must have moved the box to set off the trembler; he was in very close proximity, on his hands and knees, the box itself was under the bath. The fascia board had been removed, obviously by the officer: he was killed instantly. The explosion was confined to the bathroom; that was wrecked of course, but apart from the windows being blown out and the ceiling of the floor below, the main blast went upwards, the bath took most of it. The second officer suffered burst eardrums and a broken wrist."

"Is there any provable connection between the bomb and the equipment from the flat in Filbert Point?"

"Forensic still have to report on that equipment, sir, but I have spoken to Major Bendix and he indicated that the wire and springs that were found are very similar, and that the fuse used would have been identical. The full report will take another forty-eight hours."

Shenton nodded to Maxwell who got up and stood close to the pinboard. "What we have at the moment is that the bus bomb was around twenty pounds and was carried onto the bus by Baldry. It would have been primed before he got onto the bus. The second at Prentice Street was certainly rigged; a phone call was made to the Special Branch. The fact that the caller actually asked for the Special Branch and waited until he was put through to them shows that he knew something about the system. He was probably one of the men in that house. Both bombs were from the same batch of explosive, so we assume that the same bomb maker made them both. The men from Prentice Street are loose, armed and about to start either bombing or shooting. It's a fortnight since we've had a shooting; the last was on the restaurant in Jermyn Street. Before that, the Military Club and when Constable Conway was shot down by a .357 Magnum; ballistics have the pistol taken from Filbert Point and if it is the same weapon, then that's a further link. Right now we are looking for four men and the woman from Filbert Point; we have no photographs and so far no photofits. The landlord from Prentice Street says that only three men lived on the top floor; we have a description of the fourth man: it fits the description of the man killed at Filbert Point."

Shenton turned towards the SB man. "Your informer could identify the man at Prentice Street as being the same as the dead man at Filbert Point. We can settle that today."

The SB man looked even more miserable. "He has not reported."

"You have no idea where he is?"

"Unfortunately . . ."

"Is there a call out on him?"

"Any sighting is to be reported, but he was told to ingratiate himself with the Kilburn community and not to report until he made some contacts. There is the possibility that he is with a Provo agent over here; he was instructed to make any contact that he could. It could be days before he surfaces."

"There must be some way of reaching him."

"I'm afraid not."

Shenton sucked hard on the mouthpiece of his pipe and emitted a great billow of smoke, waited a moment to control his irritation and then said gently, "It really is important that we check whether or not the man in the room at Filbert Point was one of the four men in that house. I would be grateful if you could emphasise the point and arrange immediate access as soon as he surfaces."

"I will, sir."

Shenton turned back to Superintendent James who had been listening with something like amusement. "If anything comes of those fingerprints I want to know at once."

"I've already got that in hand, sir."

"Then that is it, gentlemen. This morning the commissioner instructed me to oversee all matters arising out of the activities of this active service unit. At the moment we have the bus bomb, the explosion at Prentice Street, the murder of Constable Conway and the restaurant shootings. The man at Filbert Point is also obviously connected in some way; Superintendent James will continue his enquiries into that murder with his usual efficiency. Thank you."

Shenton stayed in his chair while his audience broke up and left the room in pairs or small groups; the Special Branch man left on his own.

Maxwell waited until the room was empty. "A muck up."

"The informer?" Shenton shrugged. "They probably under-rated him from the start. The chances are that when he heard that the house had been raided he ran . . . if he was able to run; he could be having a hard time now."

"He could save us a bit of time."

"It never comes that easy, does it? Our best chance is with the military. Jimmy James has those prints out to Lisburn by now and they aren't confined to printing convicted men. If that man was the bomb maker they'll have a line on him."

"And that Detective Sergeant Milton, he should be able to do a photofit of the girl. That'll be useful."

"Then it's back to routine."

Shenton leaned forward to peer at the photographs up on the pinboard. "Did we get a reply from that Dutch commissar?"

Maxwell shuffled his papers. "No. Shall I send a chaser?"

"Yes," said Shenton as he put a match to his pipe.

# Twenty-Eight

A protest demonstration was marching towards Parliament Square. The men in the vanguard carried the banners of union lodges. Behind them came the homemade slogans on pieces of hardboard nailed to broom handles: *End Low Pay Now*; *NUPE Says NO*; and *If It's A Living Wage Why Aren't You Living On It*.

Maureen watched them pass, mostly men in khaki anoraks with fake fur collars or PVC ski jackets. One of the stewards pacing the march handed her a leaflet which she took with a smile. *Stop the Cuts. It is your Health Service that will save YOUR LIFE. If you pay PEANUTS you get MONKEYS.*

She moved to the rear of the people who had stopped to watch the men pass by, looked for a litter basket, failed to find one and slipped the leaflet into the pocket of her suede jacket. At the corner of the street she turned into the Central Westminster Library and walked through into the reading room. A few old men were sitting at one of the broad oak tables, nodding sleepily over the newspapers and free magazines. She went to the end of the room and put one of the chairs at a corner of the table so that she could not be overlooked.

She set out her handbag and the bag from which she took her newly bought writing pad, envelopes and ballpoint pen. She thought for a few moments and then wrote her letter to the president of Sinn Fein, stating that she was an officer of the Provisional IRA and that it was necessary for her to report directly to the chief of the Army Council. Having lost her line of direct communication, she was acting on standing orders in sending to him the enclosed letter which he was requested to pass unopened into the hands of the Army Council chief. She wrote her second letter to an old college friend, reminding her of the past, and saying that all she was being asked to do was to deliver the enclosed letter by hand to the Sinn Fein office in Dublin. It was imperative that the letter should not pass through the mail where it would almost certainly be photographed by the Irish Special Branch.

She turned to a fresh page and addressed the letter formally to Little Pat McGlynn, using his full nomenclature, Chief of the Provisional Irish Republican Army Council. She wrote the first paragraph quickly, reminding him of when they had last met, of John Driscoll's work, the funeral oration and pistol shots over his grave. Then she looked up and glanced across the reading room at the lined pudding faces huddled at the tables nearest to the radiators.

She glanced back at her pad and took up her ballpoint again.

"You will have been told that I killed Brendan Casey and it is true, I did kill him. I had no choice. Ten months ago, which was three years after my husband's death, I was seconded to work with Casey as intelligence officer, following his appointment as controller of active service units in London. I was given these orders by John Ryder and I carried them out to the very best of my abilities.

"I reconnoitred possible targets, I checked police strengths, I evaluated information. I also built up a collection of maps and identified sympathetic areas. I reported directly to Casey. I was not happy with the situation: I was not consulted before operations were mounted. I could see no result from the reports that I made.

"Eight months ago, Brendan Casey told me that he was moving into a new flat and that it was necessary for me to move in with him. He told me that this was because he was to be isolated from the active service unit and that the English police were concentrating on men either on their own or in pairs who lived in casual lodgings. A couple who lived as man and wife would attract less notice.

"I refused to move into the flat with him unless it came as a direct Council order and, for the first time since I had arrived in London, Casey allowed me to speak directly to John Ryder. This was by telephone on 7th January at eight o'clock in the evening. Ryder told me that the arrangement had your personal approval and had been mentioned at the previous day's Council meeting, a note being made of the fact that our living arrangements were completely separate. We took the names of Mary and Bernard Wilson. I moved into the flat at Filbert Point on 10th February.

"I greatly disliked the arrangement. I had hoped that daily contact with Casey would mean a greater involvement with active service operations, but none of my work was accepted by Casey. He wanted me as a housekeeper, took me nowhere and had little interest in my ideas. He drank heavily and made many suggestions of sleeping with me. I tried to make direct contact with John Ryder, but Casey refused to allow me to speak directly to him.

"On 7th October, I returned to the flat and found Casey in the process of making a large bomb, more than twenty pounds of gelignite, and when I came in he had fixed a timing mechanism, electrically timed by a wristwatch. Casey was furious that I had returned earlier than he had expected and also for his own carelessness: the entrance to the flat was always deadlocked if any explosives were being handled. Casey refused to discuss the bomb; I reminded him that as the intelligence officer I was entitled to know and comment upon operations. I demanded to speak to Ryder. He would not listen. He had also been drinking, which is stupidly dangerous for anyone dealing with explosives or fuses.

"Later that night he came into my bedroom with a bottle of whisky. I told him that if he did not leave I would, and make my own way to Dublin. He did not leave and in the morning said that he had been drunk and could not remember anything.

"The following day the London bus was bombed, and I asked Casey if the bomb used was the one that he had made. He said that it was not and that his bomb was with the active service unit, but that the target it would be used against had to wait because of the police activity. I did not believe him. I again demanded to speak with Ryder and he said he would arrange it as soon as he could, but that Ryder was travelling and could not be contacted.

"On 11th October, there was an incident in the adjoining flat at Filbert Court. I came into the flats in late morning and found the floor crowded with people, including policemen; the man who lived next door had been deserted by his wife and he had killed his young son and then himself. I was visited by one of the policemen who wanted to use my telephone. I acted normally, as a neighbour would in those circumstances. He was an ordinary policeman from the local station. I am certain he was not a member of the political police.

"That day, Casey came back in the late evening and told me that the courier had arrived from Belfast. He said that as if it had some special significance: the courier was Danny Malloy. At first I did not know who he was talking about, but then I remembered Malloy, a young volunteer who had once acted as a courier for my husband, John Driscoll. Casey said that it was very likely that Malloy was an informer and that immediately after he had left the house, the other members of the unit had moved out.

"Casey had been drinking and drank more while we were sitting in the living room of the flat. I wanted to discuss the explosion on the bus again, but he would not listen. While we were talking he received a telephone call; he said it was from Sean. He told me that he had booby-trapped the house, and that if someone had come to set it off the same day that Malloy had made his visit, it meant that Malloy was an informer and that he had gone straight to the police.

"I agreed with Casey that for a check to be made on the house the same day as Malloy had made his visit was very suspicious, but there was something else that made me very uneasy. Casey had told me that he had removed all guns from the house, but not the explosives. That did not make sense; if no one came, the explosives would have to be recovered and that would be very dangerous and a breach of security. It seems to me that Casey knew that the house would be visited and that because the explosion had taken place there was now no way of checking any loss of gelignite which could have been used as an unauthorised bomb on the bus. I argued with him and he lost his temper. He grabbed me and I threw whisky into his face; he hit me several times and then held me helpless against the wall. It was then he told me that my husband had not been shot by the British army but that a squad directly under Casey's command had shot him and planted evidence that it was an SAS unit. I asked him who else knew and he said Ryder knew and that it was also Ryder's idea that I should be seconded to him so that he could keep an eye on me and take action if I ever became suspicious.

"I gathered from him that my husband was shot because he was on his way to report his suspicions to the Council on embezzlements of Army money. I tried to leave the flat and Casey caught me in the hall and beat me, took me into his bedroom and forcibly raped me. He was a very strong man and I was more or less helpless without a weapon. The rape was very painful and I was also nearly unconscious from the beating he had given me. I was in no doubt that he intended to kill me and that it had always been intended that I should be killed; the only question being that my death should not follow too quickly upon my husband's because it would have aroused suspicion.

"After the rape, Casey told me to get him the whisky bottle from the living room. I was naked and knew that I had no chance of reaching the entrance door of the flat; Casey's bedroom door opened in the hall and he could see if I tried to pass it. I went into the kitchen; I knew that he kept a locked canvas bag under the sink unit. I took a razor blade and gambled that I would find a weapon in the bag. I knew that otherwise I would not live through the night. In the bag I found a .22 pistol which I knew how to use. I went back to the bedroom with it hidden in a towel. Before I could speak, Casey pulled me, the towel dropped and he saw the pistol. I had to shoot him then because he was about to kill me. He did get on top of me, but in the struggle I shot him twice more and he died.

"I left the flat the following morning, taking his car, which I left in a multi-story parking block. When I left, I took my clothes and all the money I could find. Among the other things I found was a second passport for Casey, with his photograph, but in a name unknown to me, his bomb-making equipment and some bank passbooks in the other name. These amounted to almost thirty thousand pounds. I do not know where he obtained it. I left the passport and other documents which must now be with the British police. The other things I took, because I did not understand them at the time, were photographs. I can recognize John Ryder, and I believe the other man is the Dutchman who was the main contact. He used many names. The piece of paper, with the numbers, I could not understand at all; it could be anything. It is only now in looking at it, it has occurred to me that if the first numbers are international zone numbers, then the whole could be the dialling code and telephone number of a contact in Holland. The first two figures, 31, are the international code for Holland.

"I am sending you the photographs and paper because I am convinced that Casey was involved in a racket of some kind that had nothing to do with his duties for the Army. I have so far stayed out of the reach of the British police; I have no doubt that if they catch me they have enough evidence to convict me of killing Brendan Casey and will jail me for life. They would also probably try to pressurise me into turning traitor. They will not succeed.

"I have very little chance of getting away. The odds are very much against me. If the British police do catch up with me, I shall do my best to use the pistol. It is very likely that they will shoot me dead.

"While he was raping me, Casey said that my husband was shot to keep his mouth shut. He said that he was a traitor. John Driscoll was no traitor. He was a brilliant man who dedicated his life to the Republican cause because he believed in freedom. He agreed to support that cause in violence when it was obvious that debate and natural justice could not prevail. I joined him in his struggle because I believed in the same ideals. I supported him, helped him in his work and revere his memory.

"It was only on the night that I shot Brendan Casey that I learned that my husband had been betrayed and murdered by a swindler, a bully and a traitor. I shot Casey to defend myself, but he deserved to die for what he had already done.

"I address this letter to you in the name of the Republican cause. It may be that I shall be dead when it is delivered. Whoever was behind Casey has great reason to want my death. The British police will have no hesitation in shooting me down if I offer resistance and I do not intend to be taken without a struggle.

"I do not know the full meaning of these photographs or the number that I am sending to you, but as they were carefully kept by Casey they must have importance and a connection with the money he was hoarding.

"I only ask that everything be done to discover the truth of Casey's activities.

"My aims and beliefs are the same as they have always been. I know that I can never return to Ireland. My fate is either death or exile.

"God bless Ireland. Long live the Republic.

"Maureen Driscoll."

Maureen came slowly up the drab suburban street crossing from the other side of the street, alert to any occupants in the parked cars as a routine precaution against watchers. There were none, and if there were there was little that she could do about it except to be ready and to do her best to die rather than be captured.

The house that she wanted was in the middle of the terrace. She opened the gate to enter the tiny front garden and in a half a dozen steps was at the front door; she rang the bell and within a few seconds the door was opened by her fellow lodger whom she knew only as Janet: a pert, pixy face framed by long dark hair, large grey eyes, slim body, which gave the first impression that she was a schoolgirl.

"Did you have any luck?"

"Not much." Maureen tried to remember the lie that she had told. "I had to wait hours before he would see me and then I had to fill in all the forms. I have to see him next week to make a full statement."

"They're all sods," said Janet in her little girl voice. "Come into the kitchen, I've just made tea."

Maureen followed her through the passageway and into the back room where Mrs Meadows, a fat woman with abundant white hair and a round, kindly face, was leaning forward on her orthopaedic walking frame, dangling a plastic bubble into the face of Janet's tiny son who was lying in a carry-cot.

"Hello, dear; he's adorable, isn't he?"

"Yes," said Maureen, "yes, he is." She sat in one of the little wooden armchairs; a *Daily Sun* was folded over its arm and she opened it out. The front page story was about a football pools winner, page two a threatened strike of steel workers. Page three was almost wholly taken up by Miss Sunshine who was looking down coyly at her tip-tilted breasts.

"Reading your stars?" Janet was holding a cup of tea out to her.

"What?"

"What sign are you?"

"I don't know." Maureen turned the page to stare at the horoscope column.

"We always look at ours: all rubbish, dear, they say it's my day for stepping out." Mrs Meadows shuffled round until she was poised over her chair and then let herself down with a rattle from her walking frame, chuckling deeply.

Maureen put the paper down and took out her packet of cigarettes. She offered them to Janet who took one; she flicked her lighter for both cigarettes and took up her teacup again. A tabloid newspaper would make a splash of a gun murder in a tower block, so it was possible that Brendan had still not been found; possible, but not a thing to bank on. The British police were very devious.

Janet puffed out a great cloud of smoke. "What sort of hassle are they giving you?"

"Fiddly things. I need my birth and marriage certificates."

"Yeah, you need those. I made sure I brought mine with me. I brought everything I could think of. If only I could have got my hands on the house deeds."

"It shouldn't be too difficult. I'll get copies."

"Your face looks much better, dear," said Mrs Meadows. "The swelling's gone down and the bruise is fading."

"It's yellow really; I've put pancake over it."

"You're a very pretty girl, dear."

"Thank you." Maureen smiled at her with genuine affection. She got up to set her teacup on the draining board and flicked her cigarette ash into the sink.

"Have you had anything to eat?"

"A sandwich, but I'm not hungry. I'll make myself something later."

Janet had her baby out of the carry-cot and was looking at him with a mixture of fondness and puzzlement. "I've got to make Jason's feed."

"You go ahead, I'm having a bath. Don't bother with the washing up, I'll do it with mine."

"Thanks. Damn, I've left his powder upstairs."

"I'll get it. Where, the bathroom?"

"No, it's in our room, the blue bag by the bed."

Maureen took her bags up the stairs; her room was at the back of the house, over the kitchen, looking down on the unkempt garden. She dropped her bags on the single bed and slipped off her jacket. Janet's room was on the other side of the landing, opposite to the bathroom; it was larger than her own, but more crowded, with a large bed and big old-fashioned wardrobe and a dressing table with a jumble of bags and boxes.

She left the door ajar and skirted the bed. The blue canvas bag gaped open, crowded with jars and packets, cotton wool, vaseline, creams and gripe water. She picked up the tin of baby powder and looked around; two suitcases lay open on the floor with baby clothes spilling from them. A writing case on the dressing table; she went across to pick it up and listened to the vague rumble of voices below her and then snapped the clasp. A spillage of papers, forms, notes, letters from a solicitor, a child-allowance book. The bottom pocket had a small folded wad of coloured paper: a new birth certificate for Jason, marriage certificate and then Janet's birth certificate. Her heart leapt at the date; Janet looked incredibly young, but she was in fact twenty-eight. She forced herself to calmly note every detail, mouthing the words to herself before replacing the certificate with the others, then the papers. She put the writing case back on the dressing table and went out, shut the door behind her and delivered the powder to Janet.

Back in her own room, she took the writing pad out of her bag and wrote out the details, forcing herself to remember them in precise order. Janet Ruth Wimbush, 16th July, 1962; James Alfred Wimbush, Metal Worker, Ruth Mary Wimbush, nee Dobson. District Surrey Mid-Eastern: Sub-District Goulsdon and Banstead. She read over what she had written and then put the writing pad back in her bag.

She went into the bathroom, swilled out the bath, put in the plug and ran the water. When she returned to her room she put the catch on the door before unloading her leather shoulder bag. The pistol lay in the back compartment under a folded silk scarf. She slipped it beneath the bed pillow before she undressed; the wads of money were bound beneath her breasts and forward on her hip bones. The jeans had been strained by the extra bulk. It would probably be better if she wore a loose skirt, but that would mean a complete change of style, something for a new identity.

She put the money between the box spring and mattress of

the bed and only then took off the rest of her clothes. From the carrier bag she took out the basic toiletries that she had bought on the way back from the library. A final look round and then she took up her towel and walked naked to the bathroom.

Wiping the steam from the mirror on the door of the cabinet she examined her face. Mrs Meadows had been right: the swelling on the left cheekbone had much reduced, although still tender to touch. Her makeup had smeared in the steam and the yellow staining from the fading bruise showed more clearly. But her eyes were clear and the tiny scab on her cut lip could easily be concealed by lipstick.

Not too bad, she said to herself, for an abused lady being chased by both sides.

# Twenty-Nine

It had been forty-eight hours since Brendan had issued his instructions and more than fourteen since he had been due to reappear. Sean felt the tension more than the others; he crossed continually to the window and peered around the side of the curtain to look down into the darkly wet street before he went back to his bed and the assembled Sterling submachine gun, complete with its curved magazine, which he held like a talisman. The television set was tuned to ITV London, which was showing an American comedy programme. Liam lay slumped in a chair watching the screen whilst he drank beer from a can. When he laid the can aside he put his right hand on his thigh as if to massage his groin, but, almost without conscious thought, he caressed the butt of his Magnum revolver.

Only David was relaxed. He sat on his bed, wearing scarf and anorak, his knees tented in front of him, schoolboy fashion, reading a paperback book, his long, black hair hanging like stage curtains on either side of his face. He pursed his lips and half smiled as he read something in the book that amused him.

Sean scowled his irritation at a burst of canned laughter from the television set. "You have to have that crap?"

"What else is there?"

Sean made another trip to the window and strained to see if anyone was standing in the pools of darkness between the streetlamps. "The bastards could be keeping observation right now."

"We can't do a thing until we've word from Brendan, and that's it."

"They could have him; shit, they must have him."

"It's only two days . . . could be an accident, anything."

David had stopped reading; he slipped a scrap of newspaper between the leaves to mark his place, closed the book and tucked it neatly into the side pocket of his anorak. "If Brendan knows that they're watching this place it would be a good reason for him to hold off."

"If Brendan knew we were being watched he'd do something about it, get word to us, send someone, the girl."

David had got off his bed and in his turn looked out into the night. "There's nothing obvious, but then there wouldn't be, would there? They could be in any of those cars, hiding in the porches of the houses up and down the street or even inside the house opposite sussing us with infrared."

"You're a happy bastard."

"There's only one way to find out." David reached under the pillow on his bed and slipped out the Browning, partially withdrew the magazine, pulled back the sliding jacket, sighted, checked the trigger action, dropped the hammer and then slammed home the magazine. "If they're out there, then they're waiting for us either to fall asleep or come out; we have to give them the worst choice, all three coming out together, three directions, tooled up and ready."

"They'll blast us into dust."

"They won't get us all. You want to stay?"

"We all go," said Sean. "No bastard stays."

Liam made a long performance of carefully rolling a shag cigarette and then another of lighting up. "I'm coming, but it's all my own idea that I do. If we get outside and it's nothing, then what?"

"We get to the car." David took the key from his trouser pocket. "If nothing has happened by the time I reach the car, then I start her up; you two get in. If they're there, they'll show by then. If it's still okay, then we go west and do that restaurant. Sean can do the front, you watch the street, Liam; it's likely they'll have Specials around all the likely places. Then we'll have it back to the car park, dump the car down the alley and pick up the van." David pushed the hair aside from his face and grinned at them, looking like a mischievous child. "What about it?"

"How long have you been thinking that out?"

"Right now. Sean?"

"So long as we do something."

"Come on then, leave the light on."

"Hold it." Sean picked up the Sterling and pulled back the bolt. He held it as he would a pistol, with a finger resting across the trigger guard and concealed as much of it as he could within the flap of his donkey coat, but the magazine was too bulky and the snout of the serrated barrel protruded a good six inches beyond the coat.

"That's no good, Sean; carry it in the duffle at least until we get to the front door. If you show that thing, they're likely to fire without a shout."

"All right."

A duffle was pulled from under Sean's bed and the dismantled Sterling was inserted. Sean carried the bag over his shoulder with the last couple of inches of serrated barrel sticking out of the top, but hidden under his shoulder.

David led the way down the stairs without incident. He opened the front door in the hall and stepped through onto the top of the stone steps, his left hand with the key deep inside his trouser pocket, and the right one in the side pocket of the anorak tensed around the butt of the Browning. The light rain had stopped, leaving the steps and the road gleaming in the streetlamps like the body of a black beetle. He went down the steps and through the scruffy front garden into the street; as he reached the pavement, Sean and Liam came out of the house and quickly ran down the steps after him. David squeezed between cars and crossed to the other pavement, the others keeping level with him, but on their side of the road.

The car looked untouched; he tried his weight against the door before he used the key, and when he got the door open he leaned in to pick up a rag from the floor and wiped the rain from the windscreen. He glanced across to the other pavement; Sean was standing between two parked cars with the bag in his left hand. Liam had gone further along and was lost in the darkest patch of all, beneath the overhanging tree in someone's front garden.

He got into the driving seat and turned the key; the engine fired at the second try and he raced the engine, waiting for the oil light to fade before putting on the sidelights. He un-latched the passenger doors and pulled out into the centre of the road. The other two appeared suddenly on either side of the car; Liam got into the front passenger seat next to him. Sean jumped into the back and was still closing the door behind him as David took the car up through the gears. The far end of the road came at an angle to the main highway and they were immediately into faster-moving traffic.

"Anything?"

"Not a light." Sean was twisted round on the back seat rubbing at the condensation on the back window with the sleeve of his donkey jacket.

"Straight up then and through Bond Street. We'll make a dummy run unless there's a group on the pavement the first time; otherwise we let them have it on the return trip, okay?"

As they came off the end of the Edgware Road and joined a knot of traffic rounding Marble Arch, David kept his atten-tion on the cars at either side of him, scrupulous on his road positioning. The traffic was heavy now; it would be too easy to be boxed up here. He resisted the temptation to turn off into the darker side street and held his place until he got to the junction, deciding at the final moment to turn into Port-land Street.

"Could be company," said Sean.

David glanced at the rearview mirror. "The taxi?"

"It's sticking to us, drops back but comes again, never passes."

"Watch it now."

He turned into Oxford Street and positioned the car for a left-hand turn. "We'll go straight in once we reach Davies Street."

"What about a go at Claridges?" Liam asked.

"We'll keep to the plan; all you're likely to hit at hotels is the doorman; the archbastards are well back."

"He's still with us," said Sean and pulled back the bolt on the Sterling. "What do we do?"

"We could pull in," said Liam, "and force it one way or the other."

David kept his speed constant, watching for Bond Street underground station. "If we stop they'll box us. If that's the law then they'll have run the number and know it's a hot car. They'll be waiting for us to turn off so they can take us somewhere quiet. We'll go straight in, Sean; I don't stop, we'll do it, and then straight down and through the back doubles. Here it comes now." He turned left into Davies Street.

"He's sticking."

Sean had the nearside passenger window down, resting the snout of the Sterling on the door sill. David slackened pressure on the accelerator, dropping the speed from thirty to twenty-five, twenty, fifteen, ten; they were level with the restaurant now, its discreet canopy stretching out over the pavement. No one was standing at the entrance, no one was passing on the pavement in front of it; he caught the impression of a man in some kind of brown uniform inside the glass entrance door. He glanced at the rearview mirror; the taxi had all its head-lights up and was within a yard or two of them now.

Sean fired, placing his bursts accurately into the pools of light on the other side of the street windows, guessing where the diners would be around their individual table lamps. The final shots of the magazine hit the door and then they were past and he swivelled for the last shots and they went high, clattering somewhere into the upper stonework.

David kept his attention on the wing mirror; he could see that the offside door of the taxi was open and whoever was in back had a foot poised to step down into the road. He pumped the accelerator and put up his own headlights. A figure was emerging from the darkness of one of the doorways level with them and Liam fired a single shot and the figure either dived or collapsed on the pavement.

They reached the end of Davies Street with the taxi shadowing within six feet of them, the driver apparently satisfied to ride them, not attempting to ram or sideswipe. They could hear the sirens of the regulation cars now. Sean was cursing a stream of obscenities in the back seat; the second magazine for the Sterling which he had placed carefully along the rear of the back seat had been somehow bounced onto the floor of the car and he was crouched head down scrabbling for it.

David turned to his left, moving instinctively away from the sound of the police sirens; the street had a sharp left-hand turn and then a right. There were cars parked at the sides; all of the buildings were in darkness. The taxi still had all its lights up. Gavin leaned out of his passenger window and tried to get a bead on one of the taxi's tyres, but the driver kept it well tucked behind the Cortina. David tried a right turn which brought him into a wide but ill-lit street, past a parade of darkened shops and blank-faced buildings.

Sean had found his magazine and slammed it into the Sterling. "Pull up and I'll have the bastards."

"We've got to dump the car, the heavy mob are almost on top of us. We've got to get a couple of roads from here before we split or they'll have us like sitting ducks. Whatever happens we stick as three until we're clear of the Specials. When I reach the forecourt of these flats, just before, between the parked cars, I'll put in and we'll run through the flats, right?"

"Okay." It was Sean. "But I'm having that cocksucker behind us."

"Now!" David braked savagely, twisted the ignition key and pulled it out of the lock, jumped out of the car with the key in his left hand and the Browning in the other. He crouched close to the side of the car, thumbing back the hammer of the Browning, and then raised it with both hands, firing into the windscreen of the taxi; the headlights were still full up, but most of their power was blanked off by the rear of the Cortina; he could hear the bullets thumping home into metal. The lights of the taxi were abruptly extinguished. He looked across the Cortina and saw a figure moving from the road to the flats . . . Liam. "Come on, Sean."

David wriggled between two of the parked cars and reached

the flat's forecourt. Liam was already halfway across the forecourt to the main entrance of the flats before he hesitated and looked back, revolver in hand. David stayed on the pavement and ducked to crouch against the dwarf wall as he peered up into the gloom beyond the lights of the flats. Whoever had been in the taxi would be out of it now and making his way forward under cover of the parked cars.

Sean emerged to his left, still holding the Sterling. "Let's go."

"Through that entrance and straight out the back."

They moved warily towards the entrance of the flats, back to back, so that they could see anything moving from the pavements. The sirens wailed to an earsplitting note as a car and a van, each with blue flashers, came in at the other end of the street, nosing up to the abandoned Cortina. Both David and Sean turned and ran to the entrance of the flats; Liam was already beyond the entrance door. "There's only the stairs," he said.

Sean was peering through the door into the forecourt of the flats and David joined him, squinting at the little group that had spread themselves into a line. "Let's take the cunts on."

"Sean, we ought to run."

"Not without this." Sean stuck the snout of the Sterling through the battered doors and fired a short burst of half a dozen rounds and all the visible figures on the pavement went to ground.

"Come on!" David had already started on the stairs and Sean came back from the door, cursing as he wrenched at the bolt of the Sterling.

"It's effing jammed."

"Come on!" David led the way into the first-floor corridor, closely followed by Liam. Sean moved with them, still wrestling with the ejection bolt, finally getting it clear as they jogged down the corridor, ejecting live rounds. He did not stop to pick them up. The corridor ended in a right turn and they followed it down to a fire door with a locking bar. David kicked up the locking bar and went through it, gun in hand. There were stairs, but they led upwards. They climbed the stairs cautiously in complete darkness, David holding his hand out against the wall so that he could judge the bend in the stairs. Another door, but this one was locked on the outside.

"Go back."

"Shoot the bloody thing."

"It's steel and we don't know where the lock is. Get back up those stairs or they'll box us down here."

They went back up the stairs; Sean was first through the door and he came through it at the same instant as a blue uniform appeared at the bend in the corridor. Sean fired instinctively; the noise of the Sterling bounced off the corridor walls like a death rattle while the bullets hit the facing wall on the other side of the bend, taking saucer-sized lumps out of the plaster. The policeman had gone to ground, the revolver in his right hand unfired.

"In here." David had turned to the door of the nearest flat and hammered on it with his left fist. Liam noticed the bell-push and put his thumb on it. Sean dropped to crouch with the Sterling aimed at the edge of the corridor around which the policeman had disappeared; he could see something, an eye or whatever; someone was having a squint, but he held his fire.

David had poked open the letter flap and was saying something to whoever was standing on the far side of it; the door opened and David put his weight against it, holding his automatic under the chin of a slightly built man. He backed the man into the tiny hallway of the flat and Liam squeezed past them to enter the living room. Sean backed through the door of the flat and pushed the door closed.

In the living room Liam was standing with his revolver pointed at a very shocked and terrified woman with grey hair and glasses; she was sitting in a chair with wooden arms and seemed to be trying to make herself as physically small as possible. David allowed the man to cross over to the woman; the man patted the woman's shoulder and then turned to face David defiantly. David smiled at him and lowered the hammer on his Browning. "Nothing will happen to you so long as you do as we say."

"Who are you?"

"Irish soldiers. You've more to fear from the ones out there than of us." He jerked his thumb over his shoulder to the hall where Sean was still pointing his Sterling at the front door. "Just stay where you are and nothing will happen to you." He lowered his voice as he spoke to Sean. "Have you heard anything?"

"A bit of scratching is all, but look . . ." Sean worked the catch to release the magazine and showed him that it was almost empty.

David nodded. "We'll not shoot our way out now; we're cornered. They'll be clearing out the flats along the way with a couple of hard men covering our door. They'll not break in till they've checked and they'll know we've got these two. Our only chance is to bargain."

"And take them with us if they don't?"

David looked into Sean's eyes. "It depends. I'll have a look round."

His survey of the flat did not take long. There was one small bedroom, crowded with over-large furniture, a single small window. He pressed himself flat against the wall and took a cautious look. The flat was at the side of the block and he had to angle his head to see anything of the forecourt at the front of the building. What he could see seemed to be crowded with vehicles flashing blue lights; about thirty feet below him was a walkway with a single lamp at the far end. He could see no one on the walkway. There was a small kitchenette on the other side of the hall and a minute bathroom with a bar along the side of the bath for support for someone infirm.

He went back into the living room.

Liam was still standing by the couple with his gun pointing somewhere between them. David put his own pistol back into the pocket of his anorak and took one of the dining chairs out into the hall for Sean. "Do you want Liam to relieve you?"

Sean looked at him. "You taking charge?"

David smiled. "I'm doing the obvious; you want to do something else?"

Sean shook his head and then started as a faint shuffling noise came from the front door.

David drew his pistol and stepped close to the door. "Now listen, I'll say it once. We have two people, the couple who live here. Any move through this door and we all go. Try it and we'll put a burst through the door itself. You got that? We'll talk when we're ready, but to a top man and no funny stuff. If you think you can take us, remember we've got our jelly wired up and we'll not only take this lot with us, but the whole fucking block." He turned and grinned cheerfully at Sean who was looking at him as if he was seeing him for the first time.

# Thirty

It was late when Shenton reached the file that had been supplied by Criminal Intelligence. His eyes were sore and he put the file aside as he went through the lounge to the kitchen and ran the cold tap over his hands and then palmed the water over his eyes. He glanced at his watch as he went back into the lounge and looked fleetingly at the whisky bottle that was standing on the drinks tray on top of the sideboard. The house was absolutely quiet apart from a couple of indistinct creaks as the ceiling boards took up the expansion from the central heating. He switched on the radio, barely raising the volume above that of a whisper as he searched for a station that was playing the light orchestral music that he found soothing.

He sat down in his armchair again and tilted the shade of the reading lamp a little higher to give himself a better light. The thin file on Casey held a couple of photographs in a clear plastic envelope stapled to the inside of the covers. He took them out: one was an official photograph, much enlarged from the picture that had been inside Casey's passport, the embossed stamp of the Eire Passport Office clearly visible across the bottom right corner. The second was a shot of Casey emerging from a street doorway; he had a cigarette in his mouth and his head was partly turned as if he were talking to someone behind him. It had obviously been taken with a telephoto lens, but the definition was good and it showed the whole of Casey's upper body, his barrel chest and bull neck. So obviously a powerful man that it seemed ludicrous that it had taken only a little 40-grain pellet of lead to end his heavy presence so definitely.

Shenton picked up his warm pipe and struck a match, lovingly turning the bowl to catch the full length of the flame, tossed the match into the big stone ashtray and read as much about Brendan Casey as anyone was willing to tell him.

Casey, Brendan Patrick. Born: Belfast (Bogside) 30th May, 1948
Height: 5' 11" Eyes: Grey Hair: Brown Complexion: Ruddy
Physique: Good Muscular Development Weight: 198 lbs
Distinguishing marks/peculiarities: None

Father: John Casey, born 1918, resident Eire (Dublin)
Mother: Died 1962.
Sister: Kathleen, born 1951, American citizen, resident USA, Pittsburgh, wife of Peter Czykskiter, no known political affiliations. No other living relatives known.

John Casey has a criminal record, theft and assault. Served total of four years' imprisonment. Declared IRA supporter, not politically known. In receipt of State Retirement Pension. No other means of support, but believed to receive occasional sums from son. John Casey never visited mainland so far as known. John Casey's brother, Brendan's uncle, was Patrick Casey, active member of IRA who carried out terrorist activities, England, 1939. Patrick Casey was convicted of murder, Liverpool Assizes, 1940. He and Sean Moires, another IRA man, planted gelignite bomb on pedestrian bridge in Liverpool Docks close to oil storage tanks; bomb caused only superficial damage, but killed a married couple who were passing at the time of the explosion. Casey and Moires executed Walton Jail, 3rd June, 1940.

In 1964, at age 16, Brendan Casey became a junior member of IRA in the Bogside Brigade. Was employed as a barboy in various drinking clubs. Known to have visited Eire, Dublin, Ballsbridge, Cork, in company of IRA officers during period 1965–1968.

In 1969, defected to the Provisional IRA together with his brigade officer John Ryder (file 76894/47). Casey led a large gang who committed various acts of violence and extortion, mostly protection rackets in drinking clubs and pubs, but also shops and small businesses.

This money was channelled to John Ryder. After Ryder's arrest and escape to Eire, Casey became Ryder's representative in Belfast. In 1972, a court-martial of Casey was ordered because of misuse of IRA funds; it was estimated that almost half of all moneys collected by Casey were embezzled by him, also that he killed for personal ends. He was protected by Ryder who is a member of the Army Council. Reports directly to Patrick McGlynn. (Little Pat).

1974, warrant issued for arrest of Casey on charges conspiracy to commit murder, extortion, grievous bodily harm, causing explosions, possessing explosives and deadly weapons. (This warrant arose out of evidence given by Gains, Purse and Dobbin in statements to officers of the RUC.) Files—restricted DO.

Warrant still valid. Known to have moved freely in the Bogside, Derry and Andersonstown and to have one time been recommended as brigade commander, but disliked and mistrusted by then northern commander Jack Harris who was relieved of his command on orders of Patrick McGlynn, 1976, court-martialled in secret, shot and buried in "the Green Field"—this incident never admitted by Provos. Harris is officially stated to have left the country and to be working abroad on IRA business.

Casey sighted Dublin, October 1984 and Amsterdam, November 1984. Believed responsible for murder of John Driscoll, December 1985. Driscoll, graduate Trinity College, had been resident Amsterdam and believed responsible for channelling funds from American sympathisers through continental bankers, also responsible arms purchases. Driscoll was fluent in French and German. Was resident in Amsterdam, 1980–1985, together with wife (Maureen Driscoll, nee Sullivan (file 86745/71). In December 1985, Driscoll returned Eire and 14th December was passenger in car that drove over border into South Armagh. The car was ambushed and Driscoll killed, no others in party were injured. Death of Driscoll, stated Provisionals, to be the work of SAS, but this definitely untrue and was confirmed as much by both forensic and ballistic evidence. Execution approved by McGlynn and carried out by squad directly under Casey's command. Casey appears to be the one Provisional officer that Ryder trusts. 1985, Casey known to have arrived in Paris. Intelligence report that Casey left France to reside in Spain, but appears to have been in London continuously since 1986.

Enquiries proceeding.

Shenton turned back and read the three flimsy sheets for a second time before, with a final glance at the photographs, he closed the file and put it back in his document case. He got up and walked across to the sideboard and, breaking the unspoken promise that he had made to himself, unscrewed the cap on the whisky bottle and poured himself a careful half inch into a water glass. He took it back to his armchair and cradled it between his hands as he sipped reflectively. He now knew a little bit more about Brendan Casey, and what he could glean from between the lines made a familiar pattern: underneath the general bullshit of causes and political argument, Casey was just a gangster. The old familiar story of greed, with more scope than usual to operate as an extortionist and embezzler because he was in a wide-open town where a man with a gun or a big fist could go on the take in the name of the Cause.

And Casey had lasted because he had a protector, maybe an employer, in John Ryder—a smarter man by far. He had heard the name, could even, with some mental effort, remember a photograph of the man, bluish-faced and clear-eyed. Ryder for almost twenty years had been a spokesman first of a political organisation, Sinn Fein, and then of the IRA. He had stood for Parliament somewhere in the six counties, but had failed to be elected. And that was about it. He had been gun-running, been jailed and had made a spectacular escape from prison.

There would be a very special file on Ryder from which this resumé had been taken, but they would not allow him to look at that one; and Casey had been his hatchet man, working directly under his orders. He must have found Casey a valuable man to allow him to siphon off money, probably a lot of money. Was it likely that Casey had been cheating Ryder? If so, why not have him brought up before one of the kangaroo courts? Answer, maybe Casey knew where too many bodies were buried, literally. It was a tempting thought that Casey was shut up because Ryder thought he was too dangerous, but it did not really add up. Firstly, the gun; a .22 was an unexpected gun to turn up in a heavy case like this. Lethal enough at short range, but you have to be very certain of precisely hitting the spot, and these people were armed to the teeth. Casey's own gun had been in the flat, a .357 Magnum, which was a gun and a half, not only capable of killing a giant but also likely to do so if he was on the other side of a brick wall.

So why a .22? The only answer that made any kind of sense was so that he could be approached without suspicion. And Casey was almost naked; he had a shirt pulled up around his armpits and socks. The rest of his clothes, including his gun and the shoulder holster, were all in the room. In the quaint phrase of the pathologist, he had engaged in intercourse shortly before his death, so he had been there with a girl and a girl had lived there with him. The girl that Milton had seen. He reached down again into his document case and found his notes; Mary Wilson would not be her name of course. He was startled by the telephone ringing and he jumped up, almost spilling the remnants of his drink.

It was Maxwell. "Red alert, sir. I've sent a car. A shoot-up in Davies Street, the SPG's have cornered them in a block of flats. I've alerted the full squad."

"Right. No action till I get there."

"I've already told them, and, sir . . ."

Shenton had almost replaced the receiver. "What?"

"Lisburn have identified the girl in the flat. I've just had the telex—quote—'Fingerprints those of Maureen Driscoll, widow of John Driscoll, Provisional officer, Trinity College graduate, comptroller of funds channelled from USA. Killed South Armagh, 1985. Ms Driscoll no criminal record. Prints covertly obtained.' Signed Black."

"Makes sense."

"Just keeping it in the family, wasn't she?" Maxwell sounded cheerful. "Her old man gets it and she shacks up with one of his mates then . . ."

"Acknowledge with thanks."

Shenton replaced the receiver and switched off his reading lamp before going out into the hall. He turned towards the stairs and then changed his mind. His wife would almost certainly have taken her pill, and in any case it could all be over by morning. He went back into the lounge and switched the light on again to scribble a note for her. He was about to move off again when, on an afterthought, he crossed to the desk against the wall and unlocked the drawer to take out the short-barrelled chief's special revolver. He switched off the lights for the last time and carried the pistol with him into the hall.

He slipped the revolver into the right-hand pocket of his overcoat and then put the overcoat on, checked that his pouch was full and that he had his keys. He drew the bolt on the door and used his key on the deadlock, careful to lift the silent alarm switch. The door itself moved slowly, weighted by the heavy-gauge steel plate that had been set there on his appointment as Anti-Terrorist Squad commander.

He reversed the key and stepped onto the porch, pulling the door to a close behind him, turned the key twice and watched for the tiny spot of the electronic eye to light up again high in the porch roof. He stayed in the porch, leisurely filling his pipe.

Maureen Driscoll had been living with Brendan Casey, the man who, if he had not actually killed her husband, had certainly shaken hands with the man who had. Was it possible that she had connived at the death of her own husband? No, that was unlikely. Casey had been a bully boy, thief, extortionist, murderer and general turd. He had been killed because someone had got tired of his being one or all of those things. And someone who had an excellent motive was the girl whose husband he had knocked off. It was not political, just a straightforward murder enquiry. And the other, self-appointed soldiers, who shot at people when they weren't looking, had at last tried it on in a saturation area, had made the mistake of going where they weren't the only ones with guns.

His personal Rover swung into the driveway and, puffing happily on his pipe, Shenton stepped down from the porch, more cheerful than he had been at any time in the previous ten days.

The roadway at the entrance of the flats had been completely blocked by cars and police vans by the time that Shenton reached the road junction at the end. Uniformed men and women were keeping the crowd of sightseers on the other side of the crash barriers; there seemed to be a holiday mood among them, with two hot dog men setting up their stalls. Shenton sighed as he moved through and acknowledged the salute of the inspector in charge of the Special Patrol Group patrol. He felt slightly ridiculous at the explosion of light bulbs as the group of newsmen went through the usual ritual.

A couple of men with film cameras were bringing their lenses to bear on him, and he noticed the rifle microphone being aimed hopefully in his direction. Shenton touched the inspector's sleeve and led him to the other side of the protective metal of the SPG's van.

"There has been no communication?"

"Not since the first shout. We've got them bottled all right, no possible way out."

"And they haven't been heard of at all?"

"Not a peep."

"I'll go through."

The inspector led the way across the forecourt and Shenton made a slight detour towards the side of the building to look along the walkway. The angle was acute, but towards the far end he could see the figures standing against the wall, ready for anyone who fancied the thirty-odd-foot jump from the flat's window.

Shenton went through the main entrance and then up the stairs to the first floor landing. Some of the doors of the flats were ajar and the inhabitants stared at him as he passed.

"We've left these, but we've cleared everyone out of the flats around the corner; the Council have moved them into a hostel, mostly middle-aged couples at this end. The Council housing officer wants a word with you for an estimate of how long it's likely to last."

They turned the corner into the short arm of the corridor, and at the turn three uniformed men, carrying their guns in waist holsters, stood aside for them. The doors of all the flats were open except for the last one on the right, and on either side of this were two officers, the first balancing a six-foot plexi-shield on the floor and behind him the back-up men with automatic shotguns—four men. A few paces behind each man, two more men carrying Sterling submachine guns. Shenton tightened his lips at the display of fire power.

"Three others in reserve with CS grenades and gas masks," said the inspector.

"They'll be better inside the doorways of the other flats," said Shenton, "if any of them poked a nose out of the door with this lot they'd shoot right away."

"Yes, sir."

Shenton reached the door of the flat and stood in front of it. An ordinary door, probably not even solid, a frame with some kind of veneer, no visitor's spy hole, one spring lock which a size ten boot would take clean off its hinges.

He moved on to the fire door which opened as he reached it. Four more uniformed men were on the other side; a whiff of cigarette smoke from a butt pinched out at his appearance. Twenty steps down to a metal door which had been unbarred. The inspector followed him.

"They probably came down here to make the break-out, may even have reconnoitred the place without knowing it's now kept locked because of vandals. The key was with the warden who lives in the next block; his orders are on any alarm to come across and unbar the door. It can only be unlocked from the outside. So they probably came down here and had to retrace their steps, went back to the corridor and by that time our men were in the corridor. They fired automatic fire, then they dived into that flat, the one nearest to them. There were no shots and the door is intact, so Ketling or his wife must have opened it for them."

"What's outside?"

The door was opened and Shenton stepped out onto a paved area to find himself at the back of the tower block; more police wearing flak jackets grouped around another SPG van: like a bloody army. He walked to the corner of the block and glanced back along the outside walkway. From this end it was far easier to see the men standing under the windows of the flat. He strained his eyes to see at the acute angle, but all he could see was that the flat was in darkness.

The inspector waited for him to turn back and then jerked his thumb to the second block some hundred and fifty yards away. "Fourth and fifth floors, we're in two flats, four marksmen. The curtains are moved occasionally and someone looks out, but that's all."

"How many have you seen?"

"Two different men: one, the first, is young, early twenties, perhaps even younger. Long hair down to his chin, looks like a student. The second one has only shown once: early to middle thirties, fairly dark hair, pointed nose."

"Where have you got the control?"

"In the flat above; we tried the floor, but it's steel-framed and compo over a concrete skim. We can't put a drill through it without noise."

"What about the adjoining flat?"

"We have a beam microphone out next to the window; it picks up voices, but it's too diffused to identify anything. Not that they say much. We're trying to get a laser kit to bounce off the window; that would give us what we want."

"We still do not know how many there are."

"Three were sighted for certain; there could be another. They've always worked four-handed before."

"Unless the fourth went another way."

"The men behind them are certain they all made for the block."

"If he was cunning and they did not see him, they would not know, would they?"

"No, sir."

"Were all the cars in the street searched immediately?"

"No, sir."

A long pause. "I'll go up," said Shenton.

# Thirty-One

Inside the flat, the temperature had fallen and Mrs Ketling was bundled in blankets, close to the electric fire; her head was down into her chest and it was difficult to tell whether she was asleep or not. David had allowed her to use the tablets that had been in her handbag. He had counted them and checked the label on the bottle which did not identify the pills. Mr Ketling said that his wife had a heart condition.

Ketling himself was ashen-faced and looked older than his sixty-one years. He sat in the second armchair on the other side of the fireplace to his wife, shoulders hunched, looking unseeingly across the room. Liam sat on the far side of the settee with his feet up and his revolver in his lap, cushions bolstered at his back, with his eyes closed, his anorak zippered to the neck.

Ketling had told them that the heating was on a night storage system, automatically switching itself off at midnight. David had turned off the overhead lights in the lounge and the only illumination came from a side lamp which stood on a table close behind Mrs Ketling. At the doorway, in a kitchen chair, Sean looked into the tiny hall, facing the front door of the flat, with his revolver in his lap. David opened his cigarette packet, selected one of the three cigarettes, lit a match and took in two long inhalations before passing the butt to Sean. Sean rose from the chair and they stood with their heads almost touching.

A tapping noise from the window made them spring apart; Sean had his revolver up and David shot his hand inside his coat. He held the butt of his pistol, but he did not draw it.

Something was being held against the window. David put his mouth very close to Sean's ear—"Watch the door, Sean. If they're drawing us one way, could be they'll come the other."

Sean nodded and turned to crouch at the chair, holding his revolver in both hands and resting his elbows on the seat of the chair. David went through the sitting room; Liam was now sitting on the edge of the settee, large-eyed and nervous. "Keep an eye on them," said David as he passed. "If anyone comes through you shoot them first." He jerked his head towards the Ketlings and moved to the window. Drawing his own pistol, he cocked back the hammer and cautiously drew back the side of the curtain. Swinging on a wire outside the window was a telephone receiver, which, at the end of each swing, touched the pane of glass closest to him. He pushed down the handle of the side window and opened it an inch or so; he listened carefully. The immediate light came from the streetlamps, but there was also a lot of light coming downwards from a source outside his field of vision. They must have a lamp outside the living room window of the flat immediately above.

David stretched his hand through the window opening and pulled the receiver through the window until there was a yard or so of flex inside with it, and then pulled the window to and caught it on one of the notches.

He put the receiver to his ear and said, "This is the Provisional Irish Republican Army; are you ready to open negotiations?"

The noise on the line intensified before the voice came through. "This is Commander Shenton of the Metropolitan Police and there is nothing to negotiate about. I am asking you to lay down your arms and come out of the flat. So long as you have your hands on top of your heads and make no threatening gesture I can confirm that neither you nor any of your comrades will be harmed in any way. You will be arrested and taken into custody."

"You've forgotten our hostages."

"What I have just said has been dictated by their presence."

"We want a car and free passage, else they're dead."

"No negotiations," said Shenton, "there is no question of

our bargaining. I have already spoken to the commissioner. There will be no deals."

"I'm telling you that we'll kill them. Their blood will be on you."

"No, it won't. You've just said it; it will be on you."

David banged the receiver against the wall—it bounced; he put it under his heel and stamped, but the vulcanite was too tough. He was tempted to put the muzzle of his Browning against the mouthpiece and really give them an answer, but shooting was dangerous; they probably had orders to be in like Flynn if any shots were fired. He opened the window and flung the receiver outside.

Shenton winced as the crash came and pulled off the headphones.

Field pulled off his own set of headphones and turned up the amplification of the loudspeaker. "What do we do now?"

"Let it sink in," said Shenton.

"They could kill them out of pique; they've nothing to lose."

"They've been with them for above two hours, time enough to see them as human beings. If they do not kill them in the next ten minutes, they'll not do it at all."

"You seem very sure, sir."

"These men are not sadists; they see themselves as soldiers, patriots. So long as they believe that we mean what we say."

"They could think that it is a bluff, sir; there's been plenty of backdowns before."

"Then we'll have to convince them. We're not changing our mind."

"The politicians . . ."

"If they want to overrule me then they'll have to take me off the case. It will be wrapped up before that."

"Politicians are tricky."

"So am I."

"They're bluffing." Sean's eyes were bloodshot and he looked more than a little mad.

"I don't think so." David was still in his corner, sitting on his heels. "If they were they'd draw it out. We could find out, though." He grinned at the frightened face of Liam. "If we put one through the window, bring that phone in, hold the old man up at the window and put a gun to his head . . . tell them they've got ten seconds; that'd prove it one way or the other. You fancy that?"

"I'll do it." said Sean. "Open that door and I'll take the old man out; let's see if they shoot him to get at me."

David slowly shook his head. "They'll just let you walk, till you run out of ammunition or get tired. I thought maybe we could use both of them, go out as a fivesome. It isn't going to work; they've got us."

"They haven't got me."

"Ah, they have, Sean, and so what? It was sure to end one way or the other and we expected to go down, didn't we? What's it matter if it's this way or some way else? I thought we'd get shot: the Specials out there don't miss and we were sure to meet up with them sooner or later. We could shoot it out—I don't mind—it would only end one way, though. They've got us." He put his hand on Sean's shoulder. "We did what we were sent for, all of it, everything we were asked."

"I'm not just giving in."

"Whatever you like. What we've got to do now is hang on as long as we can. Brendan got crossed up, but we've got to give him, or someone else, time to clear up the room and if something's happened to Brendan, then for Kathleen or someone to get down and clear it. They'll know what we're up to; so long as we hold out here the more we're tying up the law and a few SAS men as well; they'll have a whole army out there. That's what it's all about, eh? Tie them up and make sure they remember us."

"The next time I hear a noise outside that door I'm putting a bullet through it."

"We haven't got a lot left; we'll try to put them to good use before it ends. Now, try and get as much sleep as you can; we'll take it in shifts and conserve energy. What they'll be hoping for is for us to lose our nerve. They're for wearing us down. Let's make them work a bit, don't make it too easy for the bastards."

"There has been no movement of any kind, sir?" Field removed the earphones and laid them on the desk top.

"Nor conversation."

"No sir, it looks as though they've settled for the night."

"One, at least, will be on guard."

Shenton glanced at his watch and yawned. 3:00 a.m. The flat above the siege flat had been taken over entirely and a desk and communications centre set up. A direct line had also been joined into the Post Office circuit; all officers were under instructions not to use their ordinary radios. The men in the flat might or might not possess a short-wave radio, but the gang of pressmen certainly did and were manning them around the clock in the hope that they could intercept a worthwhile message.

Shenton had already used the direct line to speak to the commissioner who, thank God, had backed him entirely: no deals, no negotiations. The policy decision made more than two years before was now under test, but the slippery politicians had gone on record at the time and they would have to wriggle a lot more before they came off that particular hook. The commissioner had asked for an estimate: three days, Shenton had replied, and there had been a heavy silence before the commissioner had ended the conversation.

He had refused to give a press conference and sent down a message that no further statement would be issued for another twenty-four hours. So that had put the block on both the bullshit areas. The architect's drawings had now become available and confirmed that it was a steel-framed building with brick infill—no joy there—and interior walls of cement block with plasterboard linings. Ceilings and floors were again concrete, reinforced with steel plates to bring up their load-bearing capacity. It would take a pneumatic drill to get through floor or ceiling.

It would be possible to go through the party wall and a supersonic drill had already been used to pierce the wall high up in the corner by the hall, and a flexible carbon rod had been inserted, complete with pin head microphone. It picked up any sound within the lounge of the flat, but was not directional. All it could really tell them was if anyone was moving or talking. Attempts were being made to insert a fisheye lens up the same carbon rod.

One decision he had not yet made was to blow out the party wall; he had been told that controlled charges would blow an eight-foot hole, with a guarantee that the force of the explosion would move inwards. The SAS men would leap into the room simultaneously with the bricks. Nothing to it, he had been assured; distract their attention at the door and windows and whoof!—in like Flynn, won't know what hit them. Shenton put the papers aside.

Marksmen from D.11 with their rifles and Gannix sights had all windows of the flat under constant observation and with a rota system that meant that no one man would have to concentrate on any one point for more than two hours. The windows were twenty-five feet from the ground and quite within an energetic leap from the window; two marksmen were posted along the wall, changed at four hourly intervals. Shenton concentrated on the plot plan; even if they did jump out of the windows, there was nowhere they could run: squad cars blocked each end of the narrow walkway and if they leapt onto the cars themselves, SPG vans backed each unit. Eight men in the corridor outside the flat itself were armed with submachine guns as well as pistols and shotguns. Overkill, the newspaper writers would call it, but then they always did. There was at least one submachine gun inside that flat, but so far no sign of the reported Armalite.

Shenton turned to the file on the flat tenants. Mr and Mrs Ketling, both in their early sixties; the woman had a history of ill health. The ordinary telephone had been cut off, sidestepping a smartass journalist who had discovered the Ketlings' name from neighbours and attempted to ring through for an interview. Mrs Ketling had a circulatory disorder, her doctor was not at home; local police were trying to get someone who could open up his surgery records. Shenton sighed.

All power, heat and water had been cut off, the lavatory would no longer be working; portable lights were trained on all windows and the door. The woman would be feeling the strain the worst of all. He took one of the indentation forms and listed: chemical toilet, screen? Then a note to himself: medication for Mrs Ketling? He passed the form across to Field and then palmed his eyes.

It was unlikely that anything would happen during the hours of darkness. When daylight broke, leave them alone at least until midday, let it all sink in. He got up from the desk and went across to the camp bed that had been set up.

"Are you all right for the next six hours?"

"Fine, sir."

"When did you last get some sleep?"

"Last night, sir, but I'm all right. It's much less wearing than normal night duty."

"You're off duty at nine tomorrow morning, that's an order. Whatever happens, you go home."

Shenton went through into the bedroom and across to the bathroom, and, against every instinct, undressed and donned pyjamas. His brain had taken over; if anything happened it would happen quickly, but not yet; they would not do anything tonight. He would have been unable to explain why he knew that, but he did know it, could feel it. The men in that room had not killed the hostages immediately, had not responded to the first actions of the police, had not replied to his call by immediate shootings. That meant that at least one of them was intelligent; the longer it went on, the more powerfully that intelligence would show itself and influence the others. It was like a game of chess, a move here, another there, in logical progression, so long as the opposing forces were rational, so long as none of them was psychopathic.

David parted the curtains and looked out onto the clear cold morning. The second tower block was more than sixty yards away and the watery sun reflected back from its myriad windows, but, no doubt, behind them the marksmen had twitched to attention and lined him up. He held the curtains to either side of his chest as he moved his head to take in as wide an angle of vision as he could. Beyond the wall of the walkway beneath him, the ground to the next tower block had half a dozen cars, some with blue lamps, and a dark blue van. He strained his eyes to see within the cars and could detect one or two shapes, but no identifiable figures; certainly no obvious target, but they would be out there all right.

He allowed the curtains to drop back into place and looked back into the room: it smelled unclean. The old man had slumped down in his fireside chair, his head bent sideways to his shoulder, mouth open, snoring quietly. The woman, awake, was sitting motionless, peering straight in front of her through those thick spectacles. In the shaft of clear light that came across the lower part of her face from the minute gap between the curtains, David noticed, for the first time, that there was a flesh-coloured mole on the end of her chin, from which sprouted splayed hairs. She had clung to the handbag on her lap, the handle clasped fiercely by those little hands with their swollen knuckles.

He went into the hall where Liam was sitting in a kitchen chair across the barred doorway, the Sterling on the floor beside him. Liam opened a bloodshot eye to show that he was awake; the black stubble showing up like a smear of bootblack. In the bedroom, Sean lay clothed on top of the rumpled bed, on his back, and with the habitual tightness of his face relaxed. David looked at him from the doorway, noticing the smallness of the body in sleep and the youthfulness of the face. Sean's pistol lay next to him on the covers.

David pressed a finger lightly below the ear and Sean came instantly awake.

"Nothing. It's half five."

Sean fumbled in the breast pocket of his denim shirt for a crumpled box of Embassy; only two cigarettes remained: he looked at them, at David, and then put them back. He found a stub that he had left in a saucer on the bedside table and lit that; David waited for him to stop coughing.

"There's half a sink of water left. A bit of tea, but no way of brewing up; take a couple of mouthfuls. Apart from that, some bread and some cheese. Two tins of fruit. The old couple didn't keep much stock. I'll have another look around, but I'd like you out there, Sean; it's daylight and Liam's not up to a sudden try."

Sean nodded and got off the bed, sliding the pistol into the waistband of his belt. David went back into the little hall and then into the combined bath and toilet. The tap he had run to get as much water into the bath as possible had dribbled rust, and the half inch or so of water was useless for drinking. He let it stay . . . if they got really desperate! The toilet was squalid, unflushed and swamped with urine over its seat and back wall: Liam, probably. He raised the lid of the cistern: empty.

He stood on the seat and pressed his head against the angle of the wall to see through the top louvre of the obscured glass in the window. It gave him a view of the acutest angle of part of the footpath and a glimpse of dark blue cloth; there would be more than one standing directly below them, cutting out any chance of a sudden jump onto the path. If they really did have explosives with them now or, better yet, a couple of hand grenades . . . . He grinned and stepped down. It did not make a fart's difference in the long run.

He went back past Liam and stood in the living room door-way to watch Sean who was helping the old lady up from her chair. Sean supported her elbows as she took her support from the back of the chair and then watched solicitously over her as she made her slow way across the room towards the hall. David's lips lifted at the corners into a half smile. His reading had told him of the technique and now he was watching it working in practice: leave the victims and their abductors in as close proximity for as long as possible. Give them every opportunity to relate to each other as human beings, reduce overt activity to a minimum and allow them to share the same tensions and hardships. So long as their abductors were not psychopaths, each hour would reduce their ability to kill.

The woman reached the doorway and he moved aside to allow her to pass, then caught Sean's eye. "All right, Sean?"

"Yeah, why?"

"What do you think we ought to do?"

"Make the bastards come for us."

"They won't unless we start shooting. They're waiting us out; hold on." He led Sean to the centre of the room and put his mouth close to his ear. "The microphones they have on the wall will not reach this far. As soldiers our main objective has been completed. We have engaged the enemy, made them mount an action against us, tied up their forces. We've shown that they have to take us seriously. The movement know where we are; Brendan has had time enough to clear everything. We've done all that anyone could."

"The boys could bust us out."

David ducked his head with impatience. "How many could they bring in? Ten? Twenty? And how many do you think are out there? Fifty, a hundred, DII, SAS with machine guns, helicopters, tanks if they want that; the whole British army could be on standby. Remember the first rule: we have no chance of taking them on in a set military operation."

"They could snatch someone, a big pot, swap him for us."

"More like it, but they never have done, have they? And I doubt it would work: the politicos would wriggle, but the police would stand against it. Taking an airliner would be a bit different, but no sign of anything up to that strength."

"So, what are you getting at?"

"It's all up to us; we can last a bit longer, another day, maybe two, but in the end that's what it comes down to."

# Thirty-Two

At the tea stall on the corner of Villiers Street, Danny Malloy bought a hot meat pie and chewed at it as he made his way down to the Embankment. His money was reduced to two pounds and a handful of small change. The cold wind coming up from the river caught his throat like a knife.

This has got to stop, this shit has got to stop. Jesus, how did it ever happen, how did you ever get into this mess. You've got to get out of this, Danny boy; anything is better than this. Telephones, they had telephones in the station. Ring somebody, report, where, who? A slapping newsbill at the abandoned tin stand: *SIEGE GUNMEN DEFIANT*. The high dark wall fell away and he was out onto the Embankment; the wind was colder and he moved into the arches under the railway line. Half a dozen uniformed policemen were on the other side of the traffic lights, close to the shrubbery of the Embankment Gardens where they had chased out the derelicts who had tried to doss down on the benches.

The groupings had begun under the arches and even after one night he could recognize some of them: The old woman with the serene face of a medieval saint who carried her two plastic carrier bags everywhere she went; the man with the surgical boot and a face the colour of lead pencils; the short, wiry Scotsman with a mattress of red hair and an impenetrable accent who wrapped himself in corrugated cardboard.

Must do something, Danny. It's got to stop. The last fragment of hardened pie crust caught in his throat and he was retching. Oh, Jesus, no, oh Jesus. His eyes watered and his throat was raw. He came up with his eyes streaming and put up his hand to find that spittle was dribbling from the point of his chin. The policemen stared on blank-faced. In the shadows, his foot trod on something that yielded and the mad eyes of Willie the Preacher, immensely tall, emaciated street hymn-singer, came into view. Fuck off, outovit.

He turned and went back up the bleak hill to the side entrance of the station. Anything, anything. He would report to Belfast, to Seamus. The telephone hood stank of stale beer and he had to support himself against the wall as he struggled to find his money; then the number . . . the Belfast code was easy, but the number . . . What day was it? He couldn't think; what about the club, maybe Seamus would switch the phone through. He must do that, Seamus. He was frightened of Seamus, more frightened than he was of Loughran. Maybe Seamus wouldn't be there, but someone, anyone, so long as there was someone who could talk to him.

He had difficulty dialling the number and then the telephone rang for a long time. When the receiver was picked up at the other end, it sounded as if the whole Irish Sea were rushing along the line.

"Yes?" came a guarded voice, heavy with irritation.

"Is that you, Seamus? It's Danny."

"Who?"

"Danny, I'm reporting . . . I'm . . . Jesus . . . I'm reporting. I need help, a place, Seamus." He waited, but nothing came. "I don't know what to do. I've been walking, walking. My money's gone."

"Where are you?"

"In a station, Charing Cross. I've been walking all over, two days now, my money's gone. I don't know where to go."

"Stay there."

"I need somewhere, Seamus. I need . . ."

"Stay there."

"Will someone come?"

The line went dead. Malloy heaved himself away from the phone; his forehead was running with an icy sweat. Across from him two policemen had appeared, moving towards the bums who were sleeping on the benches. He shambled into motion, frightened not to be in motion. His bowels ached and he clutched the brass rail by the steps leading down into the lavatories; someone had broken the padlock on the gate. Only one bulb was working. He went into the end stall, cold, stinking and—Jesus!—a gout of blood had streaked upwards along the partition and a broken syringe floated in the jacks.

He stumbled back to the main concourse. One of the bums was screaming at the policemen who had prodded him into wakefulness and the others were dragging themselves to their feet like an army of the living dead. Malloy found a side exit and went out into the bleak night.

Oh, God, dear Jesus, let me get out of this. Let it stop. Anything, I'll do anything, go back to the hut with the dirt floor, help the old lady dig the vegetables, look after daft Mary. Never complain at anything, anything at all. Just let me get out of this and I'll do anything, anything at all.

# Thirty-Three

Major Flint came into the outskirts of Belfast on the Lisburn Road manoeuvring his Triumph Dolomite skilfully through the narrow streets in heavy rain. He was adept at moving through bandit country; the index plates of the car were changed as a matter of routine and the car itself was resprayed at monthly intervals. In the past month he had grown a Mexican moustache and the hair at the nape of his neck was long enough to fall over his collar.

His tour of his field units brought nothing worthwhile, but the tip from Dublin had been precise. A personal emissary of Little Patrick McGlynn had crossed the border into Northern Ireland with orders for Loughran. It could mean a specific target, details of a new arms shipment, plans for a fullblown campaign, anything. There were a thousand ways in which he could reach Belfast, but he would have to use the roads and, in theory, that ought to make it easy to take him . . . except that theory was theory and real life was something else.

He drove on through the dreary streets, ready to brake at the first flash of light. Men driving alone were noteworthy. He had his papers ready and the check jacket added credence to his cover as a brewery representative.

As he neared the Falls, the litany staining the ruined walls and corrugated iron sheets of the burned-out houses settled into its usual monotony: *Provos Rule; British Bastards Out; Fuck the Taigs; Fuck the Queen; Fuck the Pope; After You With the Queen;* and then, the only touch of wit on the corner of Queens Street, *No Pope Here, Lucky Old Pope.*

Flint touched the button on his dashboard and the static

came rushing through the speaker of what looked like the normal car radio. "Two cars at checkpoint nine: both clean."

Flint spoke into the microphone hidden in the sun visor above the steering wheel. "Details?"

"Car one, man and woman, both late twenties, coming home from a visit to the girl's mother in St Mary's. Car two, male, thirty-five, medical doctor known personally to officer at check point. Twenty-four vehicles booked at other checkpoints. I have details."

"Not required," said Flint and switched off the microphone. He'll come through the Falls, probably already through. Loughran would not meet outside his stronghold. He'll be in one of the houses, drab, anonymous, a rat hole no different from a thousand others, protected not only by guns, but by ten thousand eyes watching every movement along the avenues of approach.

He slackened speed as he came to the end of the Falls and, instead of going forward to the crossroads that would bring him to the roadblock, he swung the car into a left-hand turn back again into Andersonstown. A light flickered briefly within the speedometer and he touched the radio switch again.

"Message from CIG. A possible taken to Station Four."

"On my way."

Flint braked and took the first road on his right, then a bewildering series of right and left turns as he worked his way back towards the edge of the demarcation area, running level for a brief time with the ironically named peace line. Once clear, he put up his headlights and doubled his speed as he made for the barricaded police station that was on the edge of the Ardoyne.

Behind him the rain continued to fall heavily on the road block at the end of the Falls Road, and ten minutes after he had turned north a blue Cortina with Antrim number plates came slowly up to the road block and had already stopped before the warning light flashed. The driver stepped out into the road without being asked and the RUC sergeant noted that he kept both hands clearly in view.

"Where are you making for, sir?"

"The Leeky Street Social Club; I'm Brian Murphy, the entertainments manager." The man offered up a driving licence folded around a piece of paper.

The policeman kept his torch on the man's face and noted that he was about five nine, medium build, dark-haired with a fringe beard, intelligent, slightly hooded eyes. His brain was already filtering out the hundred or so faces that he had committed to memory. Then he looked down at the driving licence and checked the paper which was on the letterhead of the social club with Murphy's name and position confirmed by someone signing himself as the club president; a small photograph of the man was stapled to one corner.

"How's old Slocum these days?" the sergeant asked pleasantly.

"Before my time," said the man in a neutral voice.

"And how long is that?"

"Four months?"

"Please face the wall, Mr Murphy."

The man turned without a word and assumed the classic frisking position, leaning forward so that his hands bore his weight. An RUC constable rapidly ran his hands across the body, inside the jacket, along the waistband, arms, shoulders, legs, stopping a fraction below the crotch, but not missing the thighs or buttocks. The sergeant kept his own eyes on the back of the man's head while aware that others in the team were opening the boot of the car, raising the engine hood and were examining the interior of the car itself. The army observer had already radioed the index number of the car through to intelligence at Lisburn, checking ownership and previous sightings. When the constable completed the frisking, he tapped the man on the shoulder and Murphy turned to stand quietly with his arms at his side, glancing without expression at the constable with the angle light who was examining the underside of the car chassis.

The RUC sergeant waited until the army control flashed his blue light before he handed the man back his papers.

"Will you be returning this way?"

"If we close before midnight; otherwise I'll stay over until morning."

"A wise choice. Thank you for your cooperation, Mr Murphy. A quiet night to you."

The man nodded and got back into his car, switched on the ignition and carefully negotiated the wire trestles and angled armoured car before accelerating into Queen Street. Behind him, the sergeant completed his note of the check with a brief description of Murphy and his apparent age which he put at thirty-seven.

The man's true age was thirty-two, his hair and newly acquired beard had been professionally tinted and his name was Kevin Dooley. He drove rapidly through the interweaving back streets beyond the Falls until he reached Leekey Street. He braked the car a little beyond the converted shop with its bricked-in windows that was the Republican club. When he pushed the door it opened immediately and Dooley handed the man his driving licence and letter.

"Roadblock at the Falls; asked me about old Slocum. I told them I didn't know him."

The doorman nodded and stepped aside for Dooley to walk into the club itself; a professional-looking bar, plastic-tiled floor and a dozen small tables at which men in working clothes sat drinking beer. A tiny stage had been built in one corner, barely large enough to hold its upright piano and stick microphone.

Dooley walked to the end of the clubroom, opened the far door and stepped into a stinking urinal; another door at the far end and he was in a littered yard. A dim light filtered through the curtained windows of the clubhouse behind him and he waited a few seconds for his eyes to adjust to the gloom before he picked his way past the stacked beer crates and general rubbish to the bordering fence. A broken concrete slab gave him a convenient step into the adjoining garden. Another dozen steps and he was at the back door of the terrace house which fronted the adjoining street.

As he reached the door it opened slightly and he stepped

through to stand motionless as the lights came on: a man either side of him, one holding a Sterling submachine gun. The second man nodded in salutation and led the way; Dooley followed him into the hall and then up the narrow staircase and onto the tiny landing. His guide tapped on the door of the back bedroom and then stepped aside for Dooley to enter. It was a mean room, heavy with stale cigarette smoke; blankets had been nailed across the single window and the only light was a single bulb hanging unshaded from its flex. Loughran sat behind a kitchen table that held a few papers, an unopened bottle of Powers whisky and a soup plate filled with cigarette ends.

"Kevin," said Loughran simply.

Dooley nodded and pulled the only other chair round to face the table. He brought out his own cigarettes and laid them on the table. Loughran put his hand on the whisky bottle, but Dooley shook his head.

"Malloy," said Dooley and let the name hang in the air.

Loughran took the cigarette end from the corner of his mouth and stubbed it out in the ruin of a hundred others. "When Ryder came over last month he wanted a man for London. A carrier, because Kathleen's been clocked too often. It didn't make sense. I've got no men to spare; Ryder said it was a direct order from Pat so I put up Malloy."

"Anyone else there?"

"No." Loughran's eyes dulled. "My word against Ryder's."

"What else did you talk about?"

"How the bastards were getting their information, raising money. The heat we were getting over the London bus bomb. He said it wasn't anything to do with the Army. He wasn't interested in any of my problems, told me it was Pat's orders that I supplied a man. Malloy went over the following night and that was it until he phoned Seamus from London."

"Why Seamus?"

"The only number he knew, said he was reporting for duty."

"Did you choose him because he could have been the tout and you wanted to prove it, get him out of your way?"

"Jesus, no. I don't know what he did in London, but there's

no way he was the informer. The bastards have been coming up with stuff that Malloy didn't know. Let's get this straight: I did not want to send anyone to London. I've got enough on my plate here without messing on the mainland. Malloy was spare, that's all, the one I could best do without, a messenger. And there's something else I don't get: if Malloy did tout the boys in London then why didn't he run? He's no brain, but he's not an idiot and he'd know he'd be the first in the frame if something happened to the unit the day after he was there. He'd know there was no way he could inform and get away with it."

"He could have called Seamus to buy time. Someone informed on the unit and Malloy's the only one who could. Pat wants to know why he was sent to London."

"On his orders. I had to choose a man on his orders. You think I didn't look at Malloy? I've been looking at everybody for more than a year, since the leaks started. I blanked Malloy because the leaks were over his head. He could have passed on simple stuff, like when I'd had a meeting, maybe even who with or who was on an operation after it was over. Any of the boys could because they were there or even worked it out after. But there was no way he could have given them Terry or the bank job. Jesus, they were waiting for us on that one and Malloy was across the border sorting out that poor bitch of a wife of his, daft Mary."

Dooley said nothing and Loughran dropped his eyes to stare at the label on the whisky bottle. Dooley took a cigarette from his own pack and reached across the table to use Loughran's matches. As he smoked he unbuttoned his shirt and pulled away the envelope taped across his chest. Opening the envelope he took out a photostat copy of the letter that Maureen Driscoll had written to McGlynn. "You'll read that."

Loughran tilted the letter under the unshaded light bulb and read it quickly, turned back and read the second half again. He put the letter down and looked at Dooley. "Jesus."

"Did you know Driscoll?"

"He gave the political lectures when I volunteered."

"Any connection with him?"

"I was in Long Kesh."

"You're going south."

"When?" Loughran's eyes narrowed to black beads and a vein pulsed high on his left cheek.

"By noon tomorrow; the Hegartys will take you over. A full meeting of the Council; you'll tell them what you've told me, all of it, and that really is a direct order."

"I hand over to you?"

For the first time Dooley smiled. "You hand over to Michael. I'm needed elsewhere."

# Thirty-Four

Shenton was awake, shaved and showered by seven o'clock, and, apart from a slight headache, as alert as ever. He had slept for less than four hours in the previous twenty-two and knew that he was good for another ten, but at the end of that he would need a solid nine hours' sleep in his own bed. The days when he could go forty-eight or fifty hours at a stretch were behind him.

As he sipped the coffee that the duty constable had brewed in the kitchen of the flat, he made a mental note to himself that if there was no break in the siege by midday he would return to the Yard until some definite sign was made. Or, he thought, at the end of the fourth day.

A messenger had brought over his personally addressed mail along with the routine squad crime reports. The first thing of interest was the copy of a telex from Commissariat Hojean of the Amsterdamse Recherche, which Maxwell had marked with a large red cross.

"Van Hoeck classified please refer Office. Agree man at right of photo Van Hoeck. Other man unknown. Regards."

Shenton picked up the telephone that the Post Office engineers had connected with a direct line to the squad office. Maxwell was not in the office. He asked for the call to be re-routed to Maxwell's home number, and while he waited he read the cryptic telex a second and then a third time. *Agree that the man is Van Hoeck!*

"Sir." Shenton could almost see the yawn.

"Morning," said Shenton. "When did this telex come in from the Dutch police?"

"Very late. I put in a call, but you had just got your head down."

"What did you say when you transmitted the photo?"

"Asked for any information. No mention of Van Hoeck."

"I see."

"Could be that Van Hoeck is a brown job."

"What it means," said Shenton, "is that Mr Hojean is a very bright policeman. If nothing happens here in the next three hours I'm coming back. When you get in put a feeler out on Van Hoeck."

"Through the Specials?"

"Yes. If they can't deliver I will have to ask Mr Hobson to take it up."

"I understand. Has there been any progress?"

"Nothing we know of. The fibre cable should be fitted with an optical head this morning. It looks like a matter of waiting them out. I'm sorry to have woken you."

"I was already awake; just trying to get used to the idea of getting up."

Shenton replaced the receiver and then picked up the field telephone that put him into contact with the watch officer.

"They're about, sir. Someone was moving ten minutes ago, one person; he looked through the curtains . . . the youngest of them; then a conversation between at least two people, nothing clear, just a few snatches of words. Shall I run the tape?"

"No, but report any increase of activity."

He had no sooner put down the field telephone when he was called to the landline. Deputy Assistant Commissioner Hobson was calling from his home. Shenton glanced at his watch, quarter past seven. Hobson wanted to know if there had been any change.

"No, sir, they seem to have had a quiet night; a few minutes ago one of them looked out of the window. Unfortunately, we cannot hear the individual conversations."

"I am seeing the home secretary at nine; he'll want to know how long this is likely to go on for."

"Impossible to say, except of course that the longer they

stay with the victims, the better our chances for a bloodless result."

"There is sure to be some suggestion of a frontal assault; the news media will be exerting the greatest pressure for dramatic action. What would be your best guess?"

"It is unlikely to end today, possibly tomorrow, but more likely the day after. The woman will be the crucial factor. I intend to offer toilet facilities and food later today. It depends on the balance of the men we're dealing with; the danger is if one of them has a latent psychopathic personality, the stress would be counter-productive in that case. I understand that if that is so it is likely to be the quietest member of the group, the one who has shown the least aggression so far."

"In which case . . . ?"

"It is beyond my control; the only alternatives being to mount an offensive or to give in to their demands.

"The party wall can be demolished and the terrorists killed within seconds; there's no sign of explosives. The technical people hope to be able to fit a video unit to give us a view of at least the interior of the living room sometime today."

The line hummed electronically. "Are you staying?"

"I'll return to Central if there is no change by midday. A new factor has arisen on which I would like your view, sir. The enquiry into the bus bomb has turned up the name of a Dutchman. It arose in connection with a mercenary recruiter which brought in the security service, Colonel Black. The name has been mentioned by the Dutch police themselves, but they refer us to the Foreign Office."

"Who is this man?"

"His name is Van Hoeck. We have a photograph of him with a member of the Provo High Council; the original connection was with the man who carried that bomb onto the bus."

"I'll take it up. I'll be in the office by ten." A small sigh. "I suppose you need to hold a press conference."

"I intend to have Maxwell deal with the press."

"I'll expect you at noon, then."

Shenton slowly filled and then lighted his first pipe of the day and, drawing a scrap pad towards him, made a note for the press statement. He drafted the first paragraph and then paused. The men in the flat could have a transistor radio. He scratched out the first sentence and commenced again, emphasising that no demands would be met.

He was still working on the statement when there was a tap at the door and the chief technical officer put his head into the room.

"We've got the screen fitted now, sir."

"Can we see them?"

"Two-thirds of the room."

Shenton got up and went out into what had been the living room. The cable ran through the hallway into the outside corridor. On the table of the duty officer, a VDU had been set up; the duty officer rose to give Shenton his seat. At first sight, the picture was disappointing; it was distorted so that the pattern of the table cloth on the table in the centre of the room filled most of the screen, with the matchstick legs of the furniture stretched around the edges of the lens.

"Can't we get it any better than this?"

"The lens is on the end of an optical fibre rod; it's very thin and we have to use a fish eye lens. It is centred on the middle of the room, but we should be able to get it onto the door or window. It will still have to be from above; there is no way that we can get a rod lower down into the room."

"How high in the wall is this?"

"Edge of the ceiling; we had just enough space to squeeze the rod around the edge of the party wall infill. Excuse me, sir." He said something into his hand microphone and there was a savage jerk in the sight picture which now focused solely on the door leading into the hallway. The top of the doorway showed clearly and then the top of a man's head, bulbous with what appeared to be a large nose and a tiny body disappearing into stick-like legs. Another jump shot and the same in longer focus taking up a sixth of the screen, but more recognizable.

"Can you get it onto the window?"

It was better; another long shot, but the greater distance obviated most of the distortion.

"Good." Shenton flicked his fingers to the duty officer. "In five minutes or so we'll lower the field telephone. It should come level with the end window, exactly where the camera is pointed. I want you to keep it there. Warn all officers of what we are doing and put those newspapermen in the tower block on notice. I don't care about them being there, but I want no distractions."

It was seven minutes before they were ready to go. The duty officer, leaning well out through the living room window, lowered the handset on the end of its extending cable. He held it away from the window until he heard from the observer in the tower block, who was following what he was doing through binoculars, that the handset was precisely level with the edge of the window. Then he brought in his extended arm and allowed the handset to swing in and hit the window. Shenton had the earphones on and held his finger on the volume key. He nodded to the technical officer to start the video recorder.

Liam started like a rabbit, but David merely smiled and rose unhurriedly from the corner of the doorway where he had been sitting on the floor with his back against the party wall.

To Shenton, on the floor above, he came suddenly into vision from the lower left of the screen. He went directly to the curtains at the window, turned to look at Liam in the doorway and only then drew his pistol. Shenton stared hard at the young profile, very young, little more than a boy.

David drew back the edge of the curtain with his left hand, saw the swinging handset and then crouched down so that only his eyes were level with the bottom of the window as he stretched his left arm through the curtains to slip the window catch. He caught the handset at its third bounce and then drew it inside, pulled the window closed and sat down on the floor, cradling the pistol in his lap.

"Good morning," said Shenton into his microphone and watched the profile of David break into a grin.

"What do you want?"

"It's more a question of what I think you want. Mrs Ketling is not a fit woman, as I'm sure you know."

"Listen," said David, "our terms haven't altered. You either fix a way for us to get out of here or we all die."

"I'd hate to see that happen," said Shenton, "but I have to repeat that there is no question of our letting you go anywhere. I want to make that absolutely clear, I will not lie to you. But as there is no running water or normal facilities, I think that for Mrs Ketling's sake, there should be a minimum civilised standard."

"Turn the water back on!"

"I'm willing to lower a chemical toilet, by rope from the floor above; that will give Mrs Ketling some privacy. She also has tablets for hypertension and has probably exhausted her supply by now. She will need a further supply. I want to send those down also."

"We want food: champagne and tinned lobster."

"We'll send down coffee and sandwiches."

"Get stuffed."

David left the handset hanging inside the window and retreated crabwise back to the centre of the room. Shenton watched as he put his head close to that of the second man, but he could not hear what he was saying, and despite the theory of lip-reading, it was impossible for him to guess at the meaning. The second man was scowling, the younger man turned up the corners of his mouth in a half smile.


David said, "They're stringing it out, breaking it down so that we give a bit at a time; makes it easier for us to give up at the end."

"Where do you get this stuff?"

"I read a lot."

"I say balls to it and take the bastards with us now."

"The only ones we're likely to shoot are the old couple. Not likely we could kid any of the others into doing a face-up with us. Anyway, there'll be a dozen guns out there with real marksmen behind them, just asking to shoot our balls off. I wouldn't mind if I could see some sense in it, but I can't. I still wouldn't mind in a way; what else is there to look forward to, a hundred years in the cage?"

"You'd really do that," Sean was staring at him, "show out and go down?"

"If that's what you want. I don't care for chopping the old couple. I'm not on for that, but if you want to do an O.K. Corral, then sure! What about Liam?"

Sean looked across to the big man and then turned his head to spit on the carpet. "Looks like it's up to me."

"No hurry." David raised his pistol and, using the foresight, rubbed the end of his nose.

# Thirty-Five

Maureen Driscoll emerged into the rain from the Passport Office clutching her brand new passport, hardly daring to breathe for fear of breaking the spell of her current run of luck. Her photographs, authenticated in the name of a local clergyman whose name she had copied from a board outside the Baptist church in Elysian Street, had been accepted without question.

A taxi was disgorging an Asian family outside the Passport Office and she slipped into it ahead of a sandy-haired man who was waving his umbrella a few yards up the street. She told the driver to take her to Grosvenor Square and sat back to watch the people on the pavements quickening their pace as the rain started. She opened the passport and looked at the photograph of herself in the long dark wig, then opened her bag and took out her vanity mirror to check that the wig itself was still riding naturally.

Her bag felt unnaturally light without the pistol, but it would have been madness to have carried it into buildings controlled by security guards. Anyway, it was her day; in less than seventy hours she had got herself free of a practised killer; avenged the murder of her own husband as well as blotted out the abuse of her own body; fought off a pack of jackals who were out to rob her or worse; and found a haven, new identity and worked out her escape route. A very busy lady. And lucky. It was good to be lucky, because without it the most cunning plan was a non-starter.

Stepping out of the taxi outside the American Embassy, she

favoured the taximan with a brilliant smile, grossly overtipped him and swung her hips outrageously as she went up the steps.

Dooley sat in the front passenger seat of the big Ford Taurus and looked through the sheaf of photographs. They had good definition and had obviously been taken by a camera with a good telescopic lens. All showed the same man: emerging from a house, opening a car door, buying a newspaper, and then several of him sitting at the table of a pavement café. A distinguished-looking man of slim build and middle height with even features and a full head of silver grey hair. Dooley turned back to re-examine those that showed the man full face before he finally nodded. "It's him."

The driver of the car turned back from looking out at the road: a big man, wide-shouldered and far more powerfully built than Dooley, with a mass of blond hair merging into a Viking beard. His shirt was open to the waist, revealing a deeply tanned chest with some kind of medallion on a chain. He was called Jan and he spoke the over-correct English of a superior education, but Dooley had no curiosity about him. He had been chosen by the liaison officer of the Dutch connection who had guaranteed that he was dependable, but you never knew that until the time came.

Jan turned in his seat to lift over the case from the rear seat and opened it, angled across his knee to shield its contents from the road. Inset in the foam rubber packing were three pistols. Dooley chose a 9mm FN Browning, cleared the breach and carefully checked its action before reloading.

"It's a good piece," said Jan, "but it's been used before."

"Where?"

"An American camp. The Walther is cold, if you would prefer."

"No." Dooley pushed the pistol into the waistband of his jeans and looked for his cigarettes. "He always spends the mornings in his house?"

"Always. He leaves after midday and does not return until darkness."

Dooley took out the crumpled pack of Sweet Afton, lit up and exhaled a long plume of smoke through the open window.

"You would prefer darkness?" Jan asked.

Dooley tossed the spent match out of the window. "No, let's do it now."

Jan fired the engine and moved the car onto the road; at the end of the slip road they merged into the traffic coming south from Amsterdam, and in less than a kilometre they were clear of the city. Dooley watched the flat landscape with indifference as they drove in silence for half an hour until Jan came off the main road and turned into an estate of widely spaced houses. At the end of the road, the final house had more ground than the others and a wide drive that swept across its front. Jan turned the Ford into a half circle so that he was angled towards the road.

Dooley cocked the Browning and held it inside his jacket as he got out of the car. The door had an antique brass knocker at its centre, but Dooley put his thumb on the bellpush and kept it there. A long angry buzzing sounded somewhere inside the house.

The door was opened by a startlingly pretty girl with long black hair and wearing a yellow dress. She said something in a language Dooley did not understand. Jan replied and the girl wrinkled her nose. Dooley put up the pistol into the girl's face and shouldered the door. The girl went backwards and he caught her by the shoulder with his left hand, moving her into the hall as Jan followed and closed the front door.

The hall led into a large living area built across the back of the house with glass doors leading onto a coloured patio. The man from the photographs started up from a leather armchair, clutching a sheaf of papers, but when he saw the pistol he sat very still.

Dooley pushed the girl forward at the same time he released her and she stumbled halfway across the room. "Tell her to keep quiet."

The man spoke rapidly to the girl and then looked at Dooley. "She does not understand English. I told her that she must be quiet so that no harm will come to her; that you only want

money." He raised an eyebrow. "I have little money here."
His eyes moved past Dooley to the impressive figure behind
him.

Dooley jerked his pistol. "Van Hoeck?"

"I am Van Hoeck."

"Who is she?"

"A girl, a friend."

Dooley spoke to Jan over his shoulder. "Take her and check
the house."

"Please," said Van Hoeck, "she is very frightened, let me
reassure her." He spoke to the girl again and she came back
across the room, edging as far as she could from Dooley. "I
have told her that she is in no danger so long as she does not
give any trouble. She will not cause your friend any anxiety.
She will come to no harm?"

"So long as she's quiet." He aimed the Browning at Van
Hoeck's chest. "Drop the papers and put your hands on the
arms of the chair. Now get up slowly, turn around, lower your
hands to the back of the chair. Lean over, move your legs apart.
Stay quite still."

He searched Van Hoeck swiftly: a cigar case, gold lighter, a
slim notebook with a soft leather cover, gold pen, a notecase
stuffed with banknotes, pocket calculator, spectacles in a case,
a few coins and finally, in a chamois holster stitched into the
waistband of the trousers, a Walther PPK pistol.

Dooley pulled a high-backed chair some six feet away and
dropped his booty next to it. "You will turn around, sit down.
Telephone calls you will ignore."

The Dutchman straightened his jacket and smoothed down
his hair. "You know my name, may I ask yours?"

"I am an officer of the Provisional Irish Republican Army."

"But I am a friend of your army. I have worked for its aims,
helped it in many ways. There has been a mistake of some
kind. I can give you the name of —"

"Ryder."

"Yes." Van Hoeck's eyes had narrowed and he watched
Dooley's face intently. "That is right. John Ryder is the Council
member who tells me of your requirements, which I fulfill
always at great risk to myself. Why have you come?"

"Why did you meet Ryder in England?"

"We use many methods of communication. The police and intelligence people are always active, but you are right, for me to meet a member of your Army Council would be dangerous, particularly for me. Only in extreme circumstances, an emergency, when it was more dangerous to trust a message to other means, only then. We were aware of the dangers of a connection being made between us; certainly I was aware of the danger, every precaution was taken."

Dooley took the photograph from the pocket of his jeans with his left hand and flipped it expertly so that it landed on the arm of Van Hoeck's chair. Van Hoeck studied the photograph and laid it neatly across his knee. "That is me and the other man is, of course, John Ryder. It can only have been taken in a car park in the north of England, in the town of Leicester. It was an emergency, but you are, of course, correct: such meetings are dangerous and here is the proof. It is a police photograph?"

"Why did you meet?"

"At Mr Ryder's request. I was in England for a different purpose, my other business; I have an agency for electrical goods, Japanese, first class company. I travel to all EEC countries. One of my clients is in Leicester, I meet many people on such visits. I felt that was good protection for this meeting, just another meeting between businessmen among many others. I also relied on John Ryder to take similar precautions, to ensure that we were not observed."

"Ryder has told us about the money. You have had a great deal of our money."

"I have been paid, certainly, but I have supplied a great deal of arms and equipment: night observation, radio interception and surveillance equipment. It has been of great value and put you on level terms with the British army. Such equipment is very expensive."

"Many of the arms were free."

"Arms are never free, even when the cost is nominal for ideological reasons; there is always expense when borders have to be crossed."

"And before Ryder you dealt with Driscoll?"

"John Driscoll? A good man, but very difficult. When he was your representative he insisted on meeting the supply organisation and there should be no traceable connection, informers are everywhere. At his insistence I took him to Vienna and arranged for his visit to Prague. The Omnipol man took him to the factory; he was given serious attention, you understand, it was a mark of respect and yet when he returned he made many complaints, that he was followed by the secret police."

"Was he?"

A shrug. "Omnipol is itself part of Czech security, but the arms were good, very good, unobtainable from any other source: rocket launchers, grenades. It was from there that the Klashnikovs were obtained, weapons the equal of any. Other decisions were made later that made many difficulties, perhaps as part of Mr Driscoll's dislike of that connection. An awkward man, but admirably thorough. I regret his death by the British."

"Driscoll was killed by Ryder's men to stop him reporting your embezzlement."

"That is not true. I was told that he was shot by a British patrol, that is all I know. Whoever says that I have misused money is a liar."

"If Ryder says it?"

"Whoever says it."

Dooley smiled for the first time, casually dropped the hammer on the pistol, set the safety catch and tucked the Browning into the waistband of his jeans. He found his cigarettes and lit one and relaxed back into his chair.

"Ryder is desperate; we know that he is guilty of many things. He says that all arms purchase money on the Continent went through you and that if anything is missing it must be you who is the thief."

Van Hoeck leaned forward in great earnestness. "The purchase of arms is a complicated business. Clear documentation is not possible; letters of credit, shipping manifests, all have to conceal the truth." An elegant shrug. "Many middlemen have to be paid and they do not give receipts. The only judgment can be on results; were the arms obtained, were they taken safely across the frontiers, sometimes many frontiers. The American supply became very important later, but again there were difficulties; after the FBI became active, a direct route from America became impossible. I had to arrange an alternative."

"Portugal?"

"You are well informed."

"And you were involved in the London bus bomb?"

"No. I expected an accident of some kind, not a massacre. I was told that the concealment of Baldry's death among others would confuse; that if he alone was killed then the intelligence people would search back, concentrate on his past. I thought it was a great mistake. A drunkard can be dealt with undramatically, a simple accident or a disappearance, but the way it was done . . ." He shook his head. "The police must concentrate on the man who carried the bomb."

"Ryder says it was done on your orders."

"My orders?" Van Hoeck moved his hand towards his pocket and then checked. "With your permission I would like to smoke." Dooley tossed over the cigar case and lighter. Van Hoeck inclined his head in acknowledgement and lit up a cigar with a built-in mouthpiece. "You are aware of my business connection in the town of Leicester. On a visit there, this man approached me in a bar, called me by an old name, one I used when I was in Ireland as an American. He told me that I had been photographed meeting Sinn Fein and known Council men. This man, Baldry, said that he had been one of the SAS team watching me; that is doubtful, but he certainly knew far too much."

"Enough to end your visits to England."

"Enough to end everything. I bought him drinks, many drinks; he was a drunkard, but cunning, certainly not a stupid man. I thought he was a policeman, but he said a soldier. I saw no difficulty. I gave him money and told him that there would be much more; that I could always use a professional man. That appealed to him; he said he was well experienced with guns and explosives and that he could train volunteers to use them. Ryder had to be told, of course, and his London man contacted Baldry. I was shocked to hear how he had been dealt with, so stupid."

"There has been a great deal of stupidity, particularly with money. I want to know what happened to that money and don't bother to make another speech about the arms. We know about the arms. In the past four years, the equivalent of five hundred thousand pounds has been passed through the Continental connection. We have received arms and other equipment, some services and a lot of paper, about money going through bank accounts, from one account to another."

"It is complicated, very complicated; the money has to be laundered through exchange agencies. Vital to conceal the source. It was all necessary and expensive."

"Too expensive. You are making yourself vulnerable, Van Hoeck, because we know that there has been fraud. Ryder is charged with treason, and Ryder is going to die. Those bank accounts were controlled by you; however they were set up, the control in the end was yours. I don't know how you did it or what you passed it off as, but I know you paid money back to Ryder."

Van Hoeck dropped his eyes to examine the dwindling end of his cigar and then looked up again. "I did pass money to Ryder, but not as a gift, not . . . it was for your cause. He had many contacts with English criminals. When criminals stole mailbags with British army intelligence papers, Ryder bought them and —"

"How much did you give Ryder?"

"The equivalent of one hundred and eight thousand English pounds. Not always in that currency, some in dollars, also Swiss francs. You must appreciate my position. Any money I passed to Ryder was by his direct order. I am an agent, Ryder was my only contact, the appointed representative of your Army Council. Whatever his instructions I had to regard them as an Army order."

"What happened with Driscoll?"

"The Driscolls lived here. I've told you that he insisted on meeting the suppliers himself when that was possible. He passed the money to me on specific orders, in cash. That made many difficulties; bank transactions, particularly in Switzerland are much less dangerous. If Driscoll took any money it was before he passed it to me. That is all I can tell you of Driscoll. Ryder will be replaced? By you perhaps?"

"Perhaps." Dooley dropped the Browning into the side pocket of his jacket and picked up the notecase, riffled through its collection of banknotes and stuffed them into his trouser pocket.

Van Hoeck watched him impassively. "I carry little money, but if it would assist your work here I could arrange for a payment from my bank, within the hour."

"How much?"

"Eight, nine thousand dollars; anything more would require a further arrangement."

"You are well organised."

"I have no safe here, no valuables, apart from a little jewellery of Yvette's. Paper records can be embarrassing; the notebook contains certain references that can put me in touch with anyone that I need. I use telex and subscription computer services."

"Which no one else has access to?"

"No, and if they obtained that access they would still not understand."

"I like that."

Van Hoeck walked across the room to a display of drinks on a cabinet at the farthest end of the room. "I would like to suggest that we mark our acquaintance. There are most kinds of drink here." He opened up the front of the cabinet to reveal an icebox. "Scotch, bourbon, I regret no Irish whisky. With your permission, of course. I take it that our interview is over."

"It is over."

Van Hoeck turned back to the table and reversed two crystal goblets, held them up to the light and then replaced them on the drinks tray as Dooley shot him in back of the head. Van Hoeck crashed head first onto the cabinet, scattering glasses, bottles and decanters, slid sideways from the cabinet and hit the floor with his legs twisted beneath him. Once on the floor he made no movement at all.

Dooley crossed the room rapidly and came into the hallway, gun in hand, as Jan came down from the upper floor with the girl. He had his own gun in hand, holding the girl lightly by the arm, releasing her as they reached the bottom of the stairs.

The girl moved past Dooley, pressing herself against the wall, trying to get as far away from him as she could. Dooley caught Jan's eye and then half turned, shooting the girl suddenly, and again, more carefully, as she collapsed on the floor of the hallway. He waited for her to move and when she didn't he allowed the Browning to hang loosely against his thigh. Jan watched him with great wariness.

"Pity," Dooley said.

"A very great pity," said Jan in his carefully accented English.

Dooley lowered the hammer on the Browning, checked the safety catch and then offered it, butt first, to the blond giant. "You were right, it is a very good piece."

# Thirty-Six

Ryder slackened speed as he came to the crossroads, checked that the road was clear and then put his foot down on the accelerator as he turned to the west. He checked his rearview mirror out of habit, but he was already satisfied that no one had followed him beyond the outskirts of Dublin. He settled down to follow the meanderings of the secondary road he was on and to consider why Little Pat had called this particular meeting.

Ryder knew himself to be a physically courageous man; he had proved it a hundred times, faced men determined to kill him, stayed when other men had run. He was also quick-witted, ruthless and a superlative liar; well fitted to survive in any military or political situation, but he still had a knot in his stomach at the thought of facing Little Patrick McGlynn.

Little Pat was an extremely dangerous man, not just because he was a cold-blooded killer with a streak of sadism, but because he was unpredictable, given to volatile changes of mood and abrupt decisions which he would never alter, no matter how disastrous, all combined with a chilling puritanism that judged fornication as more blameworthy than murder. Like Swain O'Geraghty who left his wife for that American girl who had come over to relive the dreams of her emigrant grandfather. Ryder wrenched his thoughts away; he did not want to recall what happened to O'Geraghty. The road was narrowing and he dropped his speed to little more than a crawl as he identified the turning, a farm lane, by its broken stick marker. He checked his mirror for the last time and turned into the lane.

The lane soon degenerated into a cart track and he was bounced along the edge of the lower fields of the farm until he came level with a barn. A man carrying a Sterling sub-machine gun appeared from the shadow of the barn and Ryder wound down the window to allow the man to take a good look at him.

"Any trouble?"

"I was clocked leaving Dublin, nothing else."

The guard nodded indifferently. "Carry on." He raised the barrel of the gun in salute as Ryder drove on into a muck-strewn yard, empty of animals except for a dog tethered at the corner of the farmhouse. Eight or nine cars had been drawn up in front of the house and a dozen or so men were standing around them. The leading figure, a man armed with an automatic rifle, motioned Ryder forward and indicated that he should put his car at the end of the line. Ryder eased his car into position, braked and turned off the ignition, leaving the key in the lock.

As he got out of the car the sky darkened and he looked up to see that heavy clouds were poised ominously above. He unclipped the holster from his belt and dropped his gun on the driving seat before shutting the door. The man with the rifle gave him a quick body search at the front door of the farmhouse and then opened the door for him.

He stepped directly into the main living room, a generously proportioned room with solid timbers and a good fire burning in the grate. Little Patrick McGlynn was sitting with his back to the fire, in a bentwood armchair, at the centre of a long dark wood table. He remained seated, the pale, glittering eyes out-staring Ryder, who nodded and turned away to acknowledge the other members of the Army Council. Michael Tomelty, the nominal president, gaunt-cheeked and watery-eyed, looking fifteen years older than his fifty-eight years. Brian Clancey, who looked as if he was still a construction worker, with the sleeves of his open-necked shirt rolled high over thick biceps. But before the construction he had been a corporal in the Irish Guards, was highly skilled with firearms and had a hard fanaticism which had elevated him to the Council at the age of twenty-nine. He was Little Pat's man all the way through and said, far too frequently so far as Ryder was concerned, that he would sooner hold a gun than a woman.

At the far left was the adjutant general, Fitzgerald, who, in profile, bore a startling resemblance to his legendary grandfather, shot dead by the Black and Tans in ambush on the road to Cork. The compact man with the thin black moustache was Miller, who held the rank of major in the Irish army, and next to him Flynn, pudding-faced, with thick-lensed spectacles, ex-lecturer in economics and revolutionary theologian. At the end of the table on the right, Ryder recognized, with a small shock, Loughran of Belfast.

Ryder took the chair that had been placed in front of the table. Each man had met his eye and none had smiled, blank distancing faces. It was going to be a bastard of a meeting. He concentrated his attention on Little Pat who was dressed, as always, with precise formality: a pressed dark blue suit, gleaming white shirt and tightly knotted black tie. His dark hair greased back with a centre parting; a slightly built man who was almost a caricature of suburban timidity, until you noticed those chilling eyes.

"We are here," McGlynn began quietly, "to hear Ryder's report. Casey is dead and the three volunteers are trapped in London. Driscoll is hunted by the British police. London has gone badly."

Ryder put his clasped hands on the table in front of him, forcing himself to keep them steady. "It started with Malloy; he delivered the money to the house and the police came, the same day. The team had left, but they had to leave the explosives behind until they found a place to cache them. I had a report from Casey later that day telling me that. He had put a trembler on the explosives just in case; he did not fancy Malloy. He was right, we know that now. Casey was killed by Driscoll; you'll all remember what I had to say about Driscoll."

McGlynn's voice became even softer. "You did not report that she was living with him."

Ryder forced himself to return the stare of those piercing eyes. "He only told me that a week ago. He wanted better cover, a man on his own, two or three men are likely to be noticed, a couple are ordinary. I agreed because it was the best way of keeping an eye on her."

"Knowing Casey's reputation for ill-treating women —"

"She was an intelligence officer, a member of the unit; he'd respect that."

"— for being careless with both women and money."

Brian Clancey decided to say something. "He was careless with this one all right."

McGlynn wrinkled his lips in icy distaste. "Driscoll has been living with Casey for months because she was told she had to on your orders."

"That's a lie."

"Why did she kill Casey?"

"How do I know? She's the one to ask."

"She says it's because Casey tried to kill her, after raping her and telling her that he'd killed John Driscoll to stop him reporting to me on the embezzlement of the funds."

Something happened in the pit of Ryder's stomach as he stared at Little Pat, fighting to keep his hands steady. Look him in the eye and keep the hands still; he could do nothing about the cold sweat that had broken out on his hairline and was trickling down the centre of his forehead.

"Driscoll was killed by the SAS."

"So we were told." Pat seemed to be able to issue his statements without moving his lips.

Little Pat nodded towards Flynn who moved the papers he had in front of him to take a handful of photostats which he passed along the table for each man to take one, and Ryder found himself looking at a copy of Maureen Driscoll's letter. As he read the first line, a finger of ice ran the length of his spine.

When he looked up, Little Pat had not moved to touch his copy of the letter which was still lying on the table in front of him. His cobalt eyes bored into Ryder's.

"It's a plant . . . rubbish . . . she's . . . a fake . . . the British . . ."

"She's not with the British police."

"How . . ."

"We know," said Clancey.

A slight flush had appeared on McGlynn's cheeks and he had his lips pursed like an old Mother Superior. Flynn passed him an envelope and he took out the photographs and slip of paper. He lined them up in front of Ryder.

"Is she right about that being you and Van Hoeck?"

"It could be, could be anybody. What does it prove? I talk to a lot of people, I can't remember them all, it's just a photograph. It's not important."

"Casey thought it was important enough."

"Who says it was Brendan who took it? You're taking the word of a traitor, a whore of a traitor who killed one of our best men."

"And the number?"

Ryder looked at the scrap of paper. "It's just a number."

"Whose number?"

"I don't know."

"It's Van Hoeck's telephone number with the international code, the numbers you dial to get him in Holland. His private number, not his office."

"Van Hoeck."

"You're a traitor, Ryder. Casey photographed you with Van Hoeck as insurance and he had his telephone number, so that he could make direct contact with him when it was too dangerous for you to do it. You were under orders never to meet Van Hoeck, that all contact for arms would be made through cut-outs. Driscoll knew how the money was being milked off and the swindle did not end with his death."

"For Christ's sake, the lying cow killed Brendan. She'll make up any story to save herself. It's the oldest trick in the world. She's . . . you'll remember what I said before . . . warned about her. I said —"

"You made her the intelligence officer."

"— because I didn't trust her. That sounds stupid, but all she did was collect information; she never knew where the unit was going to strike. She had no chance to pass it on. I couldn't prove she was a traitor. I told Casey to keep her under control, trust her with nothing." He risked a glance at the others. Fitzgerald was looking at his hands, Tomelty frowned in concentration; Loughran poker-faced, only Clancey was smiling.

"Why did you meet Van Hoeck, Ryder?" McGlynn's voice was as cold as his eyes.

"I met him only once, when we were both in England. He was there on something else. I . . . he thought his line was being tapped. It was important to discuss a new supply line, a new way in if we get the rockets —"

"Rockets!" McGlynn spat the word.

"Casey drove me there, he'd fixed the meeting, as the cutout with Van Hoeck. How, why . . . I don't know if he took that photograph. It doesn't make sense."

"He didn't trust you, Ryder, but he was your man. He should have been court-martialled over the Shabeen affair; would have been but for you. Easy to blame him now, he's dead, shot by Driscoll's widow. You've read her letter; she shot him after he'd raped her, told her he killed her husband to stop him telling us that you're a traitor."

"No!"

"I say you are. Maureen Driscoll has reason to lie, but she says too many things that tie together with what we already know. Things that she couldn't know about. You commanded the active service units on the mainland, Casey reported directly to you and he made the bomb that blew up that London bus. He wouldn't have done that without you knowing. You were in liaison with the Dutchman under orders never to make personal contact with him and we know that you did. Driscoll says her husband was on his way to report false accounting, creaming off of the American money. He was killed. You say by the SAS. She says by Casey on your orders. And all you can say, Ryder, is that she's lying. I say she's telling the truth."

"Anyone can say that. It proves nothing. I could make up a story about anyone around this table over what's happened in the past and then say prove you didn't do it. How can anyone prove that? How do you disprove a fairy story?"

Clancey came heavily forward. "The British police colour-coded the gelignite in the house with the bomb on the London bus. A direct order was given by this Council that no working-class target on the mainland was to be attacked without our direct authority."

"The London bus was nothing to do with me. Brendan's name came up the night it happened; remember, the man with the bomb fitted his description. It was decided that the man on the bus was a London gangster."

"It was you who said it was a criminal. We were waiting for further information and now we've got it. The Metropolitan Police Forensic Laboratory have proved that the explosive was the same: gelignite that was under Casey's control."

"So Casey reported to me, reported every second day. I took his reports, gave him instructions; we talked no more than five minutes a time. I don't know if he was doing what I told him."

"So it's all Casey, like Driscoll's all lies. Nothing to do with you at all."

"I don't know. Jesus, what can I say? I'm a founder-member of this Council and you're taking that bitch's word against mine. Get Van Hoeck, ask him."

"Oh, we will, Ryder, and the man asking him the questions is very good at getting answers. Right now, you'll tell us about your trip north, and Malloy, the man sent to the mainland by Loughran." Little Pat nodded towards the end of the table. "Tell us about my order that only a man from Belfast should go."

# Thirty-Seven

She leaned against the door of the kiosk to check that it was fully shut and dialled out the code for Dublin and the number. She listened to the electronic sorting gear making the connection and then the telephone at the other end began ringing: she could picture it in the little alcove beneath the hall stairs in the house just off the South Circular Road in Dublin.

Maureen held the receiver tightly against her ear, poised the first of her coins on the edge of the shelf and used her hand to bring out the cigarettes from her raincoat pocket, shook a cigarette loose and used her lighter one-handed. She squirted a jet of smoke against the glass wall of the kiosk and counted the rings: ten, eleven. She could be out, of course, shopping, in the garden, even in the bath. Though not at eleven o'clock in the morning. Jesus, she could even have moved house: fourteen, fifteen; hell, she would let it ring up to twenty and then . . . . The receiver at the other end was picked up on the nineteenth ring and her sister answered, a peevish voice.

"Bernadette?"

"Yes, who — ?"

"Are you alone, Bern?"

"I'm . . . who is that?"

"Don't you know? There could be someone listening to this call."

"Maureen . . . is that you, Maureen?"

"Please don't cry, Bern. Can you talk? Are you alone, where is everybody?"

"At school, Tom's at work and . . . where are you, Maureen . . . all the papers . . . Mum and Dad are so worried."

Maureen pressed home the second of her little pile of coins. "I'm in a callbox, so I haven't a lot of time. There's something I want you to do for me, Bern, something important, a matter of life and death. I can't ring them, the bastard Special Branch will have their phone tapped, sure to. I don't think yours is; they wouldn't think of me ringing you unless Tom—has he been up to something?"

"Tom? No, of course not. You know how he is."

Maureen pulled a face and ground out the cigarette end against her own reflection in the glass divider of the cubicle. "I know how he is." She closed her eyes to inhale deeply. "I'm taking the hell of a chance in calling you, Bern; they'll kill me if they catch me, either side. You tell no one that I called or what I'm going to ask you to do, I want you to promise that. You've got to promise. If you don't want to get involved, if you're frightened, tell me now. I'll understand, but if you're going to do it then you've got to promise. You tell anyone and I'm dead."

"Maureen, I wouldn't tell anyone about you."

"Not wishing to maybe, but I mean it, Bern, you don't tell Tom."

"Tom wouldn't —"

"You don't tell him." She listened intently to the empty line, a high-pitched electronic hum, but so far as she could tell there was no sudden loss of tone that was supposed to indicate an eavesdropper.

"All right." The voice had turned sulky.

"If the Army find me, I'm dead, it's that simple. Now what I want you to do is get an envelope and you write a name and address on it that I'll give you, stamp it as well: then you go to see Mum. You don't make a special journey, just go to see them like every Friday. You still do that, don't you?" She pressed home another coin and found that she was sweating.

"Yes, every week, Tom drives me; he'll think it's funny if I don't want him to."

"You let him drive you. You make no alterations, everything as usual, that's important, in case anyone is watching. There's sure to be someone, if not the police then a reporter, neighbour.

You go there like you do normally, show the kids off, just let it go on as normal. But during the afternoon, when you're helping Mum to wash up or something, you'll find the moment, so long as it's just Mum and you, you understand?"

"What's Mum got to do with this?"

"Everything, she's the only one who . . . she'll understand. But on your own, so that no one can hear. You tell her I called, tell her that I'm all right, that I'll get out of London and I'll contact her. That I can't move, but that I'll make it and get in touch with her as soon as I can. You tell her that I called you because her phone will be tapped, she already knows that. Tell her that I need the passbook, she'll know what you mean; tell her it's time to use the book. She'll have it hidden and she'll get it for you. It's not big, a bank passbook that'll go into an ordinary envelope. When she gives it to you, you put it into the envelope and tuck it away, in your clothes somewhere, and the next day, when you're out shopping or taking the kids to school—so long as you are not with Tom or anyone else— you post it. Just put it in a box is all and it will reach me so long as you act normal and say nothing to anybody. Dad, Tom, no one at all."

"Oh, Maur."

"It's all right, all right, nothing to cry about. You can do that for me can't you, Bern?"

"Yes."

"Got a pencil?"

"I've got that."

Maureen took a deep breath and committed herself irrevocably. "Mary Garden, you've got that? Now," she involuntarily lowered her voice, "73 Melcroft Avenue, London W.11. That address means my death if it gets to anyone else. You'll do it for me, won't you, Bern? I'm putting my life in your hands." She listened for a moment to her sister crying. "God Bless, Bern."

She broke the connection and stood for a moment breathing heavily. You planned well, John, I'd never have thought of it myself: contingency money deposited in another name; I might have got round to that, but I would never have been too clever and kept the book. I would never have thought of lodging it with my mother. That was shrewd, John; you knew my mother was the one who would guard it with her life and tell no one, not even her husband, once you had sworn her to secrecy.

She lighted a cigarette and opened the door of the kiosk. You were right there, John, but what about my sister and her tight-arsed husband?

# *Thirty-Eight*

Kevin Dooley slept for most of the journey to Paris, coming awake as the train ran over the points outside the Gare du Nord to find that daylight had faded and that all that the blank window of the train had to show him was his own reflection: a thin-faced, hollow-eyed man with a stubbled chin. Rain was also streaking down the window and he did not have a rain-coat; he just hoped that whoever was meeting him knew what they were doing, had something organised.

After Jan had delivered him back to Schipol Airport he had made his check-call to his control number, only to have the voice at the other end cut him short, abruptly order him to report to the European office: the connection had been cut before Dooley could reply. So something had happened and something important for Little Pat to pull him off the plane to Shannon.

There was a sour taste in his mouth and he groped auto-matically in his pocket for a cigarette before he remembered that he had finished the pack on the taxi ride to the railway station. He looked at his watch: 8.33, but that was home time and you added an hour over here, so 9.33. His stomach rum-bled and he tasted bile. Jesus, he was hungry; he had had nothing to eat since the roll and coffee Jan had bought for him in the airport cafeteria twelve hours ago.

The train ran smoothly into the platform and all the other passengers in the compartment were on their feet, putting on their coats and getting their bags together. When the train stopped the compartment rapidly emptied. Dooley joined them, working his way into a group so that he went through the ticket barrier amongst them. Around a dozen people were waiting outside, but none of them looked likely. He moved past them onto the concourse. Always keep moving. Quite a lot of people, all with wet raincoats or dripping umbrellas. And then he did see her and knew her at once, a dumpy woman with a lot of untidy grey hair and the air of a harassed housewife.

She walked across in front of him and he followed her to the side entrance and out into the dimly lit road. The rain was drenching down and his hair was plastered to his scalp by the time she had fished the car keys out of her bag and opened up the doors of the small Renault jammed into a line of illegally parked cars.

"Hello, Kathleen."

"Hello yourself, Dooley."

"Got any cigarettes?"

She gave him a pack of Gitanes from her bag and cuffed the condensation on the windscreen away with the end of her sleeve. While Dooley lit up she got the car going and pulled into the road, drove to the end of the street and in a couple of turns they were hidden in the Parisian traffic.

"What's up, Kathleen?"

"London." She shook the mass of hair from her face and peered through the clouding windscreen. "You're going to London tonight for Maureen Driscoll. We know where she is, but she won't be there more than a couple of days."

"I'm on the red list in London."

"We'll alter you. I've got the gear together; been dashing about like a blue-arsed fly all day. You'll be met by Dennis and he'll take you to Malloy. That's your first job; Dennis has got him in his garage. Pat wants to know who was running him. Don't use that control number again, it's tapped. The Dutch report you give to me and I take it to Pat."

"What do I do with Driscoll? Anyone can top her, Dennis —"

"No." She turned the car across the run of the traffic in the best Parisian manner. "What Pat wants to know is if her letter was the truth; he wants everything she's got on Ryder."

"I got plenty on Ryder from the Dutchman."

Kathleen concentrated on getting the car through a narrow back street made even narrower by cars banked over the pavements, before moving into a long street of tall, old houses. "If she is telling the truth then you bring her back."

"In my pocket?"

"She's got no choice; if she stays in London the police will take her and if she disobeys then we'll get her. She'll agree, probably be glad to, but it'll take a few days to set up, maybe four."

Dooley lit another cigarette and opened the side vent of the passenger window to toss the match out into the pelting rain. It was a very long street unbroken by shops or any kind of life. Kathleen finally stopped the car outside a house with stone steps leading up to a solid front door and a multi-buttoned entry-phone. Dooley followed her up the steps and waited while she found her keys and opened the front door. They walked up two flights of narrow stairs and then along a long corridor. A thin Arab padded silently past them as they turned a corner into a shorter corridor. Kathleen unlocked the first door and led the way into the room, a simple room with a bed, a wardrobe and a handbasin. Two suitcases were on the bed.

She threw back the lid of the first suitcase and took out its contents: a dark blue suit, still with its store tags, black nylon raincoat, a shirt, string tie, singlet and underpants. "I couldn't get shoes; you'll have to do with the ones you've got." She dug further into the case and brought out a small tape recorder, a packet of throwaway razors and a towel.

"Where's the passport?"

"Here." She took it from beneath one of the bed pillows. Dooley examined it carefully; a British passport issued three months previously, no visa or entry stamps. It described John Winter, Engineer, born London, May 1959; the photograph showed him with his hair combed forward and wearing heavy-sided spectacles. He ran his thumb along its edges: genuine.

"O.K. Where's the glasses?"

She handed them to him and he crossed to the mirror by

the side of the handbasin to try them on. They slipped down to the end of his nose.

"It's only while you go through immigration."

He threw his glasses back on the bed and took off his jacket and shirt. "Any hot water?"

"Should be."

He used the heel of soap on the washbasin for lather and one of the razors to scrape off the stubble, wiping his face; he combed his hair across his forehead and Kathleen snipped at the ends with nail scissors. He put the glasses back on and examined himself in the mirror. It would do. The jacket of the suit was loose and the trousers a trifle long in the leg, but no more than he usually found in store-bought clothes.

Kathleen was sitting on the edge of the bed, smoking, with the passport in hand. She gave him a final, critical survey. "It'll do. What's your name? Where were you born? When?"

"John Winter, London, 1959."

"Your new contact number is on this envelope, the name and address are Driscoll's, it's a room she's got; there'll be a landlady, other lodgers. Here's the ticket. I've got to get you to De Gaulle in an hour."

"I'm starving, can't we get something to eat?"

"No time, I've got to get your report." She handed him the tape recorder.

Dooley helped himself to another of the cigarettes and sat down on the bed with the recorder. He thought about it for a couple of minutes before pressing the button, but once he started he spoke steadily in a monotone, recording everything that Van Hoeck had said, mostly in the Dutchman's own words. It took eight minutes and then he switched off and handed Kathleen the recorder. She ejected the tiny cassette and tucked it away somewhere inside her dress.

"Who was the girl?"

"I don't know."

She looked at him for a moment before reaching into her voluminous handbag to take out a wad of banknotes. "Five hundred pounds; anything else you need, ask Dennis."

Dooley added it to the money he had taken from Van Hoeck

and shoved it into the inside pocket of his new suit. "You read that letter she sent to Pat?"

"Yes, Pat gave it to me, wanted to know what I thought. It's true where it matters, one or two things she's made sound better, maybe."

"What did you think of John Driscoll, Kathleen?"

"Driscoll?" She moved around the bed, throwing his discarded clothing into the empty suitcase. "Driscoll was all right, but he didn't make many friends. He was a college boy, too clever for his own good; clever without being cunning. And full of himself like the college crowd who joined in the sixties. Thought you did it by winning debates, but, Jesus, could he talk, spun words like a silver mist, the Irish disease. Pat didn't like him, not serious enough for our Pat. Hadn't paid his dues. I remember the way Pat looked at him that night when Clancey put the British royals up as a target." She found a bottle of duty-free whisky under the lid of the suitcase. "You want a drink?"

"A small one."

Kathleen took the water glass from the handbasin and poured him half an inch. "Driscoll said they were interchangeable, put one down and another dozen popped up and that all they would do would be to use it as propaganda right across America. He was proved right, wasn't he, when Mountbatten got hit. Driscoll's idea was to make them look ridiculous, no shooting, no martyrs, just get a couple of buckets of lion shit so that when they came trotting out of Buckingham Palace, all ponced up, the horses get a sniff of lion and they're off like the clappers, crystal coach and all, on one wheel all the way to Aldgate Pump."

She took a hefty swig from the whisky bottle and hiccupped. "I reckon they should have given it a try."

Dooley took a tiny sip from his own glass. "You didn't think that the Brits took him?"

"Jesus, no. Driscoll could talk his way through any check point. He'd never cross through bandit country and if he was jumped by an SAS squad he'd never give them cause to shoot him; wouldn't have a gun anyway." She took a more cautious drink from the bottle. "One time I thought it might be the UVF, but that wasn't on, either; they wouldn't have kept it a secret."

"Who did you think it was?"

"I didn't know, did I? Anyone."

Dooley was watching her closely. "You thought it was Pat."

She put down the bottle and pushed back the mop of hair hanging across her face. "Yeah, I thought of that, too. It wouldn't have been the first time one's been blamed on the Brits," her lips twisted, "for strategic reasons."

Dooley nodded, poker-faced, and got up from the bed; he put on the raincoat and checked his appearance in the mirror above the handbasin. He put the passport in his jacket pocket, the spectacles and almost empty packet of Gitanes in the side pockets of the raincoat.

"Let's go if we're going."

Kathleen recapped the whisky bottle and threw it with everything else into the second suitcase. She moved rapidly but meticulously around the room, checking the wardrobe, under the bed and then using her handkerchief to wipe the handbasin, the bedside table and Dooley's glass before finally wiping the handle of the door as she opened it for Dooley to walk through with the suitcases. They went along the corridor in silence, down the stairs and then out into the rain.

# Thirty-Nine

It was midnight when Kathleen cleared Shannon Airport, passing through immigration in the company of four nuns whom she had been in conversation with on the plane. She recognized both men waiting in the car outside the terminal; and as she got into the back with her suitcases, the car moved off without any of them saying a word. She had bought the usual duty-frees and she stuffed them into her capacious shoulder bag, throwing the plastic airline bag through the window as soon as they cleared the airport.

She dozed off as the car made its way north and did not wake until the car was bumping along the lower fields of the farm. Guarded lights were shone into the car and then they were in the courtyard. The car was stopped again outside the farmhouse and she got out, leaving her bags. The door was held open by the man she knew as Big John who escorted her to the door of the farmhouse, followed her in and shut the door behind him to stand with his back against it.

Clouds of stale cigarette smoke hung heavy in the room and the long table was littered with ash. Little Patrick McGlynn had moved his chair to the far end of the room, close to the fire; immaculate as ever, he had a file of papers on his knee and a pair of wire-framed spectacles on the end of his nose. He got up as Kathleen came towards him and took off the spectacles.

"We'll have the others back for your report."

"Is there tea or something, I'm parched."

"In the kitchen."

Kathleen went through into the kitchen. Clancey was there smoking a cigarette and saying something in a low voice to a man she did not know.

Clancey grinned at her. "Hello there, Kathleen."

"Yourself, Brian." A kettle was hissing on the hob and she found some instant coffee to spoon into a cup on the draining board. She drank it black, clearing some of the sourness from her throat. She put the cup back on the draining board and Clancey said something to the other man before he turned to her.

"We'll be having your report."

"Sure." As she turned to leave the kitchen, she saw that the other man had turned to face the door of what looked like a vegetable store. Clancey followed her glance and gave a slight nod; that would be where they were holding Ryder.

Back in the living room the others had appeared. McGlynn was back at the table, still holding his file of papers; Clancey went by her to take his seat as she rounded the table to face them. A single empty chair facing all the others. That would be where Ryder had sat: he must have known as soon as he came in, once he saw that chair, that he would be facing a tribunal.

She remained standing while they got settled, checking them off, all except Miller. He would have left so as to appear in an official capacity elsewhere; a very careful man, Mr Miller. Clancey was fiddling with a cassette recorder: Japanese, Kathleen noted, the same model as she had used herself.

McGlynn closed his file and looked at her. "This court-martial is in resumed session and we will hear the report of Captain Reardon."

Kathleen stood slightly more erect. "I met Captain Dooley as instructed and informed him of the chief of staff's further instruction. I supplied him with new clothes, passport and checked his new identity. He recorded his report on his work in Holland. I then took him to the airport and saw him onto the plane for London."

"His report."

Kathleen took the cassette from her coat pocket and passed it over to Clancey.

"You'll be driven back." McGlynn nodded to the man on the door who stepped aside and opened the door for her.

When she had gone Clancey inserted the cassette and pressed the button on the recorder; a few seconds of silence and then Dooley's flat voice emerged tinnily from the speaker. Loughran stuck a fist under his chin as he lit another cigarette from the butt of the one that he had just finished. Flynn put a hand on either side of his head and stared at the table; Fitzgerald tapped away with the end of a pencil and Tomelty threw himself back in his chair, blowing smoke at the ceiling. Only McGlynn sat motionless.

No one spoke as the tape unwound to its end and Clancey switched off the machine. "That's it."

McGlynn stirred. "Anyone with anything?" He glanced around the table. "We'll take the vote."

Tomelty blew out a stream of smoke. "Guilty."

"Guilty," said Fitzgerald, still tapping his pencil.

Clancey grinned wolfishly. "Guilty, the bastard."

Flynn raised a hand and then dropped it. "Guilty."

"Guilty," from Loughran at the end of the table.

McGlynn nodded. "Unanimous, and the sentence is death, to be carried out immediately."

Clancey put his large fists on the table. "Is there anything more to be got out of this, the money?"

"You can try, but he's to be dead by daybreak." McGlynn got up from the table and signalled to the man at the door. "You'll stay till it's over, John; report to me in Dublin."

The others rose from the table and began moving towards the door; McGlynn put a hand on Loughran's arm.

"You want to handle it? He was fixing to put you under."

"I need to be back, there's lots to do."

"And room to do it now we've cleaned the stable."

"Yeah."

McGlynn looked first at his watch and then at Clancey. "You'll command; do what you like, but he's got to go by first light."

Clancey sat down at the table again and watched them all

leave. He lit a cigarette and smoked it through as the cars in the yard outside revved up and moved off, their headlights moving across the front windows of the farmhouse. A silence and then Clancey got up and flipped the cigarette end into the peat fire.

"Okay," he said to the man by the door, "let's get him."

# Forty

When he heard the footsteps coming up the stairs, Danny Malloy drew his knees up to his chin in a self-protective ball. Not again, no please, no: the light was switched on, dazzling, a single unshaded bulb shining down directly into his eyes . . . could not see, but he knew they were coming near, right up to him; he tensed, waiting for the boot to thud into his back.

"Get him up," said a voice he had never heard before.

Four hands pulled him upwards, but he could not stand.

"Untie him," came the same voice.

A knife sliced through the tape holding his wrists and he was pushed into a chair. The raised bruise on the left side of his face had closed the eye completely and the open cut on his cheek was rawly painful.

"You've been in the wars, Danny."

Malloy screwed up his right eye. The man who was speaking looked out of place, quite small and dressed like a bank manager in a dark suit, collar and tie. Malloy tried to say something, but it came out as a grunt.

"Get him something to drink."

A mug of water was pushed into his hand by someone he did recognize, the tall grey-haired one they called Dennis. Malloy took the mug in both hands, but even so most of it slopped over his knees. The small man took the mug from him and poured something into it. As Malloy raised it again he smelled whisky, and this time he did get it to his mouth.

"Cigarette?" The man put it into his mouth and lit it for him. Malloy could see the others now: Dennis and behind him the big ginger bastard who had done most of the beating.

"Okay, Danny, let us get this sorted out. You've changed your story since you rang in: first, you were walking about for three days, then you got picked up by the police, held for a couple of days and then they kicked you out."

"I thought—after the house—I thought they'd think I'd informed, but . . ."

"The house was raided the same day as you went there."

"It wasn't me. It wasn't—I swear . . ."

"Where did the police pick you up?"

"By the river. I didn't know what to do, at the back of that station where the drunks sleep. They said, well, they just said who are you, what are you doing, like they do, and took me in."

"Who questioned you there?"

"A sergeant, he said; he wasn't in uniform."

"What was his name?"

"Smith, Sergeant Smith—there was another one—tall. I didn't tell them anything. I swear I didn't."

"But he got your name, where you live, knew you were from Belfast?"

"Yes, I told him I came over to work. I've worked here before."

"O.K." Dooley got up and looked around the old storeroom. "We'll get you somewhere better than this. Get washed up and I'll see you downstairs." Dooley went down the steep stairs into the workshop below and waited for Dennis to join him.

"I say he's lying," said Dennis.

"Sure." Dooley lit another cigarette. "Once they got his name and address, the Lisburn computer would show up PIRA. Least they'd do would be an exclusion order. Get the van."

"Do you want me?"

"You're driving me. Malloy in the van with the others; we lead in your car. Where's the gun?"

"There's one under the seat, but Billy's got . . ."

"One will do. Find somewhere open, away from houses but not too far out; I want to be back in an hour."

"You're staying at the house?"

"Yes," said Dooley, "and tomorrow I'll need a car, something straight with the right papers, legal hire."

"You want us tomorrow?"

"No, but I might bring someone back with me."

Malloy came down the stairs followed by the others. He made some attempt at a smile to Dooley.

"Okay, Danny, you're going back in the van." Dooley smiled easily. "You'll be all right on this one. It's not so far."

# _Forty-One_

At four in the morning it is still dark on the east coast of Ireland and the wind that comes in from the sea blows from the northeast and is bone-chillingly cold. The road south from Dundalk runs parallel to the coast, but is punctuated at intervals by minor roads that cut across the scrubland bordering the sea. There is a particularly desolate stretch east of Drogheda, without a house of any sort. The road moves through a flat salt-drenched scrub with great stones bordering the sea. Only the gulls live there, sheltering from the wind in little hollows scratched out from the bleak scrub heavy with salt.

The gulls became restless, a new note in the wind, a note not unlike the wind itself, but with a mechanical pitch; they roused to rise in screeching protest into the sky as the headlights of the leading vehicle scrunched its way from the little road into the slight hollow in the scrubland.

The second car nosed carefully up to the rear of the first and both engines cut. The leading car dimmed its lights, but kept the headlights dipped into the ground, facing towards the sea. Four men came from the cars, one with a rifle who went to the edge of the hollow, looking back across the minor road by which they had come. Clancey led the others into the headlights of his car; he had the collar of his sheepskin jacket turned up against the wind. Ryder was pulled forward by the other two, his hands tied behind his back. Ryder had lost his jacket and he stumbled badly as he was pulled into the light of the headlamps, his mass of grey hair falling across his face. His shirt and trousers were crumpled and stained; the men who controlled him were uncaring and as they brought him forward his foot slipped on a slimy stone. They held him upright and pushed him into the glare until he stood, swaying unsteadily, in the full glare of the headlights.

Clancey came forward to face him. "John Ryder, you know me and know that I am an officer of the Provisional Army of the Republic of Ireland. You have been tried by court martial on a charge of treason against the Irish people. You have been found guilty and sentenced to death. The sentence will now be executed. You will have a minute to make your peace with God."

Clancey nodded to the men holding Ryder who pressed hard forcing him down to his knees; the smaller of the two took a bag from his pocket and dropped it over Ryder's head, hooding him. Clancey moved to one side and waited a moment for the second of the two to position himself behind Ryder and raise his pistol. Clancey waited a little longer and then raised his hand. The executioner fired at point blank range into the back of Ryder's head.

The gulls that had settled themselves back into their nests rose again in a protesting cloud from all around them. Ryder had pitched forward at an awkward angle and the executioner crouched low to straddle his body to fire again.

Clancey moved away from the headlights towards the back of the car where the man with the rifle was still watching the road. He opened the door of his car and got inside, away from the wind, and lit himself a cigarette. The executioner and the smaller man had taken shovels from the boot of the car and were attacking the scrub at the side of the hollow. Clancey glanced at his watch: 4.08 a.m.

# Forty-Two

The rain reached London just in time to fall upon Arthur Milton as he stepped out of his car at the rear of the East London police station. It hit him in the back of the neck as he stooped to turn the key in the driver's door; the rest of it hit him in the face as he crossed the twelve yards to the station back door.

He was wiping his face with his handkerchief when he entered the CID room and signed the book at 9.01 a.m. There were three notes on his desk and a wad of overnight crime reports. He lit a cigarette as he skimmed through them, and, while he was reading, the very young Constable Read came in from the main corridor. It had been a busy night: eight cases of mugging, one suspected assault and seventy-three reported break-ins. Eighteen cars had gone missing. Seven cases of serious criminal damage. Someone had smashed in the window of a local shop which had been displaying photographs of the Spurs football team. Critics are everywhere. Almost all of the break-ins reported a lost video recorder. Milton sighed and looked across at Read who, without his helmet, looked about twelve years old.

"What ones do we go round to, Skip?"

"About all we can do is to get the best men to drop a form in." Milton scratched his ear. "It's an epidemic, like measles. Don't know why they're so keen myself. I never see anything on the box I want to see once let alone twice."

"You can get some good films on video, though," said Read. "When I'm on lates and put the box on in the afternoon, all you get is a woman doing flowers or a kid's programme."

"Yeah, well, I don't suppose they're all being knocked off by blokes on night duty. You'd best hang on while I see if Mr Gardner wants something different."

Milton crossed the CID room to tap on the door of the glass cubicle of the new divisional inspector.

Inspector Gardner had, until recently, been a CID sergeant in a neighbouring division who had had to accept a return to uniform in order to step up in rank. He was a formidable-looking man with the build of a gorilla and a misshapen left ear which, according to folklore, had been chewed by the madame of a brothel; Gardner never told anyone that he had been born with it. Milton found him a great improvement on the previous bureaucratic Inspector Durant.

"It's getting a bit out of hand," said Gardner, skipping through the crime reports. "Seventy-three break-ins in twenty-four hours. They don't seem to pinch anything except TVs and video recorders."

"It's about all they've got; not much family silver around here."

Gardner squinted ferociously at Milton and then nodded casually. He knew about Milton, several years older than he was himself and stuck for however long it was to his pension as a clapped-out detective sergeant.

"Had a lot of it on my old patch. You can always get a quick fifty for a recorder. Could be an organized ring, I suppose. Know any bent electricals?"

Milton looked at the ceiling. "Not really; no one on the markets sells recorders that I know of. There is old Simmo, he keeps a shop over the back of Broadway. He used to be a receiver, but nothing much now. He's a bit fly and recorders have serial numbers. A load of steam irons is more in his line, but he does do a line in pirate videos, blue stuff according to some of the boys and I suppose he could be tempted."

"Worth a knock, then. Twenty-seven of these break-ins are in Filbert Point. Anyone likely there?"

"You know how it is," Milton said, getting into a slightly more erect position. Gangs of yobbos hanging about the walkways all day. They knock on a few doors and do those on spec when there's no answer: you can get into any of them with a screwdriver. The way it is mostly, the neighbours don't want to know even if they do hear it."

"Yeah," said Gardner, "all those blocks are frightened city, and you know all about Filbert Point, don't you?"

"Everyone knows about me and Filbert Point."

"Happened to me once when I was still on the beat. I was called in to a sudden death, eighty-year-old granny living alone who died sitting on the toilet. Nothing to it; natural death. It was in one of those little terraced houses, fag paper walls, built round the turn of the century; looked out on a railway line. I called on the bloke next door, looking for friends, relatives, you know, and he only turned out to be an escaped convict, didn't he. Bloody heavy mob raided the house on a tip three days later."

"I know the feeling," said Milton.

"I bet you do, except yours was a terrorist. Expect you to have x-ray eyes or something, don't they, so you can read 'terrorist' written across her tits. She was just another bird in a tower block, right?"

"She was a bit different," said Milton, "ten times more intelligent than the rest of them."

Gardner laughed. "Dead suspicious for a start. You had much of a hard time on it?"

"I got some lip when I went up to Central to do the photofit; asked if I'd know her the next time, stuff like that."

"Sod's law," said Gardner, "no one ever beat that. Have a look round Filbert Point, Arthur, and do a number on this Simmo. We'll get the beat men to give a form out on the others."

# Forty-Three

Major Flint headed south of Belfast along the main road leading to the border; once clear of the suburbs of Belfast the country opened out into arable land whose pattern had probably not altered in a thousand years. He was driving a battered transit van, filthy and hung with wisps of straw, a vehicle that was common to any farmyard or market town. His tweed jacket was worn over a crumpled shirt.

The van had been wired up in a hurry in the Lisburn military workshop and he had his radio with its transit microphone built into the door pillar. But there had not been time to plate the bottom or back the doors. The radio worked, but he was likely to move out of range of Lisburn once he neared the border. His Browning pistol was clipped high under the dashboard and he had two sets of papers: his military pass concealed in a slit at the back of the jacket lapel.

It was a chancy operation that he had had to put together in a hurry. His top informant had not rendezvoused. And his call from London had alerted him to Van Hoeck being found shot dead in his home in Leiden. And the offering, the goat, Danny Malloy had also finished up dead in a ditch on the outskirts of Banstead. Something had gone very seriously wrong and who the hell knew what the Dutchman had told them before the end?

He turned off the main road and almost immediately ran into a road block: a Saracen had been drawn across the road some thirty yards ahead, whilst a second had reversed off the road into the gateway of a potato field. A small stone wall ran along the edge of the field giving cover to three squaddies who were all watching him, with automatic rifles on their hips. Flint noted that they were Greenjackets. A sergeant was in the middle of the road carrying a Sterling submachine gun in a body sling.

Flint drove slowly within a yard of him before braking and switching off the engine. He offered his false driving licence.

"Get out."

Flint got out, keeping both hands well in view. The sergeant handed the licence to his back-up man.

"Open up."

Flint went to the back of the van and opened the rear doors, then stood back as the sergeant leaned forward to poke around the half dozen or so empty sacks that had been thrown into the back.

"Put your hands on the roof, spread your legs."

Flint put his hands on the roof and submitted to a cursory body check which ended when the back-up man came forward to report the reply that had been radioed back from the Lisburn computer room. He was given back his driving licence and the sergeant dismissed him with a jerk of the Sterling's muzzle.

The public house was at the edge of the village, a flat-fronted, cottage-shaped building built of the same stone as that of the dry stone walls edging the fields. A couple of battered cars, two farm wagons and a jumble of motorcycles had been parked on the beaten earth at the side of the pub. Flint parked with the nose of the car angled into the road and checked that he had some change in his trousers pocket; he lit a cigarette before speaking quietly into the concealed radio.

"I'm at Sheeny's . . . going in now."

He did not release the receive button. Outside the van he stamped his boots on the hardened mud and put the van door on the silent catch; it would open at the slide of a finger, but to a normal grasp would appear to be locked.

The bar was a couple of cottages knocked together and a cement floor covered by matting: a hard-drinking pub for men who liked hard drinking. Flint bought himself a Powers and beer chaser. He took no notice of the men at the end of the bar and sat by himself, smoking and looking through a copy of the *Dundalk Reporter*. He felt eyes on him once or twice, but as soon as he had finished his drinks he left and returned to the van: it all looked the same, but a touch of his thumb told him that the driver's door had been used. He looked casually around; no one had followed him from the pub and none of the cars parked at the side seemed to have any occupants. He tossed his cigarette and ground it down with the heel of his boot as he opened the van door with his left hand and leaned forward to reach the Browning beneath the dashboard. He released the safty catch and thumbed the hammer.

"Nothing violent, Major. I'm in the back."

Flint slid into the driving seat without turning his head. He wound down the window and took his time lighting another cigarette while he watched the door of the pub: one of the men from the bar was standing in the doorway. As he put the van into gear, he watched the man in his wing mirror; the man made no move towards any of the cars, but remained looking at Flint's van as he drove it behind the hedge.

"A man around thirty, gumboots, red-checked shirt, taking a lot of notice of us."

"That's Camul, sort of self-appointed intelligence man, no ranking. He clocks everyone who passes through, notes their car numbers, dresses tough. He's a sizeable lad."

"But nothing special?"

"Jesus, Major, would anyone special be that obvious?"

"You sound cheerful."

"If I do there's no reason for it; things are getting rougher by the hour. It's time for me to retire, I think."

Flint concentrated on his driving and said nothing. The man in the rear of the van was a very special informant, vital for the checking of information and early warnings. He was also a mercenary, simply in it for the money, without loyalty to any side at all, a professional, rare in the ranks of internecine warfare.

"Something's happening in the South," he said.

"Is that a fact . . . what is it?"

"There's been a High Council meeting for sure. Little Pat

called Loughran south, but you'll know all about that. For a court-martial."

Loughran's been court-martialled?"

"You're jumping to conclusions there, Major, and we've business to settle first, haven't we?"

"It will be handed over before I leave the van, so long as there's value."

"Hold it, a car's coming up behind."

Flint put his hand down on the Browning and held it against his thigh as he concentrated on his wing mirror: a low car with wide tyres, half of it hidden, a Mercedes.

"The driver's Flanagan, dairy farmer, flaunting the profit he's making out of the Common Market swindle. He'll pass you on the straight."

Flint turned the final bend and waited for the Mercedes to sweep past him; as he glanced down at his dashboard display he noticed the red dot above the tripmeter and depressed the button.

"Your position T4."

"Half a mile from the border," reported Flint, "I'm turning back on the Dundalk Road."

"Listen Major, Loughran was called for a full Council meeting; it was Ryder's court-martial."

Ryder! Flint swallowed and tried to make his voice as casual as he could. "Why Ryder?"

"He was caught with his hand in the till; McGlynn got a letter that pointed to Ryder. The details I don't know, but if Ryder was court-martialled on Little Pat's orders there'll be but one end to it. Loughran was called to give evidence. It was on Ryder's orders that Malloy went to the mainland, you see, a double bluff of sorts: if Malloy informed then it was supposed to be down to Loughran. Looks as though Ryder was a shade too clever there, but he's had a good run."

"Do you know what happened to him?"

"I guess he's either dead or wishing he was. One more down for you, Major."

Flint realised he was sweating. "Who'll take his place?"

"That'll take a week or so. A man was sent to Holland as

well: Dooley, no doubt to have a talk with Ryder's Dutchman, so he'll be vanished as well. And Dooley went to London."

"Why London?"

"He's gone to pick up Maureen Driscoll."

Despite himself, Flint allowed the surprise to show in his voice. "They know where she is?"

"She phoned her sister and the sister's husband told the boyos. Lovely, nothing like keeping it in the family, is there? Up by the hedge, Major."

Flint pulled the van into the side of the road, close to a beaten track which led to dilapidated outbuildings of a small farm. There would be a van, a car, hidden among them somewhere. "In the sack behind my seat," he said over his shoulder, "five hundred dollars. I'll be in touch."

He waited for the back doors of the van to close and then drove off immediately. He caught a glimpse of the stocky figure in battered trilby, rolled gumboots and mud-stained dungarees turning towards the track and then he was past the hedge and on his own again.

# Forty-Four

Shenton finished his tea, replaced the cup in its saucer and took up his pipe, conscious that the others were waiting for him to say something. The bank of television screens in front of him showed three different angles of the living room in the siege flat and the duty technician worked on the controls, fine tuning the focus to concentrate on the human figures that they showed. Sergeant Field was waiting patiently by the window with the telephone and its coiled extension. The third man, standing easily to Shenton's right and also looking at the television console, was the major in command of the SAS unit: a young man of no great size, he wore the ubiquitous black dungarees without any badges of rank.

Shenton took his time lighting his pipe, checked that it was drawing smoothly and tossed the spent match into the waste basket.

"It could panic them."

"Pressure," said the major. "It's the third day, they're not likely to do anything that they wouldn't anyway. All it does is let them know that we're there."

Shenton waved the smoke away from his face and stared at the screens. Mrs Ketling was still in her armchair, swathed in blankets and apparently asleep. Mr Ketling was in the armchair facing her with only the top of his head showing, making it impossible to see if he were awake or not. The fat gunman sat slumped on the settee, leaning on his elbow with his eyes closed. The third, older gunman was out of the room and the young one sat as he had all morning, on the floor beneath the window, reading his blasted book.

"How much noise?" said Shenton.

"Not much, could be that they'll hear nothing. If they don't, it gives us another way in, if they do . . ." he shrugged, "they'll be facing the bathroom, deciding whether to fight. If they turn back to the old couple . . ."

"You blow the other wall."

The major nodded. "And that's it."

"It?"

"The wall goes and so do they."

Shenton's instinct was to do nothing and wait them out indefinitely; they had to come in the end, but the woman was visibly sinking and this was the third day. He bit hard on the mouthpiece of his pipe and made up his mind. "Very well, I'll talk to them when you're in position."

"Thank you, sir." The major left the room and turned back to the screens. Nothing had altered. The fat one had given up, there was no question about that, which left two, and the older one who kept prowling around the hall was feeling the pressure all right. It was the young one who was the enigma; he obviously had deep inner resources and which way he would jump would be an intellectual decision. He had been kind to the old lady, but that did not mean much with a convinced revolutionary.

Field stood up by the window. "They're in position, sir."

"Lower the telephone."

He turned back to the screen and watched the telephone receiver appear, dangling at the end of its cord to bump gently against the window. The gunman closed his book, first marking his place with a scrap of paper before getting unhurriedly to his feet and slipping the catch on the window.

"You're late," he said into the telephone, "did you oversleep?"

Shenton overrode him. "How is Mrs Ketling?"

"She's all right. Those pills you sent make her drowsy; she's all right. Both of them are all right, so far."

"You've been there for three days, conditions must be unpleasant. You must come out eventually, there can be no other solution."

"There's always another solution."

"Even more unpleasant."

"Your way's a lifetime in prison. I might prefer mine. There's the old couple as well. They're the reason we've not been shot down already."

"You have to realise that there is no question of you using them to bargain your way out; absolutely none at all."

"We could shoot one and find out. We've nothing to lose."

"I am the senior police officer here and I am telling you that a full unit of the SAS is all around you. If there is any shooting, a single shot or anything else that suggests harm to Mr or Mrs Ketling, they will come in, not us, but the SAS comes in shooting to kill. Not one of you will come out of that flat alive. That is the only alternative you have to surrender."

David slammed down the telephone and let it drop to the floor. He turned to look into Liam's blotched face and smiled. Sean appeared in the hall doorway. "There's a noise; someone's fiddling about with the wall."

"Probably a drill, setting up to chop a hole through it."

"I'll chop the bastards!" Sean swivelled the Sterling back towards the bathroom.

"They just told me: the SAS have moved up, any shooting and they'll come in, through the wall, the door, windows, maybe the floor as well. The man just told me."

"He's —"

"Lying? What's the point! Sure it's the SAS, who else would they use? No, it's them leaning on the wall out there."

"Bastards." Liam's face had paled to a mottled grey.

"Bastards, and soldiers, no prisoners. We can end it right here, shoot the old couple or just put a bullet in the wall and in they come. It'd be a quick way to end our troubles all right. We might even get to take one with us. Or---"

"Or?"

David grinned wryly. "Jail, and wait for the amnesty, escape maybe, live in hope and all that."


Shenton heard the shout of "bastards" and saw the smaller gunman swing the Sterling back to the wall, but the micro-

phone heads pushed into the wall picked up little more than
a rumble. A laser gadget had been set up on the opposite tower
block which was supposed to pick up the vibrations from the
windows and translate it back to speech, but no one seemed
to be able to get the angle right.

The fat gunman had collapsed back on the settee again.
Shenton tensed as the one with the submachine gun turned
back into the room, but he was talking to the young one who
smiled and turned back to the window, already taking the
book from his jacket pocket.

His outside telephone buzzed and he picked it up.

"A call from Central, sir: Mr Hobson."

"Right."

"What's happening, if anything? I'm on my way to a meeting
of the crisis committee."

"I think we're close to break point. One has definitely given
up. It's between the other two and it's a matter of face—-neither
wants to be first. It might go through tonight but I doubt it."

"Yes. The Dutchman you were interested in, Van Hoeck.
There's a signal from the Dutch police about him. He was shot
dead yesterday and they want to know what our interest was
in him. I'll leave you to answer that. And that missing informer
turned up, he's dead as well, shot through the head and
dumped in a ditch outside Banstead. Ring me as soon as anything breaks."

"Yes, sir." Shenton waited for the line to clear and asked
the operator to get him Maxwell. When he came on the line
Shenton told him to signal Holland. "Say our interest is that
Van Hoeck's name came up in an enquiry on terrorist groups
as an arms supplier. Ask if they can find anything to connect
him with PIRA. There ought to be papers or a safe deposit
somewhere."

"Will do. You heard about Malloy?"

Shenton grunted. "If we don't get to the Driscoll woman
first she could go the same way."

"Might not be a bad idea," said Maxwell. "They don't mess
about, do they?"

"I'll be here until further notice," said Shenton and put the
phone down.

# Forty-Five

Flint reached the motorway and drove through the morning traffic fast and skilfully, his eyes moving constantly from the road to the rear- and side-view mirrors, automatically checking any vehicle closing in from behind or about to draw alongside.

"ETA in five minutes," he said, leaning his head towards the hidden microphone. He made a racing turn into the secondary road leading towards the military camp and bumped gently up to the security gates, braking to a halt at the guardhouse. He waited while the picket guard came cautiously forth to check him and the vehicle and then he drove into the security compound. Inside the main building he ascended to the first floor and identified himself to the watchman who operated the electronic security grill at the entrance of the forbidding concrete corridor that contained the combined offices of all the security agencies operating in Ulster.

In his own room he checked the recorder attached to his direct line telephone: no one had called. He threw off his jacket and opened the security cupboard to take out his bottle of whisky and a carton of his private stock of American cigarettes. He sat down at his desk and poured himself a heavy shot of the whisky and lit a cigarette; after a few minutes he got up again and operated the combination lock on the filing cabinet within his security cupboard, took out two files and re-locked the cabinet. He went back to his desk and sat looking at the two red-striped folders without opening them. He finished his drink, picked up his second telephone and asked the security switchboard operator to get him London.

When the call came through he asked for the extension and lit another cigarette one-handed.

"Black," said the voice, and he flipped the scramble switch.

"Flint. Ryder was court-martialled last night."

"What charge?"

"Fraud was the main one. McGlynn got a letter from London which could have had something else in it. Our friend didn't know who it was from."

"Driscoll," said Colonel Black, "she was always the danger."

"Looks like it; she's still in London. They've sent Dooley for her."

"To kill her?"

"We don't know, but it's likely. Why else would they send Dooley?"

"They wouldn't risk him in London just for that, there'll be questions they want answered."

"She couldn't tell them anything about us. All she could tell them is about Casey. It's all gone now."

"Did Ryder tell them anything?"

"I doubt it. Whatever they did to him it would only have made it worse. They would have got his money out of him if it was reachable, nothing else. He'll be dead by now."

"Yes," said Black, "so Loughran's in the clear."

"And back in Belfast."

"A complete failure." Black's monotone became even more clipped. "Report here on Friday."

"Yes," said Flint and the receiver went down at the other end.

His cigarette had burned to a stub and he lit another. An absolute and complete balls all round; Van Hoeck, Malloy and Ryder all dead and Loughran, the target, back in Belfast with reinforced authority.

He flicked open the first of the files on his desk: Danny Malloy. A few notes, mostly of the small payments that had been made and a plastic envelope of black-and-white photographs showing Malloy in a street riot, throwing bricks at a police cordon, kicking down a barrier and hurling a petrol bomb; all taken at the Divis Street riots. He had been thrown into the general remand cells and the undercover man put in with him and the other rioters had fingered Malloy as the weakest and most likely to turn. Malloy was scared of not being allowed back on the mainland where he had worked in a car factory. He wanted to send money to his wife in southern Ireland who had gone off her head when their child had been born and who lived with her mother in a cottage out on the west coast.

He had followed instructions and joined the Provos, but had risen to little more than messenger. Flint came across the note that Malloy had insisted that he make about money being sent to his wife, hesitated for a moment and then put it aside with the rest.

He poured himself another shot of whisky; he could feel its effect on him but was past caring. The whole thing was shot to hell, two years of intense conniving work up the spout in a few hours.

The second file was the more important by far: all that was on record on the most important informer that they had ever had in the hierarchy of the Provo High Council. He held a handful of flimsy payments records, £98,000 in two years. There was no reference number and the code name, Redwing, was used only in messages to London as a guarantee of the quality of his information. There was no photograph in the file or anything else that pointed to Redwing's true identity. Only he, Black and the head of the Secret Intelligence Service knew that Redwing was John Ryder.

"Greedy," said Flint, "just too bloody greedy." The whisky glass wavered over the file. "I told you that many times."

# Forty-Six

Maureen Driscoll stubbed out her cigarette in the saucer at the foot of her bed and stood up, smoothing her denim skirt about her hips. The pockets that she had sewn in the crepe bandage had rearranged the money around her body so that it no longer rode lumpily across her stomach. More evenly distributed it thickened her hips, but gave her greater freedom of movement; if she wore the raincoat unbuttoned it would be unnoticeable. She rose up on her toes to see herself at an angle in the mirror in front of the dressing table before putting on the black wig and tinted spectacles in which she had been photographed for the new passport.

Satisfied, she took off the wig and switched on her little transistor radio to check the time signal. The time signal was followed by the news and she raised the volume a fraction; the siege had been pushed to second place: it was still a stalemate. She flicked off the set and checked her bag, safety catch high and loosely covered by a handkerchief. Her new passport, with its picture showing her in a black wig, was in the front compartment, contact lenses in their little case, loose money, spare cigarettes, cosmetics and the other passport showing her as Mary Wilson. She had to get rid of that, fatal to leave it in the room, nowhere to burn it, dangerous to throw it in a dustbin, amateurish to leave it anywhere it could be found.

The thing to do would be to push it through a drain; duck down behind a parked car and slide it through the grid, just so long as, Jesus, so long as she got rid of the right one. She pulled up her skirt and pushed the new passport with its precious visa into place within the folds of the crepe bandage across the front of her stomach. She tried sitting down, stretching this way and that until she was satisfied that it was secure, even if she had to run.

She picked up her raincoat and looked around the room. It was time, more than time, she had already stayed longer than she should. A full day in the hope that the letter would come with its magic passbook. She gave a final look round the room; she would take nothing, the clothes, case, shoes, radio. Goodbye to Mary Garden. Everything she needed for her new identity had been bought in the chain stores along Oxford Street and were in their new suitcase, lodged in the luggage office at Victoria Station.

Her rent was paid to the end of the month and she would write, no, she would telephone, a sudden call back to the North, that would give her a week's cover. And after that, even if the police got involved, this room would tell them nothing. She would be just another nomad lost in the big city's whirlpool.

She rolled the black wig loosely before putting it into the raincoat pocket, fluffed up her own hair, checked herself one last time in the mirror and left the room.

In the hall, she opened the front door as quietly as she could and pulled it gently to a close behind her until the latch dropped. The little gate was open and she went out onto the wet pavement. She walked less than a dozen steps when she heard her name and she spun round, her hand going automatically to the bag.

"Dooley," she said stupidly. He was standing less than a yard from her, his left hand lightly draped across the top of the open door of a tan Sierra, a slight boyish figure in a white raincoat and black sweater.

"Get in the car, Maureen." He stood away from the door. "We've things to talk about."

She moved towards him holding the shoulder bag with her left hand, her right searching under the flap. He did not seem to notice, had already turned his back to walk behind the car to reach the driver's door. She got in the car and watched him warily. There was no one in the back, no one else in any of the other parked cars.

Dooley slid into the driving seat and put his left hand on the ignition key. "You'd better close your door."

She pulled the door closed with her left hand. "Where are we going?"

"Just a drive." Dooley fired the engine and pulled away from the kerb. He drove up to the end of the street and turned, apparently aimlessly, into the first side street before reaching the main road and tucking in behind a bus. He released his right hand from the steering wheel and produced a pack of cigarettes, shook them in her direction before taking one himself. He used the dash lighter.

"How did you find me, Dooley? My sister, that husband of hers? The silly bitch told him?"

He puffed out a great cloud of smoke and fanned it away with the back of his hand. "Does it matter?"

She had the bag on her lap, her hand still on the butt of the pistol. "What do you want, Dooley?"

"Either fire that damn thing or drop it. I'm in a hurry with a lot to do; no time for games."

"God." She took her hand from under the flap, but still clutched the bag, like a talisman. Her brain was trying to encompass this new disaster; Dooley of all people, the quiet killer. What had John said about him—the best of them all, the man who had everything, except a soul.

"So you wrote Pat a letter telling us all about Ryder and Casey." Dooley gave her a quick grin. "You must have been reading Pat's mind; a nice bit of timing there, Maureen, pictures and all. A clever girl, I've always said."

"Why are you here, Dooley?"

"To find out what you're up to. You write your letter to Pat, but no other contact. Why didn't you report? Why is the unit in that tower block and you out here? You hide out on your own, sending for money through your sister, tell her to tell no one. So what are you, Maureen, traitor, informer or what?"

"Jesus Christ, if I was an informer would I be in that house trying to get my half-arsed sister to get my money to me? I'm on the run, Dooley, from the Brits most of all; they've got my photofit plastered all over this town, didn't you see it?"

"I saw it." He snapped the end of his cigarette into the road.

"I had no way of contacting the unit; Casey never told me where it was, he never allowed me any contact. I told Pat all that in the letter."

"Yeah." Dooley shook another cigarette loose from the packet with his left hand. "So you killed Casey, got yourself a place, stayed clear of the police, kept your nerve. You've handled yourself pretty well. But you weren't coming back to the Army, were you, Maureen?"

"After killing Casey? Ryder would have me gunned down before I got both feet on the ground."

"Forget Ryder, he's gone."

"Ryder's dead?"

Dooley nodded indifferently. "Pat sent me to decide what to do with you."

"You've been sent to kill me."

He gave his first genuine smile, showing all his neatly regular teeth. "Why now, Maureen, if I'd been sent for that wouldn't it be all over by now?" The very softness of his voice was chilling and she knew he was speaking the exact truth. She had dealt with Casey for all his bruiser bulk and physical power, but this softly spoken, neatly dressed student figure was far more deadly. She had a gun and they were driving through thick traffic in one of the best-policed cities in the world, but she just knew, was absolutely convinced, that if he wished it she would be dead, right here.

"I told you Ryder's gone; Pat believed your letter. It fitted in with other things, anyway. You won, Maureen, and Pat wants you back. I'm here to take you back."

"I can't go back. I'm wanted for murder. What use would I be?"

"It's not your decision. I told you, it's an order."

"The oath to death? There's nothing left. I've nothing left to give."

"No one resigns."

"For Christ's sake, Dooley, can't you get it through your head? I don't believe it anymore."

"Don't you now." It came out as little more than a whisper and his eyes had narrowed as he half turned in his seat, steering with one hand.

"Not the aims: foreign domination, the injustice, freedom. Of course I believe in all that; but what the hell is going on? What's Ulster now—just a lot of poor sods fighting for a share of each other's poverty. The hundreds that have been killed, maimed; what good has it done, what has it made better? I've spent my youth, seen my friends die, my husband, for what? Is one son-of-a-bitch the better for it?"

"It's a war, people get killed in wars. Did you think it was all making speeches and singing pub songs? I remember the college boys marching about in '68; they thought you did it by singing the songs. "We Shall Overcome." And then they got their heads thumped in by the B Specials. So they ran. Overcame fuck all. No one took any notice until we came with the guns. They took notice then, all right."

"What good, tell me one good thing that comes out of it?"

"Well, now, you're the bright college girl, you should be telling me. The Prods walk soft now; they don't come into the Falls to burn us out of our houses anymore, do they? No more rigged ballots; their fake parliament's gone. And the British can't pretend it's nothing to do with them anymore, leaving us to kill each other. For forty years the British population were taught that Ulster was a pimple on the arse of the British Empire. They know what it is now, all right: a rebellious colony that they can hold down only by force, and every British soldier we kill gives us his family. They know he died for nothing."

They drove on in silence.

"And Pat wants me back—what for?"

Dooley shrugged. "It'll take a couple of days to fix a passport and then you'll go."

"Where are we going now?"

"Casey's van is still missing; he'll have left it somewhere round the Filbert Point flats."

"What van?"

"He used a van to move the lads to a new place that night. He got it from Dennis and knowing Casey he could have left something in it."

"It's more than a week, the police will have it."

"No sign of that; they'd have been in contact with Dennis for a start. It'll be in a parking space round those flats or in a side street, somewhere near."

"The police could see me."

"They'll not be there now."

"A neighbour, anyone."

"They only see what they expect to; I've proved that many times."

Milton had got nowhere at Filbert Point. Two hours of patient questioning had turned up nothing new. All the break-ins had been on the fourth and fifth floors, between eleven in the morning and two o'clock in the afternoon. Each of the doors had been forced by a heavy screwdriver and two youths had been seen knocking on doors, asking for their Uncle Charlie. They were white, of average height, in jeans and anoraks; one had long hair.

Milton got into the lift and put his notebook away with a sigh. It was all too easy; a couple of little creepers knocking on doors when men were likely to be at work and the women trekking to the shops; screwing those doors where there was no answer; in and out in a couple of minutes. On the ground floor, two women, encumbered with shopping baskets and small children, watched him leave the lift with guarded hostility: men moving through the flat-blocks during working hours usually meant trouble, official or otherwise.

As he went through the main doors, he found that the rain was heavier than ever, turning the dreary forecourt into a shallow lake. He turned up the collar of his coat and tried to find a way past the worst of the puddles to reach his car, which he had left on the end of what looked like a permanent collection of rusting cars and vans. As he fumbled for his keys, a car swung across the forecourt, spraying water everywhere. Milton stood to one side and the car rounded the line of vehicles at a much lower speed; as it came level, Milton looked down through the half open passenger window into the face of a girl who was wearing spectacles with large, tinted lenses. She was a pretty girl and she reminded him of someone, a girl he had met somewhere, or maybe it was just the glasses. He finally got his key in the lock and was opening the door when he became aware that the car was turning: the girl was out of the car, walking back towards him.

He stood there with the door open, trying to remember who she was, and as she took her hand from under the flap of her shoulder bag, he did remember. There was something different about her hair, but there was no doubt, it was her all right. She brought out the gun and held it low, levelled at his stomach, shielding it with her body from anyone who might be looking out of any of Filbert Point's thousand windows.

"Stay where you are, Sergeant, especially your hands; keep them just as they are."

The car drew alongside and a slightly built man in a white raincoat got out. He came behind Milton, looked inside his car and noted the handset.

"Where's your personal radio?"

"I'm not carrying one." Something hard prodded the small of his back.

"You will walk to the car and get into the passenger seat. You will do it carefully, keeping your hands in front of you, and when you are inside you will put your hands on top of the dashboard. Any sudden movement and you are dead."

The girl stepped aside and Milton found himself walking toward the Sierra. He got into the passenger seat and put his hands meekly on top of the dashboard; there seemed to be nothing else to do. The girl got into the passenger seat behind him and the man crouched at the open door; again that hard object prodding the small of his back and the man was searching him one-handed. He did it rapidly, throwing whatever Milton had in his pockets onto the floor of the car: notebook, wallet, warrant card, cigarettes, coins, pen, handkerchief, everything except the handcuffs.

"Put your hands behind your back."

Milton swung them wide, but the man was already out of range. He's good, this bastard, Milton thought. The handcuffs went over his wrists and then the safety belt was pulled across his body and clipped home. The little man slammed the door and went round the front door of the car to the driver's side. Milton watched him push in the ignition key and fire the engine; they drove off at once and within a couple of minutes were edging into the traffic that streamed across the turnpike into southeast London.

The shock was passing and Milton looked through the rain-spattered windscreen at the trucks and cars moving around him. The girl seemed to sense something. "If you try anything at all I will put a bullet just there. Believe that."

"I believe it."

"Why were you at those flats?"

"Checking on break-ins. It's my job."

"Where's the van?" said the driver.

"What van?"

"Casey's van."

"I don't know."

"It's stupid to lie to us," said the girl.

"I don't know anything about a van." Milton tried to ease the pressure on his arms by pushing against the seat belt, but it was unyielding. He was very near death, there was no doubt about that. An insignificant-looking man and a slip of a girl, but their very quietness was convincing; when it came to it they would kill him, dead, just like that. He was surprised to realise that he was not frightened; he ought to be pleased by that because he had always taken it for granted that when it came he would be like any man. And he had been frightened, oh, many times, particularly in the early days: the Mason gang with their knives and shotguns and mad Jimmy McPhail who had carried a hatchet in his belt, ready to cut off the head of the first man who came to arrest him. It was because he was frightened that he had gone in the harder to cover fear, the fear of being hurt or maimed, mainly, but fear of death as well.

Perhaps it was the girl, a girl who was ready to kill him, but also one that he found attractive, a pleasant-voiced, sensible girl of high personal standards. A wry smile twisted the corner of his mouth; the sort of girl, by Christ, that he could respect.

The girl stirred behind him and he automatically tensed his neck muscles in anticipation. "Where are we going, Dooley?"

"Out of town."

Dooley. The name meant nothing to Milton, but if they did not mind his knowing the name it meant they knew he was not likely to repeat it to anyone else. He thought about his wife and then deliberately turned his thoughts away; it was pointless to regret anything now. All he really felt was a kind of tiredness.

A beer lorry drew level and stayed alongside for some time before pulling in ahead: *McOwen's Ahead of the Field.* What the hell was he doing here, sitting trussed like a hypnotised rabbit, being driven through suburban traffic towards his own death? In a film he would spring the handcuffs, snap the belt and kick the driver as he went over the back of the seat for the girl. The car would crash with the girl disarmed and the driver knocked out. Simple.

Except that it was not a film and that layer of his brain that he had relied on through twenty-six years of tricky police work told him that he would be dead if he even raised his shoulders.

The road widened as they began the run-up to the motorway, but Dooley took a slip road to the left, and, after another double turn, they crossed a bridge with the cars speeding along the motorway below them. At the next junction, Dooley chose a subsidiary road that was flanked by trees which, in a couple of miles, turned into little more than a rural track and finally into nothing at all. All Milton could see through the windscreen was marshland, the remnants of a drystone wall, patches of scrub and a half-filled drainage ditch, and not one living soul.

Dooley switched off the engine and lit a cigarette. "You were at Filbert Point for the van."

"I told you, I was checking on break-ins."

"How many times have you been back to those flats?"

"Today was the first time since the Green case."

"Green case?"

"He was the man in the flat next to mine," said Maureen. "He killed his son."

"And I used your phone."

"So you did, Sergeant, and got a good look at me. A great help in making up that photofit."

"Yes."

"And you just happened to be there today, is that what you want us to believe? The one policeman who could recognise me?"

"I didn't at first," said Milton, "when I saw you in the car. It was when you were walking back. I knew you then."

Dooley ground out his cigarette. "We're wasting time."

"And you'd know me even better next time, wouldn't you, Sergeant?"

Milton looked through the blurred windscreen and said nothing; there was nothing to say.

As Dooley put his hand on the driver's door she leaned across and put her hand on his shoulder. "You turn the car, Dooley." He looked back at her for a moment before nodding and then she got out of the car and opened the front passenger door. She had taken off her spectacles and held the gun loosely by her side. Dooley unclipped the seat belt and pushed hard into his shoulder. "Move."

When Milton had his feet clear of the car, Dooley hit him hard in the small of the back. He lurched out into the rain and almost fell as the girl stepped back. She motioned towards the ditch with the muzzle of her gun. "Over there." He looked into the ditch which was choked with reeds and nettles. Was this really the last thing he would see in the final moment of all?

He looked up for a final glance at the grey, watery sky and the girl kicked him hard in the back of the knee; he went face down in the ditch, his foot caught in a ball of scrub grass and turned his ankle. A searing pain shot through his leg and a flint sliced into his cheek. As he strained to lift his head up from the nettles, he found himself looking up her skirt. She was crouched at the edge of the ditch, squatting on her heels. He stared into her face and, for a moment that lasted forever, she looked back at him before putting her left hand on top of his head to turn his face away, almost gently. She doesn't look like a killer, he thought: cold metal moved across the top of his ear and then there was an astounding explosion, a scorching pain and then nothing.

Maureen adjusted her aim and fired a second time, then got up and ran to the car. Dooley had already opened the passenger door and as soon as she was in he put the car into gear and drove back across the marsh. She took her shoulder bag from the back seat and put the pistol inside, keeping her bag on her lap.

After a moment Dooley said, "You'd better put the safety on, Maureen."

"Yes."

Dooley took the pack of cigarettes from his pocket with his left hand and offered it to her. She took a couple and used her matches to light both.

"You're quite a girl," said Dooley, "you had me thinking that maybe you were something else."

"I still don't want to go back."

"There's nowhere else for you to go, not now. Whatever it was with Casey, they'll hunt you to the ends of hell for this. There'll be no resigning, Maureen, we're the only friends you've got."

She turned to stare out of the window and Dooley drove on in silence. When they reached the main road he took a different route back into London, manoeuvring skilfully through traffic that became progressively heavier as they moved into the depressed inner city. High, drab buildings, small factories, abandoned churches and defunct cinemas given over to bingo.

Dooley turned abruptly into a side street and pulled into the kerb. "Back on the main road, twenty yards or so, you'll see the underground station. You'll go back to the house you were staying in until you get the call. You don't go out, for anything at all, that's an order. It's a safe house; they'll not find you there.

"You did."

A cold smile. "You'll need a passport. It'll take a day or two and we'll alter you a bit. One of your wigs, now, you're good at that."

"And where is it that I'm to go?"

"Pat will have plans for you, be sure of that."

"And who will be taking me over, you, Dooley?"

He shook his head and bent forward confidentially. "I've things to do." Before she could react he had put his hand over hers and taken the bag from her lap. "You'll not need the gun."

He took the pistol and dropped it casually into the side pocket of his jacket, as he looked through the rest of the bag. He opened the passport and looked at the photograph that showed her as Mary Wilson.

"It was too dangerous to leave in my room."

He handed her back the bag. "Go straight there, Maureen, and stay in the house. You'll not stand a chance if they pick you up. You really are one of us now, whatever fancy bullshit you were telling yourself before, you've shut all the doors now. Without us you're dead."

She got out of the car and slammed the door.

# Forty-Seven

The siege ended at dusk. An hour earlier David led Mrs Ketling into the hall, waited until Sean had pulled away the armchair and dressing table that had been jammed against the door, and held it open wide enough for her to stumble out into the corridor. Half an hour later Mr Ketling was released in the same way, and then they waited with guns drawn for something to happen, but nothing did happen, not even the lowering of the field telephone.

As darkness fell, with its promise of another cold, uncomfortable night, David rose from the corner where he had been reading his paperback book in the glow of the spotlight from outside and, carefully marking his place, put the book into his pocket. Then he straightened himself in full view of the uncurtained window and pressed hard with the flat of his hand above his right buttock, trying to smooth out the kink in his spine. He turned his back on the window and took out his Browning, withdrew the magazine and pulled back the sliding jacket to expel the round that lay in the chamber. He rasped at the surface of the pistol and magazine with the edge of his sweater and then took each cartridge and carefully wiped them clear of prints as well. Then he dropped pistol, magazine and bullets onto the seat of the armchair.

He smiled at Sean who lay supine on the settee. Sean nodded, got up and went through the same manoeuvre with the Sterling submachine gun and his own revolver. Liam watched them with half-closed, bemused eyes. Sean took two steps, plucked the pistol from Liam's lap, emptied the cylinder in his palm and wiped the pistol clean, dropping it on the floor.

Then he rubbed the bullets on the sleeve of his jacket and threw them across the floor.

"Okay," said Sean.

David nodded. "You okay, Liam? We go out. It's over. I'll go first; if they don't shoot, you can follow."

"You tell them nothing," said Sean savagely, bundling Liam's shirt under his throat. "Nothing!"

"They'll aggravate you," said David, "keep on talking at you, accusing you of this and that. Throwing names at you as if they know already, telling you we've about told them everything. The worst bit will be when they wake you up after you've just dropped off. They'll ferret away at wearing you down; it's five days they've got to do it."

"Name, rank, fuck all else," said Sean. "Spit in the bastard's eye."

"Yeah," said Liam.

Sean kicked his foot. "Up off your arse then."

David pulled away the chair and table and threw the front door fully open; he paused and heard a click, a rustle, something, then he stepped through the doorway and turned to his left.

"Hold it!" A voice thick with tension.

David grinned. Three, four, five men, two in the centre of the corridor looking inhuman in body armour and visors, aiming automatic shotguns from a crouch, and the other three along the walls in combat stances with their Smith & Wessons zeroed onto his chest.

"On your knees!"

David got down on his knees.

"Spread your legs, you bastard! Clasp those hands on your neck."

More were appearing now. David could see the heavy feet moving up the corridor: it was an army. The voice was shouting again and he heard Sean get on the floor behind him and Liam would be somewhere, maybe not even through the door. A boot was pressing him full length on the floor. A confusion of voices and legs and what looked like enough hardware to start the Third World War.

# Forty-Eight

The darkness lifted slowly to the accompaniment of a strange pattering noise, and it was some time before Milton realised that he was alive. The insistent pattering connected up with the water that was pouring down his face; it was still raining.

A cautious movement of his head, agonising, but it moved, and he turned slowly on his left shoulder, pressing against the side of the ditch. The rain had turned the bottom of the ditch into liquid mud and, as he tried to get upright, his feet slid from under him. It took an age before he was able to get enough leverage to raise his head cautiously over the edge of the ditch. Nothing.

He got the top half of his body over the edge and rolled over on his back, pulling his knees up to his chest and squeezing his cuffed hands under his feet. It was more difficult than he had expected, his arms pulled out to their limit. The final wrench almost unhinged his shoulder-sockets, but his looped hands came free in the end and he lay exhausted on the soaking grass.

He was in one hell of a bad way: filthy, manacled and helpless in a God-forsaken wasteland in falling darkness, but he was alive. And that was impossible. The muzzle had been against his ear. For whatever remained of the rest of his life, he would remember that moment and the absolute certainty that he was about to die. It was impossible for her to miss.

He put his hands to his face: congealed blood down his right cheek and a raw patch by his left eye. He touched his right ear and winced; something had happened there, but no bullet holes. He was alive and it didn't make sense; she could not possibly have missed him, could she? Unless she had meant to.

He got to his feet and almost immediately fell over. His ankle was on fire. He tried again and took two steps before it gave way again. Jesus. He started to crawl dog-fashion towards the lights glowing in the sky of London town. It was going to take a long time.

Maureen Driscoll emerged from the underground system at King's Cross and walked the length of the main line station, weaving through the jostling crowds making for the suburban lines. She emerged onto the forecourt and hailed a taxi, which she took to Victoria Station.

At Victoria the taxi delivered her onto the main concourse. She paid the driver and pushed her way through the people in the taxi queue with their Continental suntans and jumbled suitcases. She paused at the magazine counter and carefully examined the other loiterers before moving on to the top-numbered platforms and the left-luggage counter. The attendant took her ticket casually and returned with the locked hold-all and suitcase. No one was taking any notice of her, but she was still a little tense as she made her way to the washrooms and waited for the big black attendant to unlock one of the bathrooms.

As the water thundered into the bath she took off her skirt and unwound the bandage from around her waist, releasing the packets of banknotes and the new passport, all slightly curled at the edges. She put them into her shoulder bag and then undressed completely, placing her clothes on the bench in a neat pile.

She lit a cigarette and then lay back in the water to wait for the tension to soak from her body. The full realisation of what she had done flooded through her. There was only one way to go, no longer any options, nothing to depend on, except herself, and all that she had to save her was a few hundred pounds, a new name, a passport and her wits. She ought to be shivering with fear, but she felt like giggling, a pleased and giggly schoolgirl, or as if she were slightly drunk.

Her thoughts drifted to Milton. It had been one hell of a risk, but also as though someone else had been dictating what she'd been doing. All she thought at the time was that she couldn't bear to watch Dooley kill him. She had surprised herself when she told Dooley to stay in the car. She had not even thought about shooting him, but it had really been when he was in the ditch, helpless and looking up at her with his creased face and sad brown eyes. Not even frightened, just resigned and very patient, like an old dog. Her hand had moved by itself, altering the trajectory in that very last half second. It was all jumbled up, and all she really knew was that she couldn't look forward, absurdly hopeful, to whatever was in store for her if she had killed an ordinary man. Perhaps that was it, because he was a very ordinary man and ordinary men are so rare, like a protected species, that to kill him would have been obscene.

She got out of the bath and wiped the steam from the looking glass with the end of her towel and looked at her face, pink from the heat, the short hair plastered across her forehead. She towelled it roughly and then herself. The bathroom heat made proper drying difficult and she compromised by using her tin of talc. Standing on the stool, she opened the hold-all and drew her new clothes out of their plastic bags: first the underclothes in their virgin white, bra and panties. A high-necked red shirt with matching scarf and then the black trouser suit. Low-heeled pumps and, finally, the seating of the wig over her own damp hair, separating the front fronds with her fingers and arranging the side falls so that they were level with her eyes.

She took the hand mirror from her handbag and checked that the back fall of the hair bounced on the collar of her jacket. She took out the little bottle of fluid and moistened her contact lenses, inserted them and checked her reflection again, this time against the passport photograph. Hello, Janet Wimbush.

She checked her raincoat pockets, transferring the cigarettes and matches into her shoulder bag before bundling the rain-coat itself and the rest of her discarded clothing into the hold-all, which she locked. With a final look around the cubicle, she took up her two cases and left.

Outside the washrooms one or two passing men glanced at her and she hesitated until she realised that she looked faintly exotic. She crossed towards the ticket counters and saw a pile of luggage stacked by the Continental platform. She dumped her bags and looked up at the indicator board as if she were checking the departure times. No one paid any attention to her and she picked up her suitcase and walked on, leaving the hold-all with the stacked luggage.

Ten yards on she stopped again, ostensibly to light a cigarette; when she put her hand out to drop the dead match, the litter basket also received the ignition key to Brendan's Cortina. She walked up to the booking counter and stood in line. "Gatwick," she said to the clerk.

Something like a boot prodded him in the side, and, when he opened his eyes, two figures were looming over him, shining bright torches straight into his face. He tried to move and slithered further along into the gutter.

"Bloody wino."

The second one bent lower and there was a flash of metal buttons.

"Don't smell like it."

He made a great effort to show them the handcuffs. "Milton—".

"You what?"

"Warrant card's . . . gone . . . taken . . . for a ride . . . Provos."
He could not keep his eyes open any longer.

"What's he rambling?"

"Some crap about a ride. Christ knows what's on here."

It was strange that he could hear them so clearly because the voice inside his head, so much louder, was so much less distinct. He could see the girl very clearly, her eyes were looking straight into his and she had her hand on his head.

A miracle, said the voice. I don't know why.

There was only one other customer at the booking counter. The girl gave her a bright smile. "New York? One way or return?"

"Just the one way."

# Glossary

BLACK AND TANS. During the Irish Civil War (1922–23) unemployed ex-soldiers were recruited to replace members of the Irish police force, who were resigning in large numbers because of their being targeted for assassination by the IRA. The name comes from their mixture of army and police uniforms which were felt to be similar to a well-known pack of black-and-brown foxhounds. The name later transferred to a motorized Auxiliary Division of the Royal Irish Constabulary which committed a number of atrocities in attempting to put down what they regarded as a rebellious province.

BROWN STUFF. Slang for British army intelligence. The name comes from the color of their uniforms.

CUT-OUT. An espionage term for a middleman or messenger who, if caught, would be unable to provide any information about the person or persons for whom he is working.

IRISH VOLUNTEERS. See UVF.

OFFICIAL IRA. In 1970, the IRA Army Council voted to recognize the parliaments of Dublin, London, and Belfast, breaking with the traditions of the revolutionary movement which had always insisted that the whole of Ireland should be a republic. The Army broke into two wings: those who supported the decision were the Officials and those who objected to it being the Provisionals. The Officials came to be known as the Stickies because of their habit of sticking commemorative Easter lilies to their coat lapels. The Provisionals took their name because of their adherence to the ideals of the 1916 revolutionaries who had declared a provisional Irish government. The Officials have since disbanded.

RUC. Royal Ulster Constabulary. The British police force in Northern Ireland. It is about 90% Protestant.

SAS. Special Air Service. Were first formed during World War II, when they were airlifted to fight behind enemy lines. All recruits are volunteers from other regiments who are rigorously selected, with only one in five being successful. Their intensive training makes them the elite assault troops of the British army. In a civil situation they are used only in extreme cases where the police officially hand over responsibility to the military. Not being policemen, they do not go in to carry out arrests but to destroy an enemy.

SINN FEIN. A political party which seeks the same aims as the IRA but through the ballot box.

SMUDGE. To photograph covertly.

STEEL CIRCLE. A security zone in the heart of Belfast. People going in and out of this area, which includes the shopping district, must pass through gates and submit to security checks.

STICKIES. See OFFICIAL IRA.

UVF. Ulster Volunteer Force. Illegal Protestant paramilitary force formed in 1912 and revived in 1966 to resist Home Rule. A counter force of Home Rule supporters, called the Irish Volunteers, was the forerunner to the IRA.